DOLLARVILLE

Pete Davies completed *Dollarville* a few days before his thirtieth birthday, having travelled to Kenya and Nicaragua, New York and California, Wisconsin and Utah to write it. He now lives in north Wales with his wife and son and has recently published a book on the World Cup called *All Played Out*. His first novel was *The Last Election*.

'Comic, action-crammed, *Dollarville* uses the fantastical to highlight the absurdities of the modern world. *The Comic Strip* meets *Heart of Darkness*, a serious dystopia in adventure movie packaging'

Cosmopolitan

'Davies ... whose first novel was the equally subversive *The Last Election*, has a talent for shining a searchlight on the truly frightening. He writes like a New-Wave Cassandra, daring us to ignore the ominous signs of the times ... Davies' style is immensely vivid, poised at the edge of sassy and shrewd'

Newsday

Pete Davies

DOLLARVILLE

V

VINTAGE

VINTAGE

20 Vauxhall Bridge Road, London SW1V 2SA

London Melbourne Sydney Auckland Johannesburg
and agencies throughout the world

First published in Great Britain
by Jonathan Cape Ltd, 1990
Vintage edition 1990

*Grateful acknowledgment is made to the following for
permission to reprint previously published material:*

ZIFFREN, BRITTENHAM & BRANCA ATTORNEYS AT
LAW ON BEHALF OF CONTROVERSY MUSIC: Excerpt
from the lyrics to "Sign O' the Times," written and
composed by Prince. Copyright © 1987 Controversy
Music. All rights reserved. Used by permission

BELDOCK, LEVIN & HOFFMAN ON BEHALF OF INDEX
MUSIC INC.: Excerpt from the lyrics to "Blind," words
by David Byrne and music by David Byrne, Chris
Frantz, Jerry Harrison and Tina Weymouth. Copyright
© 1988 Index Music Inc. (ASCAP)

The right of Pete Davies to be identified as the author of
this work has been asserted by him in accordance with
the Copyright, Designs and Patents Act, 1988

Printed and bound in Great Britain by
Courier International Ltd, Tiptree, Essex

ISBN 0 09 977510 7

FOR TIM & JUSTIN

'I'd like to say a few words about
the international context…'

(and thanks for the atlas)

ACKNOWLEDGMENTS

My thanks first to Steve, who helped steer me from the Rosario in La Paz to the house in Managua—and to all the good people of NWAG who, when I got there, were unfailingly generous. To Lil and Jennie in particular my special thanks—*Dollarville* began when we went to Quilali.

I'd like next to thank Robbie in Kenya—in Wisconsin Scott, Jane, Ben, and Renee—in London Chris and Sian, Frances and Rachel—and David and Henry in New York.

My thanks go also to Johnny; to Pig, Dread, and Charlie for crucial assistance at the pivotal moments; to the members of the wp consortium—and to Peter and all at Upstream for leading-edge work, and some state-of-the-art times.

Finally, for her support through the travel and the trouble this book has taken, my thanks and my love to Rebecca.

CONTENTS

Part 1

THE FAR CAPILLARIES

Three things that set us free.
Guns, God, and Guts.

—Pat Robertson Campaign Button,
New Orleans, '88

1. ALPHA

Mr. Squalatush lived in a place of great beauty, tucked high among the folds of the Cordillera Entre Rios. All around him and his people, the mountains were wild and green; sheathed in cloud forest, they rose to six thousand feet above the level of the sea.

The mountains were rugged and remote, but they had not gone uncharted. The satellites had risen from Guiana and Nevada—and Mr. Squalatush had marked, with keen eyes, the tracks of these new stars. He had, of course, no idea what they were.

He had lived since birth without papers or radio or science; he and his people had been little disturbed by news, or by fabulous notions such as man in space.

Some missionaries did come, with their stories of Jesus—but these were no match for the stories of Mr. Squalatush.

He was the settlement's tale-teller; he knew all the many stories of his people and their land. They went back a long way, and new ones were always being added; and Mr. Squalatush made a good job of telling them.

Short and round-gutted, he was an animated barrel shape perched on spindly bowlegs. He bobbed up and down before his audience, spinning vivid interpretations of the changes in the weather and the movement of the heavens; he made parables of the new stars, and proved with conviction that the gods were still active.

He was an old man, though how old precisely it was hard to say; he himself couldn't have given a firm number of years, and nothing like a census had ever reached where he lived. So if you watched him making evenings pass happily with his talk, you might have wondered, was he fifty, or seventy?

But it's best to leave it at what he knew himself, that long life in a good place had left him hale and sprightly; and that among his people, only the ancient and historic Mr. Balbo was older.

His people were a small, quiet group. They went on foot, and had between them the communal use of two horses. They grew meager crops, and, if there was a surplus, the men took it to town, and exchanged it for small money to spend on beer. Bringing the money back, after all, would have been pointless—cash in the settlement was not a functional commodity.

The town was a day and a night away along tracks of wet mud, and you could hardly ever get a ride; vehicles were so rare, they were half beyond imagining.

Their homes were huts of plank and earth, with shutters of cardboard; the roofs were corrugated tin, carried back sheet by sheet on the heads of hung over men.

There was only one gun. It belonged to Mr. Balbo, who claimed that in his youth he had fought the Americans. Whether it worked, or he had any ammunition, no one knew. And no one gave them cause to find out—they were far away, and the soil was poor.

But still, the settlement had beans and basic grains and chickens and eggs, and from time to time an animal to kill. And every year came first the small rain, then later the big, which was tumultuous and long.

Then Mr. Squalatush would go on a full morning's walk into the forest and watch the surfaces of rivers shatter into dances of leaves and spray, crashing with noise beneath the downpour until the forest steamed, white and gray and green in its excess of water. And at those times, veiled in mist and vapor, where Mr. Squalatush lived was a place of greater beauty than ever.

When the mercenaries first came, they made their base a fair distance away, and the settlement was only rarely disturbed. One woman, whose man beat her, left the settlement and crossed the hills, and arrived at the base in a damp gray dawn; she stayed, living with other women in the shanty that gathered at the shiny wire perimeter. Sometimes she returned to visit her sister; she looked ravaged.

Under tutelage, meanwhile, from Argentinians and then Americans, the mercenaries passed by more and more. They took food and paid inadequately for it with money, which wasn't especially welcomed—it meant the men went to town more often, and drank more beer.

Other times when they came, they called everyone together, and explained to them the wickedness of the people across the border who were, they said, Communists. This wasn't a point of view that the villagers chose to dispute, partly because they were polite and pliable people who didn't, in truth, have much idea of what a Communist might be; and partly because the only time one of them did, he took a sound and ugly thrashing for his pains.

Then the blond American came. His name was Chester Gantry, a gleaming little man who brought with him, on a rugged vehicle called Ford, some new and exciting machines. There was a generator the size of a small goat, and a collection of fat batteries; there was a television, and a satellite dish about a forearm's width from rim to rim. He also brought a video machine; but after playing several programs on this machine, he said he'd not be leaving it with the rest when he went.

This was thought a very great shame. On one tape in particular, the story of the crucifixion and resurrection was told in tones more striking, more bold, more bloody than they'd ever heard from any previous missionary. With its stirring music and pyrotechnic effects, it was a tape they'd eagerly have watched again and again—but no dice.

Gantry was, he said, on a mission to aid them. When he left, he gave them money to buy gas for the generator; and he showed them where to tune the minidish so the television could bring them new programs. He told them when to watch, and left them with the incentive that next time he came, he'd bring them back the video. The people of the settlement were mollified, and, as he promised, the television brought them a show every night; so for half an hour each evening, they gathered around and watched.

The shows were not, like the videos, Bible stories, but featured instead some truly glossy and fascinating individuals. They stabbed their fingers at the camera, ferociously uplifted; they sprayed spittle over microphones in ecstatic, one-to-one contact with Our Lord; or they relaxed on cozy sofas in dewy-eyed togetherness, discussing wickedness in humble, grateful, hushed, and harmonious tones. They were, thought Mr. Squalatush, the most extraordinary people.

They were also—and he was joined in this conclusion by the great majority of his people—a novelty that rather rapidly wore off.

The healing power of Jesus they could, as a concept, accept; that he was alive and almighty in the United States seemed, on the other hand, an extravagant notion—and it didn't help the corn grow. So the men went to town and drank the gas money. No more gas, no more programs; people shrugged, and got on with their lives as they'd always done before. The equipment sat unused, getting dirty, and collecting its first rust.

Mr. Gantry, when he returned, was extremely angry. And things became, very suddenly, very frightening.

"Who drank the money?"

They stood gathered around the tailgate of the truck called Ford. Chester Gantry, though a slight man, had a powerful, wraithlike, golden yellow presence; he reminded Mr. Squalatush of the more sinister local spirits that lived in the canopy, shimmering with energy, unshaven and slightly manic—he stood before them on the back of the pickup and stared around the silent assembly.

Toward the clearing's edge, a troop of twenty mercenaries lounged at the border of a row of plots. They chewed dried strips of beef, and cleaned their guns.

Behind Gantry, the squad leader *Jefe* Scarskull leaned against the cab of Ford and examined his nails, one foot crossed lackadaisically over the other. He sometimes looked their way, and he had the eyes of a dead man.

Nearer, though somehow less threatening, two scrawny men stood flanking the tailgate, their heads reaching to the level of Gantry's thighs on either side of him. They stared vacant-faced into the group, assault rifles angled across their chests.

"Who drank the money?"

Mr. Squalatush's group numbered seventeen adults, among whom nine children lurked, sucking thumbs in their mothers' rough skirts. Of the five teenagers, one was plainly scared; another scuffed about behind the group, acting dangerously indifferent; while the only girl showed, too plainly, her fascination with one of the better looking mercenaries. She stole a string of furtive glances away to where he lay with his fellows, tossing her now and then a faintly sneered little wink, or, raising his head with sensuous eyes half closed, indolently blowing her a lazy hint of a kiss. The girl's mother looked the other way. The last two teenagers stared steadily at the assault rifles—Belgian FAL's—yearning to be also thus heroically equipped.

"Who drank the money?"

But among the seventeen adults there was consensus. Everyone, of course, knew who among them had gone to town, and been legless for days afterward. Sallow and embarrassed, they had returned one by one as each, separately, reached one hangover too many and their bodies said, enough. One—the most notorious of their beer fanatics—stayed to the very bottom of the bottle (and the very end of the money), sleeping in the gutter or the jail, whichever was available;

and he returned, days later, to add with bleary incredulity to their fund of stories of how the town was changed since the mercenaries had come. Why, there were ten, maybe even a dozen trucks called Ford there now; and there were also, he confided to Mr. Squalatush (who did not go, and was reprovingly dismayed) whores. He'd had, he triumphantly leered, the both of them—but could remember very little of either transaction.

There were a lot more than two whores, out in the shanty by the mercenaries' main base. There was beer, of course, but also rum and bourbon and a pinball machine.

One of the men took his money there, where he drank less copiously, less joyfully, and alone. He'd gone, thinking he'd beat up on his woman who had left him and meaning, with a sullen pointed pointlessness, to sleep afterward with other whores; but he found her so bruised and cowed already, he offered to take her home. She didn't come back. The money Congress had voted had ended in her pocket; she was hooked and high on that humanitarian aid.

And all of this was known, along with other beer-fogged and rumor-milled embellishments and inventions. All seventeen knew who'd done what, and all seventeen were in undiscussed but immediate and natural agreement that it was invidious to single out individuals. It was just the way some men were, and trying to change them—it was like asking the horse to lay eggs.

Moreover, the way they saw these things, it could be said that since those who didn't go didn't stop those who did, well, surely in that case, in a sense, they'd all drunk the money?

"That money," said Chester Gantry, "was not your money to drink. Nor was it mine. That money was the eternal property of the Ninth Church of Apostolic Redemption in the City of Angels, gathered up in God's Holy Name by good and Saved souls for your spiritual benefit, and held on this earth always and only in the Trust of Jesus Our Savior to further His Work. And you drank it."

The assembled group stared, impressed, at their toes.

"You drank that money," said Chester Gantry, "and that was Sinful." Then Mr. Squalatush saw Mr. Balbo stepping forward; and he began to be scared.

"As I understand it," said Mr. Balbo with a reasonable but, also, an ever-so-faintly disdainful degree of respect, "we are, Mr. Gantry, free men and not Communists, as you say the men who live in the south and the west are." He paused, having laid out a position—and it was only courtesy to await agreement on that position before proceeding together any further in conversation. But Gantry simply looked at him, and his eyebrows were raised impolitely.

Mr. Balbo continued; and the people stood quietly bow-shouldered behind him, suspecting, uneasily, that he might be leading into uncharted territory. He said, "I accept that we are not perfect people—but surely, aren't all God's people imperfect?"

In our own stories, thought Mr. Squalatush, even gods have failings, and suffer pride and conflict and misfortune. . . .

"But we are imperfect," Mr. Balbo went on, "because we're free. And if you or, as it may be, God, freely give us what at first you called aid—surely what is freely given us, is ours freely to do with as we please? Freely even, as we're not saints, to drink? We're not, Mr. Gantry, much used to money; we're poor, but it's been our habit to drink it when we have it—there's not much use in it otherwise. And if that's wrong, well, God, as you tell us, will judge us in his time."

"The time of the Lord," said Gantry, "is now." He put his right foot up onto the rim of the tailgate, and leaned forward with clasped hands and empty eyes to look down on Mr. Balbo. His voice was softer than ever as he continued. "I say to you, His Judgment is presently upon us; and time, as His Hour draws nigh, is short. So is it not then true—ask in your heart—that we must welcome Our Maker in our lives, and lose no precious second to do so? For if we do not, will we not surely be chastised?"

Behind him the *jefe* unfolded his crossed legs, stepped away from the cab of Ford, and strolled silently closer past one of the guards; his low-gaitered boots stroked through the dust. In front of Mr.

Balbo he pointed across the clearing and said, "That your hut over there? That your hovel, old man?" And when the old man said yes, he walked over and went inside it. There came a quiet clatter of possessions being randomly tossed about.

Gantry went on, with relentless smiling unction. "Is it not also true, that when we make peace in our hearts with His Son who is Our Sweet Savior and Lord Jesus Christ against that Awful Day—is it not then true that all we have becomes His? So that for all that we harbor and covet and keep and hide from Him, for all that is His that we misuse—such as money granted with His Love to buy the means to hear His Message—will we not then be punished for that keeping and misusing?"

"It might be true," said Mr. Balbo. He was quite calm, looking up at the American, though his white head shook a little with age. "Or then again," he said, "it might not. I wouldn't know."

"You doubt God's Word."

Mr. Balbo thought hard and then seemed, in spirit definitely, if not actually in his shoulders, to shrug. "I only doubt, which is my right as a man, that you alone may speak it."

The *jefe* came back, now standing directly below the American, right in front of Mr. Balbo. He held up as evidence Mr. Balbo's gun—an ancient musket which, if it had ever fought any Americans, had probably done so in the Spanish-American War. The *jefe* said, "Atheism is Communism."

Mr. Balbo began, "We're not discussing either—" But by then Scarskull had stepped forward, setting aside the old gun and drawing from its leather holster his Colt. Mr. Balbo seemed barely to resist. He was turned with a firm hand on one shoulder sideways around before the group and then pressed, peculiarly slowly, to his knees.

Jefe Scarskull set the barrel of the pistol against the back of the old man's head, and blew his brains out through his face onto the earth.

The dead body fell forward. The *jefe* stepped back in the silence, clicked the catch on the Colt, and returned it to its holster.

"Who," said the *jefe,* "drank the money?"

The only noise was the sudden scream of a monkey, answering echoes of the shot.

"You"—the *jefe* pointed at Serra, a haggard, chicken-faced father of four who looked, with the bags beneath his eyes, a likely candidate for the crime (the Sin). But before Serra could be further singled out (his eldest was only seven) Mr. Squalatush stepped forward. If he was, after Mr. Balbo, the oldest man there, then he should be next to speak up.

Hearing his voice shake, he said, "Mr. Balbo did not go to town. Mr. Balbo spent no money. . . ."

The *jefe* seemed about to step forward again; everything proceeded at the pace of dream. Mr. Squalatush saw where the seams in the man's combat jacket were here and there coming apart as his body, squat and muscled, moved in the sun like a lizard's. He saw the coffee-colored skin of his cheek and his chin all marred with scars—but Gantry reached down to touch the *jefe's* shoulder, and spoke absolution and instruction.

He said, "Leave it, Scarskull. We will not discuss it further. But you"—he gestured to Mr. Squalatush—"will now take charge and be responsible. We'll give money regularly, and you will, regularly, buy fuel for the generator so the television can work. You'll find, in town, that the supply's now steady—I've had a pump brought in. But then, as I've told you"—smiling—"we're here to help."

He was turning away when he added, "But in view of your transgression, God tells me you'll not get the video yet."

The mercenaries began laying out their forward base camp the following morning. Fit men and boys were informed that they were to help on this job; they'd be given, it was unspecifically promised, food for their work. There would, of course, be a chapel.

And the television began again. Its voice was a greasy clamor, staining the silence of the beautiful place where Mr. Squalatush and his people had lived, for so long, in peace.

2. ECTO VIII

Against a glimmering backdrop of stars near and far, the world is festooned with necklace upon necklace, tiara upon amulet of satellites—the planet's brooches, pinned to the mantle of gravity. They glide by in the crackling vacuum, spitting blipping gobbets of data. Here, watching Tyuratam, is Aquacade, successor to Trackman 2; there, monitoring the launches out of Plesetsk, two Rhyolites hang gleaming; and listen on this big Elint to the KGB man, lugubriously blackcoated, barreling down wide avenues in Moscow; he checks in with the wife on a Japanese car phone to ask what he's getting for dinner. Instruments measure and analyze; tapes turn, and lenses click.

You can see the Great Wall up here, and in the southwest, the plume of pollutant from the Four Corners power plant. On a dusty Sonora back road in cloudless desert, the naked eye picks out the speck of a truck, charging desperate at *el norte;* there's a pinprick of flame for one second when it hits the electric fences, explodes, rolls: more illegals, dead on the spic line.

The Chinese launch a Long March 3. It arcs up in the darkness, inviting contracts from Belgium, Australia, Iran. A fundamentalist satellite—but then there's this host of them already, hustlers rabid for the Lord, beaming prayer and propaganda at every state in God's own union and far beyond. He shall come, they say—hand on the book, finger stretched trembling at the camera, passionate beads of sweat under studio lights—He shall come with sword and flame, and the sky shall be fire. . . .

The big birds hang sparkling on the lip of the earth's gauze-lit drapery, shimmering where they turn, tossing sharp splashes and dry beams of brilliant reflected sun into the blackness. They are, these things, of the rarest minerals, of most precious alloys, of filaments of silicon and nuggets of plutonium, cosseted and sheathed in fine plastics and foils—a banquet of inorganics.

The spore that lands on Ecto VII has drifted for eons, aloft in galaxies of fire and cloudy gas for many times the lifetimes of planets. The gravest disasters of our midget world—our cataclysms and our wonders too—are mere dots, small as a border incident, beside the torments of matter and antimatter that the spore has negotiated. Fission and fusion, the births and deaths of suns, have tossed it imperiously through void upon void. It's been swept up, deflected, and flung through the nebulae like a stone from a sling-shot by the whirling heave, the centrifuge, centuries wide, of a black hole's catchment. It's been buffeted by explosions worth a billion volcanoes, and slept for eternities in the gulfs between stars. It's the size of a pea—and has wandered infinity past places, races, creatures unimaginable of iron and flame and stone. On high mountains and dry plains, in vast metal cities and over seas of inky, burning orange, in tempests of combustion and trackless deserts of green ice glinting with shadows beneath its path, blood and carbon were, forever, spilt and torched.

The spore passes Pluto, Saturn, Jupiter, and the cold far sun falls on its smooth dull shell. It finds our feeble gravity and bumps, with the faintest little clatter, into a solar power panel at the tip of one of Ecto's hydraulic wings.

It sticks there, warming to the scent of chemicals and compounds, of electrical action in glass neurons and synapses, in ganglions and optic fibers from Osaka and San Jose. Signals, pulsing from, to, and around the earth, activate the slow hard atoms of the dormant baby pebble thing inside it—and the rock beast, ever so gradually, is admitted to the conversation of men. Or, at least, he's admitted to game shows, weather channels, home shopping, soccer on Globewide, preachers, politicians, porn on 69, news, ads, coded spookspeak instructions for bombings and coups—the whole tacky clutter of the American psyche. . . .

Ecto VII hangs, geostationary, over the crumpled fabric of Mexico, covering the three quarters of a million square miles of that country and beyond to north and south—and is now home to the rock beast, coming alive and tuning in.

The arrival does not go entirely unnoticed. The satellite reports to a grass-topped dish-dotted bunker, tucked away at one end of the Kalero Megacorp's airstrip on the Stockton Plateau—and it reports, automatically, that swatch C47/2/01 on sun plate nine has become marginally misaligned. But when the telemetry comes in there's just the one tech on duty, and he's very bored. He knows, yawning, that there are thousands of those little dazzle-dappled swatches, guzzling sun energy; and always one or another, here and there, jolting fractionally out of true. So he files the data, unremarked and fast forgotten, under minor malfunctions, and goes back to the fashion tips in an out-of-date *GQ*.

In orbit, the beast grows slowly in his tiny spore, stretching its fabric, scraping with his hardening body mineral particles off the inside of the shell. As the flakes float about him, an ore-rich dust, he nibbles into them with a leisurely enjoyment. He feels stone veins warm and expand, rocky joints twisting and crackling into shape, flexi-metal thews bending into an Erector Set musculature; his fiery microheart stokes up with new reactions, and sends lava through chinking arteries skeined with most rare and sinewy crystal. He is tic sized—but will grow in layers and accretions of fantastical space matter, and will split open his shell—and then begin, thrilled and gleeful, to eat the wondrous fabrics of Ecto VII.

The preachers were repetitive and insistent; but Mr. Squalatush and his people soon gathered that it was obligatory to watch them all the same and at least to talk, whatever you believed, as if you acceded to their message. Some, of course, really did come to believe it—which was disruptive, because they came to mistrust each other and even when they could talk freely, now argued. One would say, I'm Saved—and then others would ask, from what?

From all the bad people in the world, maybe—because the world, said the shows, "right through to here in our backyards, right to the core of every gatherin' of the foetus-murderin' *lib-rulls*," was riddled with all kinds of bad people, with infidels and heretics, with Communists and fellow travelers and generally Libyan and I-raynian kinds of people—as a result of which, making ready for the millennial confrontation was, they said, very much now the order of the day.

The television was called Hitachi, and it brought to the settlement a regular roster of preachers. One such was the Rev. Jose Lee Pepsi, of the Calvary Elected on the Gabriel River Freeway (hard by, as he often pointed out, the Los Alamitos Naval Air Station, where our boys were making ready whether you were or not). And Jose Lee, he had a making-ready speech he'd rock into like an F-14 off an aircraft carrier.

The speech ran, at first steadily rising in volume and pace between tense, spit-dripping intakes of breath, "Oh, yay, for I say He shall come, He shall come among us from on high, and in His Hand shall be a shining sword to cleave our darkness asunder, and on His Head shall be a radiant crown of His blinding heavenly charisma to light His way, yay, and I say"—his voice dropped to an apocalyptic whisper; droplets of sweat bobbled with quaking urgency on his upper lip—"He shall come. He shall come. He shall come, and we must, oh, yay"—he flung back his head, neck writhing with sinew and tendon, eyes closed and lids fluttering in ecstasy and abandon, the voice a screeching appeal—"*lay bare*, I say *lay bare* our very souls, I say *chisel off* the very *barnacles of iniquity* on the keel of our being...." Jose Lee gasped, panted, paused; put trembling, out-stretched fingers to his shining temples and muttered, sublimely incoherent, "Oh, thank you, Lord—I hear you now—you shall come—I welcome you, *thank* you, Lord." Jose opened his eyes; he smiled abruptly and winningly at you, the viewer, as if clicking from a trance; and proceeded in a voice now calmed and unctuous, "Well. Well, well—truly it is well. Truly"—he shook his head in humble wonderment—"Truly I am blessed, for Jesus speaks through me. I say He was with me—just right there now He was with me—and He wants you to call this number...."

And as Jose Lee gave his toll-free, Mr. Squalatush was several times heard to mutter under his breath, "Jesus, who needs it?"

Gods, said Mr. Squalatush, were in his experience firstly plural, not singular—and secondly, not remotely interested in the dead rising from their graves, in skies of fire patrolled by awesome hosts of angel militia, in Final Battles for Jerusalem or any other damn place. Gods, said Mr. Squalatush, hung out in organs of the body, in your crops, in trees and flowers, or in the homes of pregnant women. They could, certainly, be frightening if they took up residence in a jaguar or in a storm; or they could equally well be truant and mischievous, distracting you from your purpose to be their fool, leading you lost and astray around the forest a while until they tired of the game, and gave you at dusk your path back home.

And at other times they could be dancers and magicians, pulling from nature's false-backed cabinet a spray of plumage, an eruption of orchids, a prism hanging in the waterfall's haze. Sometimes, said Mr. Squalatush, after it rained, the air in the soaked-through canopy was dense with mist and steam, with fragrant motes of dislodged and drifting bark and pollen; the greens of the leaves were glossy and multitudinous from lime to emerald, from dragonfly to jade, from chili to cornstalk; and everything waited in a suspenseful pause, waited to be sure that the rain was truly past and not teasing—until clouds cleared, mist lifted—and then, there! the first shaft of sun burst through, and then another, and then another, great pillars of opaque and glowing light swirling with insects, flashing off the leaves, spreading through the green of the canopy a translucent wash of sparks in flame red, purple, richest blue, until it grew so bright you could barely look on it, and the chorus in your ears of birds and monkeys grew wild, exultant—and those were the times that the gods came with gauzy wings and silver manes down the sunbeams, a soundless torrent of illuminated joy. Mr. Balbo once claimed he had seen a man rise weightless like a spirit full thirty feet skyward off the ground, when the world at such a moment had made him so happy. But then, they had shot Mr. Balbo.

And they babbled on Hitachi . . .

And the weather grew more changeable. The river ran crazy at Rapido Pansik, and, it was told, on the coast there'd been snow— unimaginable flowers of white falling for the first time ever until, the next day, things flipped over and the sky fried off the wet with a hotter heat than most people could remember. . . . If He comes, thought Mr. Squalatush, He'll not much like what He finds.

He sat, grumpy and bored and begrudging his time, in front of Hitachi.

"For all our fellow Christians in the Isthmus, a big welcome, and here's some great news. . . ." The woman announcing was shiny as a well-polished apple, and her smile was relentless. If a butcher had garrotted a lamb on the occasional table by her knees, that smile wouldn't have shifted one inch.

The news was that Kalero Megacorp, that great exemplar of the American way of life, had recently launched a new satellite, Ecto VII, and among its many other duties and functions, Ecto VII could now relay more efficiently than ever before from the City of Angels to you, the blessed viewer, the best and the latest on the Good Lord's intentions.

Then there was a chunk of corporate PR, the voice-over much

obsessed with the Lord's miracle gift to us of His technology. And the outcome of all this, Mr. Squalatush realized with mounting dismay, was that there could now be not half an hour, but two whole hours nightly of the Good Lord's Word. The prospect was appalling; and meant, also, a big hike in the fuel bills.

The settlement was fast learning the many wonders of a cash-based economy. The store established by Mr. Gantry's mission sold a great number of things never before seen in the region. There were fertilizers and pesticides, tools and torches, Bibles and prayer books, and soft drinks in such numbers it threatened the trade of the town's two bars. It was said, also, that if you looked right and asked right there were guns in the back room, and cocaine. And, of course, there was the gas pump; above all, there was credit.

It fast became clear that the money Gantry gave was not sufficient for the purchase of the supplies his regimen made necessary. Apart from running the generator to watch TV, they were now also expected to learn the use of pen and paper; which they would, of course, have welcomed, had it not involved the constant copying down of improving tales from the pamphlets the TV promoted. And the acquisition of these and other things was only possible through the creation of debt.

The last time Gantry came, he told them how they stood, economically, in relation to the mission store. They stood, it transpired—he was as persuasive an accountant as he was sinister when preaching— near fifty dollars short. With interest, he said, at the local wage rates, that made twenty-five man-days of labor. Except they'd also need boots and packs—which they could have at a discount of, say, an extra five days' worth of work.

And it was thus that Mr. Squalatush and his people became the mercenaries' mules, trekking for weary days in the wake of their murderous incursions.

Gantry wasn't seen again, though rumors of his appearing from time to time around the neighboring provinces were spread in the town with the whispered furtiveness of a ghost story. But Dandy Royle, when he came, was an altogether better proposition.

Dandy rolled past the mercenary camp—which now like a cuckoo's chick had grown to dwarf its host, spreading wire perimeters, locked stores, and drill grounds into the forest—and pulled up in the center of the original settlement. Ignition off, he sat back, slapped his palm down on the door through the pickup's open window, and said with feeling, "Whoo-ee. Yoh. Hah. Ho-o-la."

He looked about him at the gathering and curious children; he leaned away inside the cab, rummaged in a cooler, fished out a beer, and snapped off the ring pull with a swift casual twist. Then he paused, opened the truck door, and said, "Well hi, y'all." After stepping down he bowed and went on, "After-sales service, at yo' service. So would ya kindly show me to yo' ee-quipment?"

Dandy was large, young, cheerful, black, and permanently distracted throughout the time of his visit—not least because he smoked voluminous quantities of the mercenaries' grass. He was, he told Mr. Squalatush, a Kalero tech just come to make sure that their gear worked right. And he'd brought, to their enormous delight, a video machine. They couldn't keep it, he explained—it was his personally, he ported it around all the Isthmus ground stations for nights, he said, when he couldn't find good programs beaming down out the sky—but they were welcome to watch with him, if they so desired, any choice they wished from among the tapes he also carried.

Mr. Squalatush therefore asked him, would he not be watching the preachers?

"You kidding?" said Dandy Royle. "Hey look—you tune in to something worth watching, sure, I'll watch. But don' give me no preacher shit, no way—I mean, don't tell no one, old guy, but me, man, I'm a *Darwinist*."

The subtleties of this last piece of information escaped Mr. Squalatush. He was intrigued, instead, at the dawning realization that it was possible to adjust Hitachi and, as a result, watch other and entirely different material. So he asked Mr. Royle would he show them how Hitachi was tuned; which Mr. Royle set promptly about doing with a whistle, a hoot, and a fresh can of beer.

He found them Globewide Satsport—and, with a happiness from which suspicion soon evaporated, they got glued to the soccer. The Kalero-Globewide Football Fest, at which the Hispania Cup would be contested, was just then imminent—the people of the settlement were enthralled. Mr. Squalatush, in particular, found the soccer quite exhilarating, and watched the buildup with a singular intensity.

With time they grew adventurous, and became channel hoppers. Royle explained to them that their dish—a product, said a little plaque, of Vidivici (Field) Inc.—wasn't geared to pick out too many signals; and those transponders up there were anyhow, he said, busy-busy. But still, they pinned down a soap or two, and a weather channel; and the Globewide signal was clear.

Now to those among the group who'd decided, either wholeheartedly or tactically, that they were Saved, these backsliding joyrides round the airwaves were the acts of shameful orgiasts. To Mr. Squalatush and others, however, they not only provided viewing that was altogether more congenial and entertaining, but also, unexpectedly, made possible a more friendly level of contact with the mercenaries. The soccer—provided of course that you supported, as the mercenaries did, the California Squad—was a way to sit down with them, without thinking all the time they might kill you.

From Tripoli to Islamabad, they were waving nukes in each other's faces like there was no tomorrow. And maybe there wasn't . . . the tele-priests were greatly excited. The Nile, they avowed, was drying up; there was famine and a plague of locusts—He shall come. . . .

In the settlement, they were rather more relaxed—especially after Mr. Squalatush asked Dandy, "Where's Mr. Gantry preach now?"—and Dandy let slip a new datum.

He said, "Shit, old guy, Gantry ain't no preacher—he's a Kalero high up, he's top zeck, he only do that preacher thing on vay-cay-tion—it's the way the man *relaxes.*"

And Chester Gantry was sitting, right then, in a bunker on the Stockton Plateau, viewing the latest strange footage from the cameras on Ecto VII. . . .

Dandy, red-eyed, with a beer in his hand, tuned Hitachi into Globewide. Jose Lee, tonight, would have to settle for being taped—because it was, tonight, the announcement of the California Squad's team for the first game in the first round of the soccerfest.

They gathered around, and up it came:

CALIFORNIA

Archimedes

Zero   De Souza   Petulan   El Foco

Garrapatal   ?   Capistrano   Flor

Volcan   Chiriqui

proud to be supported by
Kalero (Holdings) Inc.

Approval was expressed with a collective sigh of anticipation at the selection of Volcan and Chiriqui, the two Andean goal scorers—a pair known popularly as "the eagle and the ghost." Studio discussion, meanwhile, focused with relish on the choice of El Foco, the once-Venezuelan *libero* and hit man who now played in San Diego. It was said he carried a list in a black book of every striker he might meet; and marked against their names symbols for the split heads, wrecked ankles, or twisted balls he wrought when they did meet. He was a card, that El Foco.

But the big story was, of course, the question mark. The defense was hard as iron, and the attack was sharp as knives—switchblade fast—but the team lacked a maestro in the middle, a midfield commander to run the play. So the question was: would Singani fall to the inducements and take a citizen permit?

The rest of the squad had all long ago done that, shipping extended families up across the Hispanic line on five- or (if their agents were good enough) even ten-year passes—and depriving in the process one colony after another of the cream of its teams. South of the line they called it theft; in California they called it the operation of the free market.

But Singani, the master playmaker, had not, as yet, agreed to cross the line, and still played for the Torreon Titans—even though there was now on the table, to bring him over, not only a house in Carmel, but a restaurant too. Still, it was widely assumed that even at this late stage he would surely go over, get instantly naturalized—and that the California squad would, as a result, then walk through the soccerfest. After all a permit, said the mercenaries, was like the virgin in the best room in the brothel.

Satsport—"brought to you by Kalero, we're all the world needs"—trailed an interview with Singani on this issue of the day, "right after these words." But then a drug flight went over, a small plane, a low quick shadow above the treetops, and Hitachi lost the signal. There was a general groan; people kicked out their feet from under them, stood, and meandered away as, despite all Dandy's prods and twiddles, Hitachi stubbornly refused to relocate the signal and sat, blandly hissing, on its duckboard.

Dandy found a cop show, but the signal was lousy and the picture murky. He said, "There must be a lot of activity tonight"—and there was, indeed, a lot of movement in the mercenary compound; they could hear *Jefe* Scarskull barking orders—then, inadvertently, he tuned to the preachers' channel. The station ident sat stationary on the screen:

Coming next on the Love Beam

The Right Rev. & Blessed
JOSE LEE PEPSI

in Jesus' name
call
213-555-2000

The background was a bright queasy video pink. Dandy's face where he knelt in the colorwash off the screen was dismal, pallid; when he stood, his grin was a crimson crack in the shadows under the awning. The generator hummed further off in the night; and they heard, faintly, gasps from the forest where the mercenary lover boy had his pre-sortie way with the girl who'd once admired him. Dandy, resigned, stepped back from Hitachi, between a couple of the Saved who'd waited, in hope of watching just this; he pulled a joint from his pocket and lit it, a flare burning round his face, then shrugged and said, "Well, sock it to me, Jose Lee."

Fanfare. Lights. An orgasmic choral outburst:

Feel His love, how sweet it is,
His love thrusts in and makes me whole,
Feel His love, how sweet it is,
His love jets out and fills my soul.

Jose Lee danced down the steps at the back of the stage past the howling choir and arrived at a trot into the living room set, where acolytes and assorted assistant charismatics lounged in beatific expectation. He wore his white shirt open and his sleeves rolled up, showing a chinking-clunking mass of gold chains, gold bracelets, gold medallions—even the frames of his spectacles were gold—and the applause was tumultuous; welcoming whoops and hosannas rang around the audience. He held up his hands to still the noise; he cocked his head in a greeting wink to the camera; he said, "We-e-ell, whoo-ha!—don't Jesus love that gospel salsa?" (Cries of Yay! Amen!) "And yoh!—ain't Jesus with us here tonight?" (Hallelujah! Praise Him!) "And are we gonna put your soul in touch with the Sweet Lord Jesus Our Savior tonight? I say, we are! I say, we are! Whoo! Hey now, Bob, Claymore, Esmee, Mary-Jill, how ya doin'?" Jose passed around the sofas clasping hands, embracing—Mary-Jill's cheeks glistened with tears of joy. "Oh Mary-Jill," he gasped, and his eyes shone out over a vision of silicon-and-surgical loveliness, "how fine, Mary-Jill, how sweet it is to have you among us." He paused, he turned on his mark, the director cued in the close-up camera, and Jose's face grew dark with shame at the Evil One— "because I can tell you people, Mary-Jill was in the pit—ain't that so, Mary-Jill?"

Cut to Mary-Jill sobbing convulsive at the memory on the sofa, repeating and repeating, "Oh, I was, I was, I was in the pit but now praise Him I am Saved."

"And I say to you, Mary-Jill was in the pit, Mary-Jill was low in a life of iniquity, I say to you this girl's sweet lips had sunk to slobber at the very staff of Evil, this girl's being was spotted and stained and writhing in lustful perversion in the grasp of Beelzebub the Wanton—and yet see now" (he turned to her) "she is Saved" (she rose) "see now" (he opened wide his arms) "Jesus fills her with His Love" (she fell into his embrace; cue close-up on Jose with trembling lips speaking to you personally from the heaving shoulder of the Saved Mary-Jill, *pianissimo*) "and I say to you He shall come, He shall come. . . ."

"He shall come," mimicked the stoned Dandy Royle, "and in His bank shall be all yo' money, and in His garage fifteen fine vee-hicles, and in yo' wife He shall come. . . ."

All around the clearing it was jet dark now. The forest was a deep, shifting shape all about them. Away at the compound, the big wire gates rattled open, and a vanguard squad came out toward the settlement. Their steps were a slow-growing whisper through dust and grass. "This place," said Dandy, "it's like a place where dead people live. I'm for the hammock."

He moved away into the night. Mr. Squalatush turned back to Hitachi and saw Jose Lee and all his paraphernalia abruptly vanish from the screen. "He shall come"—*click*. But the TV wasn't dead, nor yet was it reverted to the normal dud gray-white buzz of a lost signal, because some new sort of signal was there—and Hitachi was suddenly radiant, energized, glaring white. Then, slowly, it gave an amazing sigh of enormous pleasure, a deep, unsteady exhalation, a sound like the loose, pattering slide of scree, rocks clacking and slipping against each other; and when the words came, the voice, ample and low, was like the echo of stone splitting far away in dark caves.

Grown to fist size, the rock beast, wriggling his delighted tungsten miniteeth into the juicy filigree, the caviar alloys of an Ecto VII transponder, had realized that his now half-inch-wide mouth was wrapped around the signal to some ground station down there. He could talk to these guys, and no problem—he had fluent Spanish, albeit of a televisual nature, acquired off all the signals he'd grown up listening to. So he said—roughly translated—"Well confiscate my rosary if this ain't the *strangest* long distance you *ever* did receive. . . ."

Mr. Squalatush stared, bright lit by the glowing television, at this extraordinary mystery. Working overtime, his head went hunting an explanation: If gods hang out in trees and animals, then presumably they hang out in machinery too; this is, ergo, a tech spirit here; this is a new god come to talk to me on TV. . . .

The rock beast said, "Hey now! Nice to be with you people! And let me tell you, I will be down off this thing to make close friends with you all just as soon as I can."

He shall come, thought Mr. Squalatush.

The sound of the approaching squad's boots grew louder, crossing the clearing now from behind the other side of Hitachi.

The rock beast realized he was only sending down words, when these people needed picture data too. He paused and did a head sift through all the signals whizzing around him; a zillion silicate brain cells shuffled and sorted in a binary mayhem. The airwaves, it struck him, were awash with half-dressed women—if that's what they wanted, let 'em have it—he sent down an image of a stockinged temptress, and wondered how that'd go down.

He shall come, thought Mr. Squalatush, in the form a porn queen?

Jefe Scarskull pulled the wire out the back of Hitachi, and Mr. Squalatush blinked in the sudden silent dark. The *jefe* had two flashlights—he tossed one to Mr. Squalatush. "OK, old man, no more preachers for now—I want five carriers. Round 'em up and get your backpacks—we're gonna go shoot shit out of that Commie El Coco, just the same way we done it last year. We leave in half an hour. So be ready."

Before they pulled out for El Coco—Mr. Squalatush's bowlegs half buckling under the weight of all that nonlethal aid—the old man made sure to slip out from the video the tape they'd set up to record Jose Lee. Because if a god could appear on TV, he could, presumably, be rerun on video. . . .

The rock beast sensed that the connection was broken; he shrugged, and clicked off elsewhere around the satellite on his dainty quartz talon toes, sniffing out new metal tastes, and randomly tuning in, as he went, to news of the soccerfest. Singani, he noted, had not yet made up his mind.

3. EL COCO

You couldn't say Charlie Fish actually *hated* soccer—he was, in every way, too nice a guy to hate anything in particular. He felt for the game, instead, just a dull and melancholy aversion; and if the reason for this was perhaps not reasonable, it was at least understandable, and simple enough.

The last time he'd made love with Suzie, his on–off lover of some years—a mournful, sweet, and valedictory coupling—Singani'd been running rings around some hapless team of Anglos on the silent screen behind them, where they lay by the fire on his living room floor. So the game was associated, in his mind, with that loss—with his long failure, as he saw it, to wean her from her cherished bad habits of criminality and shady dealing and to make of her (he was, in so many ways, peculiarly old-fashioned) a respectable woman. Now, when he saw soccer, he ached.

It had been, of course, a doomed enterprise—the more stuffy he got, the further she drew away. Eventually, as he came close to thirty, he made one last, almost consciously hopeless play for some commitment on her part: He bought a house, and asked her to share it with him. She came around to inspect it—it was a cozy terraced two-story on the border between Traderstown and the Heart—and she announced, with characteristically brutal simplicity, that tonight would be their last evening together. The invitation had, finally, driven her away.

She was not unkind—in her own way, she felt sad for him too, that he had (in her eyes) grown older than his years, with his misplaced integrity—but like she'd told him, again and again: There was no room in Dollarville for decency. And if he couldn't take her the way she was—free, reckless, a nighttime operator of scams and backhanders, a girl who ran with the times, and rarely did good without first thinking through the fun factor, the profit, and PR—then he couldn't have her at all.

They settled up their affair warm and naked by the fire; he felt that even the termination of their relationship was conducted with all the coded, fix-it finesse of some black market arrangement. On the television from half a world away, Singani danced across the Astroturf, foxing his way through the tackles, looking up and then, effortless, stroking long passes inch-perfect to the feet of his frontmen stalking like big cats through the panicky herd of the opposition's defense.

On the field of his heart she'd stepped that lightly for years, making similarly graceful incisions—and Charlie Fish couldn't bear, anymore, to watch the game that he'd loved as a younger man.

Suzie had been tall, blonde, strong, striking; when he'd first seen her in Clubland he'd been awestruck. He was a big man himself, and together they'd looked like angels. But the bar where first they met, like too many others, was owned by the man she called her godfather, the man named Grief—for whom she worked, she said, as his lieutenant, his facilitator, his chameleon girl.

Shifting Grief's gangland consignments of drugs, of stolen hootch, pirate videos and car stereos, of forged concert tickets and counterfeit transit passes for all the cantons of Dollarville, she was unpindownable, vanishing like a ghost around the town from one disguise to the next. She could be Asian or black or Hispanic, she could be Miriam Patajoli in the morning, and Consuela Hernandez after noon; but whoever she was, as Grief thrived, she was less and less Charlie's—if she'd ever been his at all.

He tried to tell himself the break was, therefore, for the best—but that, of course, was a bitter joke. Her parting words, said with sorrow in his doorway as the security electronics went *peep-peep, peep-peep,* echoed now every evening in his empty little house. "You're boring," she told him.

"I'm honest," he told her.

"And you're broke."

It was true that Charlie Fish wasn't a guy well-equipped to make big money. But Jimmy Baines was loyal, and the work Jimmy passed him kept Charlie, barely, solvent. So in the wake of Suzie's exit, he was glad when Jimmy offered him a free working holiday—a research trip to the Isthmus.

They were at a PR party in the Big Aloha. Charlie had written the videowall elements of Jimmy's client's presentation. The client was a manufacturer of garden tools—and in among the surfboards dangling from the ceiling, the profusion of plastic palms growing from piles of sand on the varnished board floors, the jukeboxes artfully concealed in the wrecks of crashed cars in the corners, there were now lawnmowers, strimmers, weeders, pruners, hedgecutters and chain saws making mayhem in thunderous close-up, an orgy of toppling vegetation on screens all around the room. Against a thumping background of manly electro-beat, Charlie's scripts for these products praised them extravagantly on a vigorous bass voice-over. On the videowall—sixteen monitors set up four by four behind the dais where the speakers made their pitch—weeds were mashed, long grass shredded, debris chopped, and hedges shattered, while models bearing cocktails passed among the crowds of buyers from the garden centers, and the speakers boomed and thudded, extolling "power at your fingertips," "robust performance," "the quality you need at a price you'll like."

There was something rather desperate about the whole event, and the gray sacks under the eyes of both buyers and sellers showed it. It had been a dog of a summer, the worst in memory, and in hardly a garden Charlie knew of had a weed or a flower survived through the parching glare of the rainless months. In his own garden, he'd been forced to emergency measures, building what was virtually an oxygen tent to keep his herbs alive. Still, business must go on. Charlie stared around the cavernous smoky room, watching the men in their suits weaving through what the place's decor leaflets described as "Resortiana"; their faces reflected palsied shades of lime and emerald off the hyperactive massacre of greenery on the screens.

Jimmy arrived beside him at the bar. After ordering a drink, removing from it a froth of paper umbrellas, plastic monkeys, and logo-topped swizzle sticks, and then downing it in one, he said, "Hey, Charlie. How d'you fancy a trip to the Isthmus?"

It was, he said, like this. The summer might well have been a monster; but it couldn't last for ever and there'd be winter soon enough. And after a summer like this, what might *that* be like? So, said Jimmy, the travel operators were gearing up with new deals for the coming season—and he just happened to have an interesting little outfit come in the doors of his office at Vidivici PR the other day. They wanted the works, the whole package—a conference, a promo video, literature, ads. "You interested?"

As he started briefing his old friend about the job, Jimmy felt a familiar pang of mildly irritated worry. It wasn't that Charlie'd never written for the travel trade before—he was an efficient scribbler, he could make any old dreck sound good if he had to—but that the boy, instead, had an inexplicable problem. If he thought a job was sleazy, he'd actually been known to *turn the work down.* . . .

Jimmy, right now, had deadlines that wouldn't wait while Charlie had a tussle with his conscience. For sure, Jimmy was a man who thought, whatever else, you should stand by your friends; but sometimes, this particular friend didn't make that too easy. Still, you try. He ordered more drinks and laid out the background.

Tourism, he said, had topped 10 percent of all world trade and was still climbing—the range, the variety, the fantastical inventiveness of the holidays on offer to the monied of Dollarville was staggering. There were sport holidays, wildlife jaunts, amusement parks, gambling blowouts, and sex safaris; and now an intriguing new niche market developed by a handful of thrillingly go-ahead young entrepreneurs whose tag line was, "As close to reality as you dare to go."

You had really to be the devil-may-care type to buy in on these trips; it was danger for kicks. At the top end of the market, through the tinted windows of four-wheel drives and light planes, the rich men of Dollarville watched the poor of other places scratch through huge and eroded landscapes, the earth broken and bleached by battle and weather. You heard boasts over dinner of the deserts, famines, migrations, the murdered places they'd visited, of the disused dams and airports from the development days that they planned, casually, to drop in on next season. Suffering had become a spectator sport. And even the just relatively wealthy—Group B kinds of people like Charlie Fish—could now buy in on it, economy class.

The obvious markets were already sewn up. Any hot spot that combined with its Thrill Appeal some outstanding scenery—the Andean conflicts, or the moonscapes of central Asia—had quickly got pricy; while Africa, for exotic pain, was in a class (and a price bracket) all its own. People with sketchier incomes, therefore, came into the market with the second-rung outfits. And it was these people that Jimmy's new clients now wanted to reach.

They were a tour operator called Frontline Ricochet, and they were investing their attentions on the Isthmus because—said the marketing plan—for scenic splendors and the odd dash of an impressive ancient culture or two, the region was undervalued, and its potential underexploited. Above all, its wars were small, complex, fragmented, unpredictable, and generally maintained at the precise kind of low intensity that made them perfect for tourists: i.e., dangerous, but only a bit. After all, where's your profit if half your customers don't come back? There are limits to these things. You don't parachute people into the very heart of the conflict; the insurance costs would be debilitating. You just put them on the watchtowers around the edge. . . .

Jimmy had a feeling that Charlie was curling his lip. He looked around the sweaty room at the lurching buyers beneath the blaring screens and wondered whether maybe, after all, he should have taken this job to a different hack.

But if Charlie didn't look like he was paying the fullest or most enthusiastic attention, it was only because he was reading the company's old brochure that Jimmy had laid before him on the bar. It said, "For the person who can take it to the brink—for the people not scared to say, I was there when the fighting was fierce—come see the lovely Isthmus—and feel the truth, naked and untamed, about the way men are."

"Sure," said Charlie Fish. "I'll do it." He could use a week away from his empty house.

Jimmy thought aloud, and spoke aloud, over the howl of a flotilla of lawn mowers advancing in serried ranks across the videowall. "Charlie, if you're bothered, you know, selling holidays where the attraction's watching third worlders out killing each other—"

"Look, Baines, I ain't Francis of Assisi—I'll do the job. I could use a break." He asked, "Is it any more crazy than selling lawn mowers in a drought? When can you get me the passes, the paperwork?"

Jimmy shrugged. "Tomorrow, the next day at the latest—the schedule's tight, we need this turned around fast."

So Charlie Fish got on a plane to the Isthmus, not so much a saint, after all, as just an ordinary guy, with an ordinary broken heart.

He clenched his teeth through the hollow-gutted fear of the take-off—planes these days fell from the sky like rain—and he only slowly relaxed as they settled at cruising speed, and the pilot reported on the turbulence to come. He lay back in his seat, trying to forget the hours of hunched discomfort ahead, the gracelessness of air travel—and remembered then how, one autumn, back when transit out of Dollarville had been easier to come by, he and Suzie had gone hop picking. He remembered how the tiny barbs on the stems of the big plants stung your skin. . . .

On the in-flight entertainment screens, they were interviewing Singani again; he'd still not made up his mind about crossing over to California, as the Hispania Cup loomed. Charlie shut his eyes and went resolutely to sleep.

The brochure he'd read in the bar, and which it was now his job to research and update, made many bold promises—but the nub of the matter was that Frontline Ricochet would guarantee you authentic danger, and all the genuine discomforts of life in a war zone.

The holiday, thought Charlie, at five-thirty in a chill and damp dawn, sure lives up to the promise. The sound that had woken him was mortar fire.

He lay fully clothed beneath thin blankets on an inch of foam mattress atop a bare cement floor. His mouth was dry fur; around the rest of his body, in his joints and on his neck and in the base of his hair, he felt that grubby, cold-sweat tingle—too much cerveza last night; too much Flor de Cano. You've got, after all, to have fun on vacation.

For hours while they drank, the rain had come down like thunder in the dark, in unrelenting torrents. Along the sides of the yard, instant waterfalls went skidding off the corrugated roof through the broken, rust-gaping gutter, crashing in jets onto the mud and the concrete—and the soaking air had roared. Through open shutters in the glassless window frame, Charlie, sitting up, now saw bony chickens pecking at the banks of the great pools that had collected while he slept.

His fellow venturers slept on. The mortars were an unsteady muttering of small dull cracks and thumps around the hills above the village, a tinny and inadequate noise if you compared it to the rain; but, he thought with forced bravery, a noise he'd have to get used to—after all, it was his own fool notion to take this job.

Aching, he wormed up from his blankets and went out in his socks onto the front veranda. He held his boots, the zips and buckles tinkling, in one hand. Outside, he leaned against the wall and hitched them on; they were artfully prescuffed gray leather with sharp-pointed toes and had looked, in the Mode Zone back in Dollarville, quite perfectly mean. Here, they were merely ridiculous—an object among the peasants of disbelieving, politely derisive admiration. But then, he felt ridiculous all over. He wore a white safari jacket, also bought specially so that he could look and feel, on this trip, like the daredevil reporter he'd dreamed of being when he was a kid. "This is Charlie Fish, on the Isthmus front line"—asking to get shot at because you can hear his boots a mile off, and his jacket shines out in the forest like a Mercedes in a Mud Alley slum. . . .

He settled down on the duckboard porch and watched the lightening sky. The little town was Quilali, on the so-called Communist side of the border; and its main street in front of him—a rutted dirt strip more used to horses than to vehicles—had been churned into an inches-deep morass by the rain. Two girls came stepping through it toward him, both with the stretching lankiness of early teenage—one had a rifle. They smiled when he nodded hello.

He asked, "What's the gun for?"—and felt immediately idiotic as if he'd asked, in a restaurant, what the cutlery did.

"I borrowed it," said the taller girl. It swung, long and unfamiliar in her thin hand, the shoulder strap trailing on slick earth—and she gestured loosely back toward the militia office, where a man in rough uniform waved lazily from a rocking chair on the porch then let his face fall back beneath the peak of his cap. The mortars chuntered on, intermittent.

The other girl told him, "It's for school. We're doing a play; the teacher wrote it." She shrugged. "It's not loaded." But then they got coy, and turned away to go and act in their play. And what would it be about? About mortars making ripples and rents in the surface of the now-blue sky above wet, gray-green hills and gouged valleys; and about being poor—Charlie shuddered with the cold, it was supposed to be bloody tropical here—in a world where the rich, no longer content with messing you about from afar, now paid hard money, as well, to come on holiday and inspect the results. . . .

The pickup arrived to collect his little group, and they went bouncing away down the ruts through the scrub; it grew denser as they went, and soon became forest. The guard who sat on the tailgate held his AK-47 lightly in his lap. Charlie's rice and beans breakfast churned sullen in his gut. It ain't, he thought, no school play now.

Top of today's itinerary was El Coco, a cooperative maybe sixty kilometers from Quilali. Fifteen months back the mercenaries had attacked it—coming down in the night, killing the older men, and kidnapping the young. An alert watch had got the women and children away—but it was reported by the Ricochet rep, with promotional relish, that the genitals of the men who stayed and died had been parted from their corpses. Also, worksheds, machinery, a makeshift clinic were all torched; and slogans were daubed on one surviving wooden wall in blood. They spoke of freedom.

El Coco, beyond San Bartolo, Panali, Las Parcelas—which had itself been raided only recently—was at the furthest edge of safety. The rep leaned forward and called, over the noise of their passage, "You'll sure get your money's worth this morning." Charlie tried to ignore him. Paranoid, he'd grown convinced that the rep was CIA. He had a crew cut and, in the capital, kept grousing at the price of vegetables—but he was plenty high now. "There's been a whole shitload of activity around these valleys the last few days," he happily told them. He was like a boat captain, Charlie thought, telling clients the fish were biting.

And death here, he thought, has so many tools at his disposal. He could be knife meat or virus prey; he could go down any number of ways. He was uncomfortable—the hard, ribbed metal of the wheel cover banged remorselessly at his coccyx as they rode through fords, went jolting over rain-filled trenches and holes, over stones and rocks, and around alarming steep turns. On the track into Quilali he'd seen a sign on the precipice roadside: "19 vehicles have gone over this edge since Christmas. Don't be the 20th." But a militiaman told him later, "There's been three more gone over since they put that up." It was drivers volunteered from the capital, he said, handling unfamiliar trucks on unknown and slippery trails, spooked with fear of the bullet hurtling suddenly their way, seeing rocks flash at night in their beams and thinking it's muzzle fire, hearing bazooka in every backfire of the worn old engine—and they never even saw the sign; just put their feet down and slewed into the void.

They came down into El Coco off the flank of a high ridge-topped rise. There wasn't much to see. To their left where they stopped, work brigades were knocking prefabbed wooden housing together—"a Gift from Sweden"—in the shade of a sparse grove. The rep, jumping down first as the pickup pulled up, went to talk with the project foreman, who leaned macho on his axe haft, one foot planted by the head of the axe on a severed tree stump. Charlie looked about him; his four companions in adventure stood, stretched, creaked, exchanged small nervous laughs, and clambered down after the rep.

Beyond the grove and the miniature house frames, the compound was a flat, cleared area of scrubby grass. Charlie rolled over the tailgate, dropping lightly onto wet earth—he was a big man, but far from graceless—then he walked away, toward the center of the clearing. It was about the size of a soccer field; and in its middle there stood against the skyline, totemic, the charred carcass of a burnt-out tractor, part keeled over on its broken back axle.

From the dismally kitsch-gothic aspect of its rusted and tilting cabin, stranded beneath a wide sky of low gray clouds, he half expected to find—as in a movie—a skeleton marooned in death on the rotted foam and leather of the driver's seat; but as he came near, he only saw the odd bullet hole: sharp-edged circles punched through the metal. Sighing into the sky, he leaned against the ruined machine—he had a sudden sense of it being as eloquent in its testi-

mony as Ozymandias—and was then distracted by voices from the
further end of the clearing.

Turning past the wreck, he saw a clutch of old lean-tos, ramshackle but reassuring; figures moved about between them, clothes
were hung on a line, and behind them other people came and went
over the far lip of the ground. Charlie, crossing in their direction,
saw trees growing dense where the ground sloped away and the forest began—and he also saw one taller person among the moving
people, a Western girl. Hands in his pockets, looking away at the
hillsides to either side—the sense of danger and exposure made the
place feel peculiarly silent, and the voices carried to him as if thinly
echoing in an airless chamber—he went, sauntering, to log on to an
authentic, real-live-war-zone conversation.

"I'm only asking you to pretend."

The girl had a pair of cameras clack-clacking around her neck.
Two men, campesinos, sat in front of her on a rough bench, exhib-
iting embarrassed and uncertain smiles. Part shy but also, it seemed
to Charlie, part vaguely injured pride, one of them told her, "I'm not
taking down my trousers for a gringo."

"Even a coffee gringo," the other man chipped in, smirking
slightly. The girl, Charlie noticed, had a tan, and must have been a
long time around the Isthmus—have to watch for that melanoma.
She spoke good Spanish.

She said, "I'll not be anywhere near you." She showed them a
zoom lens, its workings not easily explicable to these countrymen,
dislocated and generally aggrieved. It was as if they were prepared
to believe that the work in hand was worth doing in some way; but
that what it actually required from them personally was just way too
strange—and so, regretfully, they'd not wish to participate. Still
waving the zoom the girl told them, "You can go right away over
there, in the high grass"—she pointed where she meant—"and I'll
stay right here; I'll take the picture right here. I mean, it's not like
I'll be examining the size of your ..."

She'd meant to be light about it, cajoling—but realized too late that her inadvertent forthrightness, born of well-meaning frustration, was entirely indelicate. Offense, saw Charlie, was quietly but definitely taken.

"Hey, *compa*," the first man said to him as he came near, plainly seeking to enlist the support of another man, "the woman from the government wants we should go pretend to take a shit. So she can take a picture. I never heard such a foolish thing." He laughed, trying to sound confident; but the unsettling peculiarity of the request still defeated him.

The girl looked at Charlie. She had jet black hair in full shiny curls, and was blithely beautiful. She shrugged and said, "I need a picture of what you shouldn't do when you go to take a crap." She passed him a script on a clipboard. From what Charlie could see, it was laid out like the videos he wrote for the megacorps back home. She told him, "I'm making a slide show about sanitation. For the health ministry."

Charlie nodded. "Uh-huh." He checked the script. It was simple, direct, to the point—he'd write it that way himself, if somebody asked. Except he'd never had for a target audience a countryside's crop of undernourished refugees—and he wondered what they'd make of other programs he'd written, about systems architecture, satellite networks, investment schemes—not top of your mind, that stuff, when your kid's dying of diarrhea because the water's filthy.

"I came here to be a nurse," the girl said beside him. "And now I make amateur documentaries about shit houses." She wandered off, snapping odd shots without enthusiasm of a stray bantam or two.

Charlie read a few paras of voice track down the right of the neatly numbered shot list; he wondered what sort of "creative treatment" he'd have gone in for himself—"Hey, *compa!* Why not build yourself the latrine of a lifetime? That's right, folks, we're talking state-of-the-art installations from the leading edge of latrine technology." He smiled winningly at the two campesinos and said, "Don't worry, guys, I'll do what she wants. It's not a big deal."

He went after her to say he'd stand in. He could go home and tell Jimmy he'd had a walk-on part in the revolution. And the two men on the bench tapped their heads, as they'd often had cause to, at the mysterious ways of the gringo.

She stood on the lip of the ground and pointed to where she wanted him to go. Behind the sheds on the compound's edge, a path dropped down the exposed dirt slope; he skidded down it to where it narrowed, snaking into tall thickening grass and bush. The rich-leaved trees grew bigger before him, deeper toward the river; he stepped through the prints women made passing that way to collect water, the wind whisking fat droplets off the wall of green as he approached it. Stopping, he looked back to where the girl, eyeing up her frame through the lens, waved him on a touch further; he slid off the path and away a bit into knee-high, tangling dense shrub, rooting around a few yards to find a clear enough patch. Then, seeing she was gesturing OK, he undid his belt and fly, and hunkered down on his haunches as if to drop off a good one.

When the first shots cracked out, Charlie had a millisecond of not knowing what the noise was or meant; then time stopped down into cold, hard, echoing freeze-frame. About ten meters ahead of him, as the damp wind chilled on his white buttocks, a bullet hit with a quick flat *puck-pung* into a tree trunk; he saw a small shower of splinters break softly open. With his trousers around his knees he dived flat.

He didn't remember his life flashing before his eyes the way they say. He was, instead, held stiff as with rigor mortis, not by fear or surprise but by an utter, absolute, staring-eyed alertness. It was incredibly silent; the world was grown cavernously vast, hollow, intense. He felt each individual fallen leaf and blade of grass that twitched against his tensed bare thighs, heard each single grain of dust and earth that shifted under his arm, his side, his hip where he lay. He heard, it seemed, every molecule of matter separately moving, as if life had become an echoing great cave....

The shooting began again, stop-start-stop, deranged, rhythmless, ruthlessly brief little shouts of hard sharp drill noise—chisel on brick; it came from ahead, to his left. A bird lurched low and screaming through the branches of the trees. He saw, madly vivid at the stem of a huge branch in the canopy, the exploding orange bloom of a massive tree orchid, heavy fronds of emerald flopping down from around its hold on the bark. It was staggeringly beautiful. Remembering in a rush all the things he'd hoped to do and see in this world, he thought, Well, Death, meet Charlie; Charlie, meet Death. Then he thought, Hey, my trousers are around my knees here. You can't kill a man when he's taking a shit, *this is private.* . . .

The heartbeat slowed; the booming of it in his ears grew mercifully less crazy. He felt already like he'd been lying there for eons; he thought aliens could cross the gulfs between galaxies in the time he'd been frozen there, like a rabbit in car headlights—but then there grew instead a kind of stunned amazement as he realized that his body, coolly automatic, was taking over, quite independent of the racketing babel in his brain; and he found himself, without any conscious plan, making move by deliberate move to get fast and unobserved from harm's way.

The firefight still sounded; but it was not, perhaps, quite as close as he'd thought. His hands, he realized, weren't shaking a fraction; everything was steady and precise. He reached down, lifted his hips, and slipped up his trousers. Grit and dirt fell in around his pelvis and his boxer shorts, but he noticed it only in the abstract—just one more unpleasant sensation, a new but integral part of the holiday experience.

Belt buckled, fly zipped, he lay over on his stomach, peeked up his head, and, limb by limb, set off worming on forearms and flat legs through the thicker grass toward the corner of the rise where the compound banked up. He couldn't go back the way he'd come—straight up the slope beneath the sheds—the path had target written all over it. He aimed to get around to the far side of the bank away from the shooting, sticking, where he could, to the deepest rim of the vegetation, keen for the cover—but also wary of who might be in there, squinting down the barrel, eyeing him with unshaven mercenary grin as he crawled in the hairlines. . . .

His boot buckles tinkled irrepressibly; as the noise of the guns faded he got his first inkling, if anyone saw him, of what a ridiculous figure he must look, coming on for all the world like a grunt in a Nam movie. . . .

He edged his way through the grass around the corner of the slope; then, raising his head, he saw before him a raggle-taggle tenting of black plastic sheets thrown messily over rough timber A's. Beneath it, people cooked and ate on their floor of earth, and slept on it with their dogs, chickens, a pig or two—oldsters, dulled mothers, pot-fat kids with stick limbs. Where were all the men? The shooting seemed to have receded now, and the people were entirely oblivious to it. Charlie, like an idiot Neptune, rose silently from the grass in his safari jacket.

A little girl who saw him pointed and wailed; but the people, otherwise, were trying hard to keep smiles hidden behind their hands. Approaching, he stopped and looked about him. He saw no blood-lusting mercenaries, bursting scraggily blue-uniformed with knives and rifles from the forest. The women moved between pots and pans and skimpy bundles of clothes; in a blackened kettle, water steamed over a fire. Looking up, he saw the camera girl at the top of the slope above him, grinning broadly.

She called, "I never saw such a drama out of taking a shit."

He had a strong sudden feeling that ignominy, and lots of it, was coming his way. He went up the slope part of the way toward her, gesturing behind him. He attempted to point out—"But there's people shooting each other down there."

"It's only," she told him, "the defense squad out on firing practice—but I got a wild picture, I tell you, you diving with your trousers down. . . ."

Charlie half turned away, like an embarrassed kid, idly kicking one foot at the ground; he waved his hands palms down and said, "Nah, you're putting me on"—and then he saw the girl die.

She must have heard, up where she stood, the mortar rounds coming in—because she turned partly around, partly ducking, right into the explosions where they landed behind her. All Charlie heard, tucked beneath the blast down the slope, was the instant dead *whump* of their arrival, a brief keening whistle of hot fragments through the air—and he saw something fly through her neck, ripping flesh away, pushing her over the edge with a lance of blood leaping out skyward from the ragged hole as she fell.

Charlie gaped, immobilized, at the body tumbling to rest at his feet. He heard a pattering rainfall of clods of earth and grass, and smelled bitter smoke blown his way on the wind. There was plenty of rifle fire now, and cries, and a frantic, this-way-and-that, head-holding child-gathering panic among the women in the shelter. He dropped to his knees, felled by real fear, the gut-gouging real thing, his stare fixed, appalled, at the bubbling of air and blood in the girl's shattered windpipe, the still-pumping severed artery. Her eyes fluttered, helpless and terrified and juddering in their sockets; her fingers scratched in spasm at the soil, and her arms flopped and twitched.

Charlie tore his eyes away, breathing short and hard, heaving in air. Another salvo came in, away toward the prefabs. He rose, legs trembling so badly he could barely control them, and ran through the crisscrossing flock of peasant women murmuring hectic prayers with a desperate intensity—ran, ducking and stumbling, straight into the forest, crashing by bushes and over rocks, between trees and away, down the slope toward the river. He gave no thought to where he went, he made no effort to be silent—all he wanted was out.

He wasn't too fit. All that kept him going was adrenaline and the tremendous noise behind him of more and nearer mortars, the sporadic crackling of guns, and then the air-shaking *thudda-thud* of a great fat-bellied Hind passing fast over the trees right above him, a monstrous beetle firing cannon and spitting out its rocket pods, a furious sound—giant sheets of paper torn over and over across the sky. The canister lids, blown off as the rockets leaped away, fell in a slashing rain through the leaves. Charlie covered his head and collapsed, legs gone with shock and exertion, gasping, drenched in sweat though it was cold; the muddy humus he lay on beneath the canopy was soft and soaking.

He looked up, the Hind fading, the trees still screaming with birds and monkeys above, and saw between the tree trunks the river ten yards below him. It was wide, running full to Cabo Gracias a Dios far away. He slithered down on his belly toward the bank—made it, stopped, gave up, and lay still.

Gunfire and the occasional loud report of another shell or grenade continued intermittently, sometimes still close, but mostly further away now. The racing flow of the dirty water, specked with branches and debris, paddled against the earth down the bank until it blended with the tumult behind. The fighting became quieter, steady, a familiar soundtrack; his breath grew calmer, and he wondered if he should move. Wind shunted through the treetops. He rolled over on his back and found himself staring, across a hollow little haven by the waterside, at a small, ragged, and most peculiar old man.

"Be calm," he said, "you're safe enough here."

Charlie paused, then sat up. He was, he realized, faintly shivering all over. His white jacket was now brown and wet clean through; the zips and buckles of his boots, plastered in mud, no longer tinkled. He rummaged for a clean patch of shirt to wipe his glasses. Then, putting them back on, he rose to a crouch, squatting with one hand on the earth while he looked around. "Safe?" he asked. "You sure?"

The old guy nodded and smiled with a kind of expressionless benevolence. He was bald, bar the long gray-silver hair that dangled over his king-size ears. The tanned dome of his head gleamed with some livid eczema—a pattern of soreness spread in patches on the bridge of his nose, down the side of his face, around his throat and the back of his neck. He said, "Sure, safe. River, see—they can't come from this side, nor leave by it."

"Who?" Charlie hissed, with a rather ludicrous urgency.

"Either."

"Either who?" Then Charlie, ducking instinctively, lost the answer in the noise of the Hind, thundering nearby on another can-non-chattering pass.

When he looked back up, the old man, his position unchanged, was studying him with mild but bright-eyed earnestness. Sitting on a fallen log in the shaded back of the hollow, he said, "My name is Roman Alberto Squalatush," and he put out his hand.

Charlie peered at him, blinking, then half rose, and sneaked nervously forward until the sides of wet earth in the recess more closely surrounded him; when he stopped, he stood straight and stared. He felt frightened and friendly all at once; another loud report made him wince—then he saw the man's hand was still out, and he started abruptly forward to take it. "Fish," he said, "er, Charlie Fish. Mr. Squalatush—well—hello."

"Hello there." The old man smiled some more, his etched scalp bobbing, softly shining in dim shafts of weak gray light that dropped lamely through the canopy. He loosely gestured upward with his right hand and told Charlie, "The weather's no good again."

Then Mr. Squalatush, to pass the time, told Charlie the story of how he came to be at El Coco.

"Can I ask you," said Charlie, "what"—he wondered how to put it, then somewhat vaguely brushed one hand in his hair—"what happened to your head?"

Stocky Roman Squalatush bobbed about in front of him, his bent legs like springs in his worn and flapping trousers. Hair, the same gray-silver as that which hung around his hobgoblin ears, frothed in a mat from the front of his livid lilac shirt—and he wore over it, once busy with many colors but now faded, an ancient, much-embroidered gold vest. He looked, thought Charlie, like a retired stevedore, a banana loader from some slow-paced tropic port. His nose was flat and broad, his hands tough, his face lined.

But if you stood closer over him as tall Charlie now did, you got a perfect clear sight of the shape of the bright stain on his brown skin, this truly unaccountable feature—quite probably, Charlie thought, the strangest thing he'd ever seen.

The old man had on his head a more or less perfect map of the world, a chart marked out in shiny pink disease—Asia and Siberia on the dome, down the left cheek Africa, with Europe between the eyes and down the nose, and the Americas wrapped round his neck beneath his jaw. Japan fell down the back of his head, Australasia tipped out on his left shoulder; the Isthmus was a connecting scar across the middle of his throat.

"They have things," said Mr. Squalatush, "they call crop kill mines. What the people grow here, the mercenaries poison. Now me, I'm a packhorse. They call us Marcovaloza's mules. We carry their mines—they point guns at us and make us lay them. So one leaked, when I was pulling it from my backpack over my head. It's not so sore any longer—I did cough for a week."

Charlie didn't feel there was really too much he could say.

The old man told him, "Never you mind, Mr. Fish, the whole world's a-coughing—have you noticed? It's cold, and then it's hot, and then it rains when it shouldn't." He paused, then said, "Did you know God is coming soon? I have him right here—" He began rummaging in his backpack and pulled out a videotape.

They heard the breaking of a branch, suddenly, close. They both froze; there was a long pause of echoing silence—and the background noise of the firefight, stuttering and confused, sounding further away now, filtered back in again.

Then Charlie heard a voice, an urgent whisper of command just above him up the slope from their hiding place. He flattened himself against the back side of the recess, scarcely daring to breathe. There was a crackling rustle of slow steps through the undergrowth, the sound, he guessed, of five or six men slipping past, bare yards from where he stood. Mr. Squalatush was crouched on the earth by his log; he mouthed at Charlie, "Mercenaries," and he grinned. "They always fuck it up." He seemed entirely unfazed.

Charlie rolled his eyes heavenward—each leaf shifting in the hushed passage of the men above him was clear as a bell—then he heard another whisper. "Hey—is there a way down there?"

Twigs broke under boots coming closer still; and Charlie's uprolled eyes then saw the toe of a boot stop, eighteen inches above his head, sticking out beyond the lip of the muddy overhang. He squeezed himself back into the earth face behind him; he wished he was cigarette-paper thin. He couldn't believe what he was going through, couldn't believe that he'd offered *voluntarily* to go through this—they'd gut him, they'd cut off his cock and stuff it in his mouth—he swore he'd never leave home again. The boot stepped back; a voice hissed, "It's easier further on, go on and down left." Charlie lowered his head, silently exhaling—and saw, to his amazement, that Mr. Squalatush had vanished.

The noise of the men moved away a bit, then passed around and down the far side of the hollow, growing quieter. Charlie, his body still stiff as a board against the earth, looked baffled all about him. Was the old guy—what?—a spirit? a gnome?—nah. . . . Then he saw once more the twinkling eyes, the rotten-toothed grin. The trunk he'd been sitting on, Charlie realized, was hollow. Like any other small creature, he'd tucked himself away in it; and now sneaked out from it, sniffing.

Once out, bones creaking, he whispered to Charlie, "Well, they did say, they'd lay on a show for you tourists."

Charlie stared at him.

But then the gunship roared once more overhead, shaking furiously at the treetops. The cannon yelled out *dadadadada* at the escaping squad of mercenaries beyond them by the riverside, shells punching into the water, taking out whole huge branches in crashes of flame. There was a hideous high howling from a wounded man;

and Charlie was now unmanned entirely, lying bunched in a quaking ball in a corner of mud, fingers straining into the earth by his head, muttering mad prayers that it might cover him up: He prayed to be any place other than the place he now was, his brain in a terrified overdrive, shunting through a chaos of memory, his whole life flashing before his eyes *exactly* the way they say it does—and he keened in a silent scream for safety.

But is any place safe, these Dollarville days?

4. THE RHINO GIRL

Mel thought Africa was safe—safer, in some ways, than home.

Since home was Wisconsin, you might figure, even generally speaking, this was back-to-front thinking. But given what she did for a living, it was downright loopy.

Mel was a behavioral ecologist, studying black rhino on the Laikipia plateau. The work, which she'd been doing eighteen months now, involved tracking the animals, sometimes for hours, through thick, semi-arid bush spread over miles and miles of high, rolling land—or, sometimes, following them way down into the jungly gorges to the west, where the land ripped apart and fell away into the Rift. And success in this work meant getting close enough to watch, to identify, to photograph; so Mel, daily, armed only with a ruler, a camera, and a Dictaphone, went chasing after rare dinosaurs that weighed a ton and a half and were, by temperament, solitary, and angry when disturbed.

But it wasn't true that she went entirely unarmed. Silas and Gitangata, her head trackers, shared between them an old Lee-Enfield .303; but then the poachers, whose trade was more lucrative than conservation, came equipped with the very latest quick-fire finery—laser night sights, the works—bought at the edges of all the continent's busy wars. And of course, Mel knew, it wasn't really safer than Wisconsin; she just told herself it was, because she liked her job.

She could have been managing fat, glossy herds of gene-and-hormone-primed Dairyland milk machines—but couldn't think of them as cows anymore, as animals, they were so damn *designed*. . . . It would have been too boring, too blindly, pointlessly, pigheadedly overproductive. Besides, fair enough, Africa was a tad anarchic—Mel was a girl rather prone to understatement—but the States were hardly Joy City, now were they? There were the guerrillas in the Sacramento Mountains, survivalists fire-fought the military over the dope fields in the Cascades, and black-on-barrio violence was risen to the proportions of urban war; there were car bombs in Tucson and San Antonio, every kind of bomb in Miami, and a president who went around saying the time of Jesus Our Lord drew nigh, and it behooved us to make ready with our weaponries to do battle with the Dark One. Mel reckoned, on balance, she'd take the rhinos.

Wisconsin was still relatively calm—she missed cross-country skiing in the winter, and tornado warnings, and the corn growing tall—but there were summers these days when you were lucky if it grew past your knees. All the water was in the lakes, chewing away at Door County and Green Bay and the Apostle Islands, nibbling the shore suburbs of Manitowoc and Sheboygan; down in Chicago, she'd heard, Lake Shore Drive was under water for weeks at a time.

So she thought, who needs it? when you could step out your tent into a dawn like this one. The sky was a vast ribbed roof of salmon pink, tender and bleak and enormous; just, she realized, the way it was above the prairie, with that surging feeling of a massive weight of climate and atmosphere rumbling and grinding over the big smooth land, the pumping heart of the earth machine, far from any ocean—and was she happy because, in some savage way, the plateau reminded her of home? Did she miss it, after eighteen months, more than she was prepared to admit?

She'd have the chance, in a few weeks, to find out. The funding for the project had been terminated—there was no money in the world for rhino anymore. They'd be poached, and the horns sold in San'a for thousands of dollars a time; nature privatized, asset stripped. . . .

She stared down from her hillside encampment at the land emerging out of darkness, the thorn trees taking shape, the birds waking and calling a first few tentative songs. Today, she thought, would be a good day, hot and clear, with maybe a small strong rain marching in by the late afternoon to freshen things up. She liked rains best when they came around five, when she'd brewed tea and rolled a joint. Then she'd sit in her canvas director's chair in the living tent's entrance, and watch the spectacle in comfort.

First the cloud came in, an entire and apocalyptic second landscape sweeping over the sky, an angry ceiling sliding shut above your head; then the thunder was monstrous. The belly of the cloud filled with bursts of whiteness where the lightning charged down, and the rain fell straight and hard and heavy. Afterward, there would be rainbows, and the sun in the west, falling earthward, would throw rich light like a carpet across the plateau until the land and the bush turned gold, the sky purple, the colors dense and tangible—and the world would be spirit rich, deafeningly alive with birds and insects.

Mel stretched by the embers of last night's fire. She was a tall girl, blonde, with long tanned legs, fit and strong and good-looking. In the base of the wide slow valley in front of her, an elephant, distantly crashing, lumbered toward the salt licks by the water hole. Nearer, nimble Gicheru strolled through the bush, gathering more firewood to heat water for later, when she came back from the tracking and would be wanting a shower. They'd built a cabin and a pulley system, and before tea she'd hoist an old oil drum filled with hot water above her head, and get as clean as in the finest hotel. She turned and found in her tin storebox grapefruit, mango, malaria tabs, and tea for her breakfast.

When she gunned up the Land Cruiser, and the trackers from their camp across the path came to hop light-footed into the back, it was still well before seven. She shoved into gear, and they thumped down the hill.

Battering down the red-dirt tracks, their passage scattered eland, warthog, impala, dik-dik, and waterbuck. Long-tailed flycatchers and orange-chested starlings darted alongside and away, or burst in fleeing plumes from the branches of trees. Like the masts of ships, the necks of giraffes rolled slowly this way and that above the bush as they lolloped away—and, bundling through the biomass, she was exultant, a big happy girl in control at the wheel, playing country music, singing loud for joy at the beauties all about her. Who, she thought, could ask for a better job than hers?

They checked waterholes and junctions—it wasn't rigidly fixed, but there were certain trails she'd come to think of as "rhino freeways"—and they radioed around the patrols, hoping for word of a sighting. For over an hour there was nothing; then, bouncing westward, they found a set of faint tracks. There were two animals, a mother and calf, a pair not yet named that she was keen to observe.

The trackers named all the animals that they came to know. There was Bahati Ya Kamuria, "Poacher's Luck," named in respect for a tough Pokot hunter from the north; and there was Tumbu, "Paunch," and Faru Yetu, who was, simply, "Our Rhino." But this unnamed pair had only recently been spotted. She laid her ruler on the ground by their mammoth prints and took photographs—she filed the wrinkles of each rhino's soles like a policeman would fingerprints—she muttered data at the Dictaphone—then she said to Silas, "OK, let's go."

He told her, "The trail's some hours old, *memsahib* Mel—they may be gone a long way."

"We'll try, anyhow." She was always an optimist. Rhino like to hide out and nap through the heat of the day, and she always hoped she'd catch them dozing right around the next corner—because finding them was less tense by far than all the creeping along through the bush beforehand, whispering and whistling, sniffing and smelling, feeling dung for its temperature, and branches broken where the beast had crashed by up in front of them.

But there was nothing close by around the corner today. Hushed and alert, twisting this way and that as they lost and found a broken and roundabout trail, they walked seven or eight miles. They approached, sometimes, the edge of the first slopes into the ravines, then pulled back, circled around, and went down again. They went carefully through thick stands of dry, bone-green leleshwa—haunt for the recalcitrant buffalo as well as for rhino—and disturbed, now and then, a flurry of antelopes.

It was blazing hot by the time they found the scrape, a great backed-up mound of earth where the mother'd dug in her heels for a cleaning. Signs of feeding grew more common—bushes either chomped away whole, or just picked at, with unlikely persnicketi-ness, by great secateur teeth. Then the tracks dropped for good from off the high land.

It was a different world in the gorges. They slid and scrambled down steep, rocky slopes, and saw the vegetation changing to new, denser shapes with the dreaming ease of hallucination. Above was bush, grass, scrub, hard stubby olive trees; here, fallen, was a chaos, a damp, sweat-aired, spilling-over mayhem of living and dying plants. They passed a ribbon of waterfall dropping into a butterfly-specked pool; they ducked around spiders hung on cathedral webs among the leaves with bodies big as thimbles, leg spans wide as your palm.

The traces of the rhino grew more evident. Around the base of each candelabra tree, they found a confusion of tracks where the mother had banged against the trunk, dislodging the juiciest tidbits from the tips of the cactuslike branches above; the trees, euphorbia, have white milky sap so caustic it can blind you, burn the skin off your flesh—and the rhino love it.

But there was, by now, a lot of stopping, starting, creeping for-ward and pausing and peering and creeping forward again, in a silence scattered with taut and wide-eyed gestures as they advanced.

They came on a muddy gulch; prints in the mud, clearly visible, were wet and fresh. On virtual tiptoe they followed them toward a dense bank of thickets and greenery; sneaking up to one bush, waiting, slipping forward to the next—and then the wind changed.

The mother ahead caught their scent, and, without warning, pandemonium broke out. She stomped at the ground, huge mashing thuds that shook it where Mel stood; then started barging and crashing about somewhere deep in the cover, uprooting and trampling, heaving out great breathy snorts and grunts.

Fine, Mel thought, don't want to see us today. She backed away steadily, putting more layers of bush between herself and an animal that (you always told yourself) couldn't see you too well. When they got mad, you shot away and up the nearest tree—except, backing, she couldn't find any trees. And things, she realized, weren't getting more tranquil up ahead of her. She threw the beginnings of a panicky glance behind her, and briefly saw Silas waving urgently at her to run his way; then the animal broke from the bushes, a huge lunging bulk of simpleminded purpose. The head, a fortress of bone and hide, a battering ram big as your body, topped with its double minaret, dropped down. Mel dived sideways for a clump of shrubs, felt the air moving and the ground rumbling as the monster spun at her feet. She rolled; the front feet landed on her shins.

Her scream, she realized, was more from instinct than pain; the rhino backed off. She heard the frantic ululations of Silas and Gitangata, and the first wild warning shot from the .303. The animal studied her, huffing, with a monumental dimness. She tried slowly to worm and wriggle away in the dust and dry leaves, wrenching for breath; with an eerie detachment she noted how, as the mother came to strike, the young calf followed behind in imitation.

The mother lurched forward, the huge feet landing short of her own this time—and then Mel saw, amazed, the fine long horn, surprisingly slender, pierce through both her thighs in one blow, in the left and out the right. There was pain, now, to the point of blackout; but no relief, as the head slightly lifted, and she was dragged like a rag on her back a yard forward before the horn pulled out, slicing like a rough knife out of granary bread. She managed to look down, and was pleased at how little blood there was . . . then her head fell back, her body swimming in pain, pain that rang like a bell, surged like ocean breakers. She heard another shot; then some projectile, stone, wood, then another, landed on or around the animal. She heard the heavy noise of it trotting away. Her eyes rolled in their orbits; she saw fireflies in the dusk, fingers of rock above Devil's Lake south of Baraboo . . . there were flowers by her head; there was, she realized, datura growing all about her. When the trackers got to her, she asked Silas to break her a fragment of seed and put it in her mouth.

She thought, if she was going to lie here and die, she might at least do it tripping.

Datura stramonium—punchy stuff, packed with alkaloids, atropine, hyoscine, gets straight to your nervous system—they use it in treatment against chemical war nerve agents. . . . It grew everywhere, the States, the Balkans, East Africa (or it used to—Mel didn't know how, worldwide, the weather was treating it) and was called thorn apple or jimson weed. Like bittersweet and henbane or the apple of Peru, it was a nightshade; it had oval, jaggedly teethed leaves, white, trumpet-shaped flowers, and a spiny, egg-shaped fruit, a packet full of seeds like a pepper mill.

Taking datura, one of the botany books told her, would cause "extreme hallucinations and excessive euphoria." But how much euphoria is too much? In the name of science, she had needed to know. She researched the plant's recorded effects—dysphasia, photophobia, stertorous breathing, and confusion most absolute—thirsts, flushes, heart race, blurred vision—and if you were a man, an inability to get your cock up. Then, starting with extremely dilute distillations, she tried it out on herself. It was wild material; just a fragment of a seed could give you hours of happy high.

But why, in the name of science, did she need to know these

things? Because rhino eat datura plants whole. What kind of dino-saur trip they got into on that, the mind boggled at imagining—and then it was good for asthma, it was a sedative, a truth serum. . . . She had a cartoon vision of a rhino doing a polygraph.

As it took effect on her where she lay—with Silas softly chattering at her side, the radio call gone out to raise help, Gitangata run back to the pickup to meet it—she had a revelation. She would have, she thought seriously, to evaluate this notion when sober—but consider the evidence. She was on a toilet site. Great twig-thick mounds of rhino dung lay all about her—and the datura, here, was flourishing. So, she reasoned, the rhino has itself a mad datura carousal. Some of the seed, undigested, passes through its cumbrous gut, and lands on the toilet site. Encouraged by the rich ordure, the seeds leap into new growth. So the rhino, thought Mel, like survivalists, *are growing their own.* . . .

In a bright cumulus sky, the sun was a scorching disk. The bush gleamed and rustled, hard edged with light all about her. Silas held her hand. She murmured memories of home—take the canoe up north, have a bottle of green death, go over Joe's Place in Lodi—the time she house-sat for Ben near Lake Kegonsa when he honey-mooned, and locked herself out one morning—had nothing on but a kikoi, had to walk a mile of cornfield tracks barefoot to the Halvessons to get the spare key—when Ben was back they'd ask him, "How's the crazy rhino girl?"

The sky was a big flat blue roof—she was going, blacking. The pain was steady and solid; she had no legs any more; there was only pain. Silas pinched her arm, patted her face. She said, "I'm with it, I'm with it." Help would be hours—the sky got dark, and small glints of stars began to flash in her eyes. . . .

5. EXILE

The fighting seemed over; there came only the moaning of the wounded man further down along the river; and Charlie was past the worst fear into a wide-eyed and disbelieving numbness. Here he was, in a soaking hole by a rain forest riverbank at the tail end of a fierce guerrilla firefight—with a crazy old man telling him he had God on a videotape. Charlie couldn't deal with it, not with any part of it; he felt entirely exhausted.

Still, Mr. Squalatush, his map head glaring in the damp shadows across the hollow, waved his precious cassette in the air. He said, "I tell you, it's the truth."

"I'm sorry, old man," Charlie told him, "but every word from on high has its way of being true. And look, it's got quiet, OK? I want to go home."

He pushed around the side of the leafy recess, and stepped wearily back up the slope through the trees. He was grimy with dirt and fear-sweat all over. The moans of the man taken out down by the bank were fading; Charlie thought, for a minute, that he should maybe go help—but he was too wiped out now to bother and didn't figure, anyway, that he could face more ripped flesh, after seeing how the camera girl had died. He'd tell the soldiers; he'd tell someone.

On the cleared ground at El Coco, they were laying out the bodies. Smoke drifted across the hillsides, obscuring the figures moving slowly around what remained of the shacks and barns; the prefab frames still flickered red flames at the low gray sky.

Charlie found a guy giving orders, in combat uniform, with a badge showing the red and black colors of the local army. He went over to him and waited until he was through; then he showed his passport and his papers, and told where the gunship had hit the men escaping by the river.

The guy said, "OK." He looked tired.

So Charlie quietly ventured, "Did you do all right?"

The man considered the question, then said with a kind of sad and exasperated pride, "Those people—it don't matter what the Yanqui gives them, they couldn't fight their way out of a quiet day in Disneyland. Trouble is, fucking bandits, sure, they're running away—but look what they've done here." He waved a hand vaguely around him, then pulled it up to wipe dirt off his forehead; he moved away, calling for a squad to go look where Charlie'd told him.

Charlie, left behind, caught sight of Mr. Squalatush, passing this way and that behind where the gunship had set down, blades flopping like insect wings by the ruined tractor. He went over to see what he was up to, and found him darting from body to body through the drifts of bitter smoke, examining each with a blank and emotionless stare. He looked up abruptly when Charlie drew near; he said he was looking to see if they'd got Scarskull.

Then he came closer and said, "And I'll tell you another thing, there's no video here—these Communists here, they don't have no TV. Just what sort of a setup is this?" He seemed almost angry that he couldn't prove his story. He said suddenly, "I'm going north; I've had enough. Or maybe west—I don't know." He turned and vanished into the wreaths and veils of smoke.

Charlie felt like a drugged man. He meandered through the aftermath, the place seeming silent, all its noises muffled in shock—then found he was at the lip of the ground where the girl had died. There were two craters where the shells had come in on her; looking over the slope, he saw her body'd not been collected. There was a soldier passing, and he stopped him and pointed down; the soldier slumped.

They went down to get her. Charlie held her under the armpits so her head was propped up against his chest, hiding from his eyes the crusted, flapping hole in her neck. And it was shortly after he'd lain her down that the Ricochet rep found him. Charlie thought, if he tells me I've had my money's worth, I'll kill him.

But the rep was too bothered about the other four tourists to get flippant. Charlie stared at the state of them—they sat cross-legged and shaking, smoke-blackened, heads held silently down. Like the brochure promised, they'd seen it how it was.

And he wondered, then, if the purpose of these holidays wasn't, in fact, to take you to other places so fucked-over that you'd be happy afterward, you'd be glad beyond belief that all you had to deal with was living in Dollarville.

Dollarville: love it or hate it, Charlie only knew that he was taking the next plane back.

"Dollarville," Chester Gantry mock groaned, "who the hell wants to have to go there?"

But no one around the table feels too sorry for him. There's Elmer Rayban, marketing; Rutger Mengel, space technical; Xavier Morales, group strategy; Art Levine, the figurehead Anglo chairman who represents the corporation in the media; and Ms. Benzene Filofax, taking notes.

And they all know Chester's ex-military; they all know he loves to go where the thrill factor's high, where there're knives in the street and warheads primed in the bunkers; and they know, besides, Kalero's owner lives that way, a short copter ride from Dollarville, and that Gantry has his ear. . . . Benzene, we should note for the sake of accuracy, doesn't know that last fact—the name of the owner's not known, after all, below level one in the hierarchy. . . .

The subject of the meeting was Ecto VII. The frequency with which the satellite was filing minor malfunctions had become impossible to ignore—and strange reports had started filtering in from the backwoods ground stations of signals going down, of some crazy pirate broadcaster interfering with transmission. Then the video evidence came down. Gantry called the meeting to order and ran the tape. It had a title up front: "Restricted. Levels One/Two Only."

The screen showed space, earth, stars, flashes of sun, the bright dots of other satellites around the turning rim of the world; and, closer, it showed those portions of Ecto on which the camera was posted, slipping slowly by as the camera revolved. The camera stopped; it focused along a shimmering arm of solar power panels toward a small black dot—it could have been anything, it was too indistinct to tell. The images were bleached out, edged with flare in the hard and brilliant orbit light; they were standard technoprop fare—with one difference.

Slung out at the far end of the big bird's gauzy butterfly wing— the distance made it hard to see clearly—was this object maybe the size of a small pup. As the camera held on it, it plainly moved now and then, little shifts and jerks, a stiff, arthritic sort of flexing move-ment—more automatic, mechanical, than conscious or animal. Seg-ments of glinting panel seemed to be missing here and there around the object: a robot? What the hell? They stood close to the big wall screen at one end of the conference table, peering into the pixels, flummoxed—then the time code flicked off, and the screen went blank.

They reran the tape. Was it space debris? Some stray old lost lump of Apollo or Mercury or Soyuz or Salyut? A clod of bandit asteroid? But whatever it was, it was interfering with their top-of-the-range new baby—and doing so just when that new baby was due to beam great good news from Kalero to hundreds of millions of soccer fans, from north of the spic line to the south of the Isthmus—so agreement was prompt and immediate. Someone would have to go up there. Someone—given the uncertainties of the situation—expendable. . . .

Someone—the data base turned up an appropriately trained and qualified individual—called Deke Lewis, who was based north of Dollarville.

"Enjoy your trip," said Elmer Rayban—Mengel was gone already, to prepare the launch site—and Gantry faintly smiled, his yellow eyes flashing with secret relish.

With Ms. Filofax out of the room, Xavier Morales then said to him, "Give our regards to Mr. Marcovaloza."

"Welcome to Dollarville."

Mel stared dully at the flickering electric billboard in the girders of the concourse ceiling; it seemed the power supply was unsteady and the brightness of the sign varied, as if it were ill, and slipping away.

The airport was hell. To get through customs alone had taken an hour and forty minutes. Collecting luggage took a lifetime. And that was only round one of the formalities; now she was in line at transit and immigration, to re-re-check in for her onward flight home. She swung on her crutches, arms and shoulders aching solidly.

She thought of the corn, the woods, and lakes; she'd be home soon enough. She would, she thought (ha) put her feet up—it'd take a while to work out what to do. Not a lot of work for a broken-legged rhino buff, these days. . . .

But there wasn't a lot of work, anymore, for any kind of conservationist—no profit in it. The world was beyond conservation, into resignation; money was all private now, too busy getting spent on the big last party before the machine spun apart, the eco-governor gone. . . . The local paper she bought was full of madness. The president at press conferences was now referring questions directly to God. Bombings were reported in Pueblo, Amarillo, Santa Fe; a tract of Oregon had been declared by survivalists an independent white nation; and the Beast himself, said the president, now prowled the Sierra Madre—a beast variously Communist, papist, or plain spic, depending on his audience. Elsewhere, a new McDonald's had opened in Ulan Bator; and Singani, on the back pages, had still not yet made up his mind.

Mel made it at last to the transit window. As usual with air travel, the delays by now would normally have meant that she'd missed her connection; but the connection itself, as normal, was also delayed. She watched a bored young clerk riffle through her poly wallet to confirm carrier, access, clearance. An immigration man posted out to colony screening from home came by, appraised her looks, then registered her injury; frowning, he leaned over the clerk's shoulder and lip-read Mel's data to himself. She couldn't see there'd be a problem—she was after all, group A.

Name:	Isenhope, Melinda Abigail
Born:	Madison, WI
Age:	29
Grade:	3xA1, Madison/Berkeley
Status:	US, White
Work:	Behavioral Ecologist
Zone:	1N 38W
*** risk supplement: High—credit rate: B ***	
Blood:	O
Test:	Neg
Repeat:	Annual
Creed:	Darwinist

"That thing with your legs there," said the immigration man. "You had an accident, right? In that zone way out there? What we talking here"—he flicked through a chart and pursed his lips—"Africa, uh-huh."

"I got run over by a rhino." She tried to be light about it, as if it could happen to anyone. But he didn't seem strong on a sense of humor. And sympathy? Forget it.

"That'd put you in a hospital, right?" They might, from his interest, have been talking of the weather, or the losers in the season's baseball. Another routine data check.

She told him, "For over a month. No fun."

"I bet. And you'd be needing some blood when you got in there, I guess."

"Sure, I got through a few pints"—she leaned forward, and had a prickling feeling around her neck—"so what?"

"Well, miss, right there that would be African blood, see. 'Cause you ain't credit A on your insurance here, so your policy—you follow me—wouldn't stretch to buy no clean stuff. So what you have in your body there, miss, it ain't screened the way they like it. And if it ain't screened, you can't import it. See, the way the rules are, oh, these last few months now"—he paused to study her papers, then continued with a leisurely, savage lack of concern—"it seems you been away too long to know any better, miss, but the way the rules are now there's blood in you that the US don't want. Which is to say you cannot, Miss Isenhope, go home. See here." And then he took her data cards. He fed them one by one into the terminal on the counter, and used a light pen to enter new codes onto each screen's worth of material; and when he was done, he ordered up a printout, to show how the new code had now rewritten all her options. Life fixed by menus of silicon ... He handed the paper, folded, across the counter, through a wafer-thin slot in the base of the bulletproof glass. Mel felt the airport seething and turbulent at her back. He said, "Your circumstances, Miss Isenhope, is changed."

```
*** effective immediate ***
Blood risk:   Category 2
Test:         8-weekly
Term:         5 years
US Ingress:
(under 139th Amendment)
—Denied Until Further Notice—
```

"Of course," he commented, "you'll be group B now."

Mel was utterly blank. She stared at the immigration man. But he said, with a faint shrug, "Hey—you can't argue with the computers."

She burst into speech. "You can't do this. What am I going to do here? Where do I stay?"

"Try looking at it this way. If I hadn't caught up with it here, you'd have gone on over Stateside, and just got sent right back again. So listen, go talk to the Data Bureaux. Call your folks. And if I were you"—he leaned forward, and snickered with a sudden evil intensity—"Get Saved, girl. Get you some Jesus in your life. Because a blood risk like yours, they sure won't let no Darwin type find one *sniff* of a way around that one-thirty-ninth."

He walked away; that was that. The thick and now unmanned sheet of glass mirrored the faces in the line behind her, jostling at her shoulder saying, Hey, getta move on, wha' happen.... She turned away. Watchful, weaponed-up, the military police sifted the throngs claiming access to the departure lounges. The scene was like the fall of a city—Dollarville—but they had not, she recalled, been paid here what they said they were owed; and the banks were belly-up, trade sclerotic, the regions insurgent—she was looking at a cash-flow crisis writ large in living Technicolor, and, as if seeing it for the first time she now stared, her panic mounting. There were creditors, bankrupts, aliens with straggling families all howling alike at the voucher counters, satchels and cases stuffed to bursting with wads and rolls of worthless big-denomination local money that the carriers would no longer accept. Desperate men keened and pleaded with strangers to change dollars.... The money was the same, but she was an ocean from home, stranded in the most slavish and craven of the cracking empire's outposts, like, for sure, Saigon, San Salvador—the empire's collaborators had always turned out to be shits, but this crowd, Jesus, the national past time was licking American ass.... She gasped: a blood risk in Dollarville, oh boy. She heaved for breath, felt a great hollow misery burning outward from the center of her chest—and through the terminal windows, saw the Galaxies and the Starlifters thundering in like Leviathan to shake the very air; saw troops and ordnance snaked out across the landing pans in hectic disorder. She looked across the teeming corridors and lounges of the litter-strewn airport; she saw, there were GIs among the crowds. She heard one leaning over a clerk at the tourist counter saying, "Where's the fast track to the Sex District, miss?" She wondered, who's spreading what kind of virus to whom?—and she was by now crying, unstoppably.

Charlie Fish stepped through the last customs barriers and saw, from behind, the tall blonde girl silently shaking on her unsteady crutches. He stopped with a start thinking, Suzie, Jesus, what happened? She was the same height—near six foot—and had the same broad strong shoulders. Then he saw that she was losing her balance, and stepped quickly forward to catch her.

When he saw that the girl was, in fact, a stranger, he kept the quick stab of surprise to himself, showing nothing. Instead he said simply, "C'mon, let's get you sat down."

Through tears of shock and anger Mel examined him. He was maybe six-two, six-three, a little taller than herself; he was fair, and had an open, bland kind of smile that seemed to make no demands. He looked malice free, with a take-it-or-leave-it manner that suggested he'd listen, and help, if that was what she wanted—or walk away and leave her be, if it wasn't.

He found her a seat on a cracked metal bench outside the main terminal buildings, near by where the bright-painted buses came grinding through, coughing black bursts of smoke, bedecked with their names and their prayers: *Tokyo Rider, Holy Spirit, Lucky Joe, Lord Ride with Us into Joytown*. He stood over her, waiting without impatience while she took deep breaths, and wrestled to calm herself down.

The prospect wasn't calming. Across a honking sea of cars, some battered, some glossy with wealth—a bristling confusion of limos and wrecks shimmering beneath the breathless glare of a relentless, smoggy sky—the antiaircraft gun posts lanced their barrels into the air. On security tracks around and through the enormous parking areas, armored squad carriers, matt colored and clanking, growled about their business at threatening and noisy speed, the men riding them holding stubby automatics across their chests. All about them on the paving and the walkways, men and women surged this way and that with urgent eyes and nervous purpose, teetering on the curbs, darting between vehicles. They wore rags and went in gangs, or fine suits and went with bodyguards; they wore caftans and djellabas and mammy cloth and saris and cycle shorts and T-shirts and Walkmans and trainers—and all about them the beat of the helicopters and the roar of the jets throbbed and pulsed without cease. It wasn't good, she thought.

She looked up at Charlie and said, "Thanks for picking me up back there."

Charlie looked down on her with a faint, detached little shrug; he registered the American accent, but found it softer and more pleasing than most he'd heard, and wondered where she came from. She was, he thought, an exceptionally striking woman.

"I just got told that I couldn't go home." She said it suddenly, with a gasp in the back of her voice; then got her control back with a small effort, well-hidden, but which Charlie saw and admired. She said, "So I'm stuck here. Can you help me? I need a place to stay tonight—until I sort things out."

Charlie thought of his empty house in Traderstown. He picked up her bag thinking, the world needs a good deed—after the bad ones he'd seen. . . . He was also thinking, what am I doing, she's a fuckin' American—but he could always chuck her out if she turned out to be a bad one. Shouldering the bag, he said, "You travel light."

She laughed. "Do I look like I could carry three suitcases?"

They took a cab. It was extravagant, but Charlie still had dollars left over from the Isthmus, and, anyway, found he quite liked, in a mild sort of way, to be showing off. He knew, for in-city spending, the local tender would still get by—though you'd need a wallet the size of a trash can—but the exchange rates were apeshit, and at the airport the dollar talked loudest. He told the driver that's what he'd pay in, after he learned the banks were offering twenty-eight local for a greenback, but that the driver set black market at something pushing five hundred. They edged into the traffic, and jerked and shoved their way into town.

On the central reservation, people camped on the dry earth beneath the marching line of lampposts. It was getting dark. Shanty, ill-lit, grew thicker around them; they passed Tin Can Canton, and sprawling segments of Mud Alley; the bright towers of the Heart rose up on the skyline. The driver left the windows up and locked, and they sweated in the baking car. Billboards yelled out all about them; the driver had brutal hip-hop loud and insistent on the radio. Charlie had to give the guy directions. The driver shouted at them with crazy red eyes in the rearview mirror, "If I tell you I know where I'm going, you gonna say, that fuckin' Albanian he lie to me—I only been here two weeks. You ain't Serbian, right?—I don' carry no fuckin' Serb in my cab. Anyhow where you been, hey?— the Isthmus? What the fuck sake you wan' go there for, you crazy? They have doctors there? Let me tell you thing with doctors, they take man in a hospital, chop him wrong fuckin' leg off, fuckin' doctors mister I tell you . . ." And he told malpractice stories down the intercom all the way to Charlie's house.

Charlie lived in a side street hard by the edge of the gleaming Heart. Where the street ran out into the main road, a snarling queue was built up at the access gates to that zone—a nail-bed of maniac architecture sparkling in the dusk, puncturing the sky up in front of them—but the driver, gabbling his horror tales to the beat, scraped down the edge of the sweltering jam, and turned away into Traderstown.

The right-hand side of the district's first street backed on to the walls and wire fences of the Heart's perimeter. It was a line of small terraced houses, with the road in front of them turning at the end into a cobbled, triangular little market yard. Charlie's was the next to last of the houses on that side; it stood by the corner where the yard opened out, and the clutter of stalls began around its sides. The driver pulled up; he waited to take his money through the screen, before pressing the button to unlock the back doors. Charlie paid, then helped Mel out and up the three steps to his front door. As he opened it while she hung on her crutches, he said, "It's nothing special. I just bought it a few months back, before they stopped lending money." And he was wondering, now he was back, what new region of the stratosphere his interest rates might have climbed to.

Mel looked through the doorway across an open-plan living room; past a scraggy armchair on the polished board floor, she saw a string of garlic bulbs hanging down a terracotta-pink kitchen wall. Beside her he said, "Go in, make yourself at home. I'll go buy some food in the yard before curfew comes down."

She told him, "I'm vegetarian, sorry—do you mind?"

"Hell no." He shrugged. "Half the meat's radioactive anyhow."

Several times while he cooked he made the same mistake, forgetfully asking if she'd do him some small task—change a tape, pass the red cabbage, boil a kettle—before realizing, with an apology, what it would involve for her. With her crutches against the wall, she lay resting in the shabby armchair, looking around at the maps and photographs pinned randomly to the living room's unpainted plaster wall—the kitchen was the first and the only room he'd decorated. His enthusiasm, after Suzie, had waned.

But he didn't tell Mel why he'd stopped painting the place; nor, at first, did he talk too much about where he'd just been, or why. He didn't talk too much at all, wishing especially not to press her on her own situation. It was just good to have company. He cooked up a pungent stir-fry—charging it with ginger, garlic, mustard, coriander, dill weed, and fresh chili—and then produced a good Spanish red wine, rich with that warm, old-resin texture that he'd bought off a man he knew in the yard. When the bottle was empty, they both felt good; he lay on his back on the floor, amid a confusion of wires linking the units of his sound-and-picture system—units pulled hig-gledy-piggledy from their boxes, and parked haphazardly around the room. He put on, quietly, some background salsa—and by the time he'd rolled a joint to go with coffee, both did, at last, begin to talk with a growing ease.

But still they both talked more, they knew, to themselves than to the other. They talked to record and get clear in the fullest detail, for their own sake, before memory grew weak, the sights and smells and sounds and tastes of the places they'd been; because those were places, the way their worlds now looked, that they'd not soon be seeing again. "And," he said, "after damn near getting my balls blown off, I can't say I much mind."

He told her about the Isthmus. He said America was like a rhino, an old puritan dinosaur dying out and stomping as it did so on back-ward little nations that were considerably smaller than Wisconsin, considerably poorer, and mostly swamp and rugged mountains— and he asked her, what for? What on earth was the point? Did no one ever learn?

"Look, Americans," she said, "they got hearts of gold, but their heads are full of shit; it's a country that thinks it has the best of all possible motives—and then does the worst of all possible deeds." But she began to risk getting angry, the shock boiling up again at what had been done to her. She told him, "They sure did vote for some maniacs this time. . . ."

He deflected the talk to calmer things, thinking he shouldn't have brought it up. He said it was beautiful where he'd been, that he'd got at least one good photograph to add to those already on the walls. Then he told her when he got around to painting the room someday, he was going to paper it with maps, and hang the spaces in between them full to bursting with his photographs. The new one, still undeveloped in his camera, was of parakeets, a green shower of parakeets whirling, "just whirling around the inside of this volcano I climbed the day before yesterday, while I was waiting for a plane—and they were shrieking out like nobody's business, in the middle of all these columns of smoke; and the rock was red, orange, hot, razor sharp. There was this sulfurous stink, and these birds, they were really so bright, unbelievably green, and I don't—I don't want to forget that sort of thing. It's going to be archive house, this place. I want to know what there was in my life."

She knew what he meant. She offered to have printed for him a photo or two of her own; she'd brought back a few rolls of film from the Mara, Tsavo, Amboseli. He had to choke back saying, now he knew her story, you'll have the time to develop them. . . .

They didn't talk about the blood risk. They agreed, unspoken, it was deferred to phone calls around the data departments come the morning. And only once did she burst out, "One thing I will not do, I tell you, I will not get Saved. I will not swear allegiance to any other man's ideas; I'm not a Russian, I'm an American. . . ."

Charlie tried to field the anger. He told her, "There were Russians here and there in the liberated zones in the Isthmus. Hopeless crowd—half of them couldn't even speak Spanish."

"Yeah, Russians," she told him. "Russians, spics, yellow men, men from Mars, they all got the same job—they're only there to frighten the taxpayer. So he forks out for more missiles, more space-ships." But then she realized it was futile and let her talk veer off, not wanting to face in her head the anarchic megacorps, the caba-listic God nuts who now ran her country; so she told him, instead, about where she grew up and, no longer, lived.

She told of driving thirty miles or more on broiling summer Sundays, past corn taller by far than a man through Wyocena, Pardee-ville, Portage on the hunt for ice cream. She told of the sign outside one little town that declared, Welcome to the Only Waunakee in the World. She told him of grain silos and water towers sticking out against the flat green horizon, of speedwell and huge, papery-pink orchids in brilliant bursts on the shoulders and in the woods; she described the dazzling red cardinals on the wires between infinite ranks of telegraph poles, and hummingbirds miraculously motion-less at the necks of flowers in the bed on the front lawn. She recalled for him, too, the Milwaukee Road freight trains, trains as long and slow as forever clanking, solemn and slumberous, over the bridge by her house toward the small town of Rio, pronounced, she explained to him, "Rye-oh." She spoke of four pristine white churches for some six hundred souls there—Lutheran, Methodist, Presbyterian, Catholic, no Southern rant—and of four spartan little bars on Main Street, with their infinite choice of German-style beers; herself, she said, she favored Bob's Place, but any place was fine.

And she told him of the vastness of the prairie sky, and how summer storms brought great masses of black and violet cloud in ceiling upon ceiling over the fields until the whole sky burst, and air became water, and lightning erupted in every quarter of the huge horizon; told him how the crude ticker tape tornado alerts would flicker across the bottom of the local stations on TV and tell you, maybe, if you lived in Sauk County then look out, and if you lived in North Freedom or Rock Springs, then you'd best get in the house. And she said, after storms, when dusk in the darkening corn filled as far as the eye could see with the tiny bright flares of the fireflies—it was the most beautiful thing, she said, that she knew; and she was crying.

She told him, "When you walk in the woods in the north, the trees are so tall and so giant and so old, there's nothing in between them and it's dark and it's like you're in a cathedral—it's echoing silent and you're miles from anywhere and sometimes all you hear is the wind and the forest, and then suddenly, somewhere, some big ancient tree just reaches its end and goes over and the crash of it falling sounds out all about you for hours—it seems like hours—and it's a sound like triumph because *there's always new trees, oh god. . . .*"

Charlie went to hold her as she shook uncontrollably; she heaved for breath through her tears, in physical pain and loss. Then, when she was still enough, he brought her his mattress from his bed, pushing boxes aside to lay it down on the living room floor. Then he was unsure, after tucking in sheets and blankets, how much more he should help her.

She realized what signal he was looking for; she smiled and told him, "It's OK. I can undress myself."

So he said good night, and went to sleep on the couch in his study; and he had strange dreams about a man with the world on his head, and televisions glowing, hissing at him in the night while, around and about him, the mortars flew, the shrapnel slashed in.... He had a bad night's sleep. Even beneath only one sheet, it was insanely hot. He woke at every sound from outside—when a helicopter thudded low over the house he jolted up from his pillow panting, sweating, waiting for the sound of the cannon....

In the Huey chattering past overhead, Chester Gantry flicked up the catches on his briefcase. In it were documents, tapes, a pair of complimentary tickets to the Hispania Cup Final, and a copy of the video of the something on Ecto VII. Before him through the windshield, the lights of the Heart rose up out of the night; the dishes turned, the signals flew, the electronics bleeped and winked, and things, thought Gantry, pumped nearer to their end. He could feel the change coming—the muscles of his body were ripe with energy; when he looked at his torso in the mirrors of hotel rooms in the mornings, he saw he was growing new hair and moles, as if his body was, he thought, getting the feel of the closing rhythms. He could smell the static in the air, and could mutter gleeful praise in his head to the Lord Who Shall Come with His Storm of Redemption....

Mel couldn't sleep any better than Charlie. She lay remembering a day's drive along the Mississippi and Lake Pepin, through Maiden Rock and Stockholm and Nelson and Fountain City, the great chained-together barge trains ploughing slowly by—but she'd heard the river, some summers, was half dry these days.

And she thought, for her exile, there was no vengeance big enough that she could take.

Part 2

THE PUMPING HEART

Now tell me what the Hell have we become?
Some dirty little bastards
What the Hell is going on?

FROM "BLIND," LYRICS BY DAVID BYRNE

6. DAWN OVER DOLLARVILLE

Water dried up where it was needed, and rose in floods where it wasn't. Bangladesh drowned, and Florida parched. Rivers turned, and ran in the wrong directions.

In Salt Lake City, in slow-trickling succession, street by street fell prey to the rising lake, and the torrentially evaporative microclimate created by attempts to drain it. There was a rapture of ferment on the networks; the Ark Arkadia theme park and resort, hastily jerry-built at a sensibly precautionary altitude in the Wasatch Range, did a roaring trade.

For an all-in day-entry fee of one hundred and fifty dollars, you could wander attractions like, perhaps, *Revelations,* the Movie, on the Holy Dome's 360-degree screen; or maybe sample the Great Mission Experience, a simulated chopper ride to an outer world of the un-Saved being variously smote down and redeemed by plague, inundation, hunger, locusts, and Christ's own American soldiers. But always, finally, burger-stuffed and soul-dazed, you took in the proud centerpiece, Unique in the World—the fully functional Millennium Ark.

You walked on board up a gangway over the Pond of the Floods (screaming roller coaster riders whizzed and clattered around the honeycomb of rails in a vast fiberglass Ararat beside you), and you led on a rope as you went to Salvation a pair of the trained animals of your choice. "Guests may select calves, dogs, ponies, goats, or hamsters. Llamas are available for a supplement of ten dollars. Peace be with you."

At the helm stood a computerized robot Jesus with neon halo, laser eyes, and the latest smart hand pistol in his belt. He turned to smile on each reverent family, each obese and vacuous old couple, and spoke unto them (in a voice of electric honey) a tape-looped text of scripture larded with exalted anticipation of His imminent coming. . . .

The bombings spread north into Colorado, and closed in a pincer movement from San Antonio and Miami on New Orleans; and the San Andreas got jittery. But to take their minds off it, causing loud and relieved sighs of Californian joy, Singani accepted, at last, a fifteen year ingress.

His family were airlifted abruptly from a threatened riot by the enraged citizens of his home town in Michoacán; while in the restaurant he now owned, it became instantly fashionable to drink your chilled martinis not with an olive, but with a fresh chili pepper floated in the stinging-cold and bracing liquor.

Three hundred miles south of the restaurant, at the Church of the Calvary Elected, a clandestine video was shot of the Rev. Jose Lee sodomizing the Saved Mary-Jill. A takeover bid was mounted by Pastor Ephraim Evangel of the Waco Fourteen Passions—and Dandy Royle, in the border mountains way south in the zone, was hugely amused. But Mr. Squalatush, who could find a TV nowhere, was anyway too busy with more urgent matters to care what happened, among the faraway host of the preachers.

The remnants of *Jefe* Scarskull's men were scattered into desperate marauding bands, running north to escape the mop-up after the engagement at El Coco. Twice he'd had to cower down on the sopping earth as danger passed close by; he knew there'd be no job in the world worse than that of a slave on the losing side. And what do you expect, if you create an army of mercenaries for no clear or good purpose, then spend half the time pretending they don't exist, and the other half running them like you couldn't run a piss-up in a brewery—but that, of course, is the CIA way.

Mr. Squalatush had a clear enough purpose: to evade recapture. So he moved west toward the centers of population, and prayed to every god he could think of, prayed hard that he'd not cross paths again with those savagely angry and spectacularly cruel groups of men. And he prayed in particular to the new tech god who lived in Hitachi, whose silken-stockinged image he still carried on his stolen cassette—prayed to this god partly because he was new; but also, partly because other, older gods seemed vanished or retreated from the forests he passed through, and the hills he crossed.

But he knew, it was the disturbance of the men who came here in war that displaced the spirits of the land, made refugees even of the gods of that region. . . . He trudged on until he came to a tarmac road, and turned south along the shoulder. The sun was shining brighter. As he walked on in the open, the map of soreness itched on his scalp.

No more video material came down to the Stockton Plateau. The rock beast had eaten the camera.

He was, by now, a good eighteen inches long, and a foot high at the top bauxite tip of his shoulder. Beady eyes of glass and gemstone glinted in the harshness of orbit light; his jet-black body was spangled with joints and sockets of priceless alloy, and his flat back had the deep luster of polished heavy metals. He felt great.

And he was enthralled by the beauty, the precious smallness of the blue-green-brown planet that hung beneath him. The planet his own species came from was massive and ghastly; in rock beast language, as far as we can approximate a translation, it was called Fat Hot Red Big Blob, No Luxuries; whereas the baby planet he'd now come upon was, plainly, paradise.

Equally plainly, its inhabitants were mad—but still, he continued his attempts to communicate with them. Each time he gnawed his way into another juicy transmitter link (the energy of the signals buzzing in his acid spittle like sherbet mixed with Coke) he slipped his greetings down the airwaves in a vocabulary learned from preachers and commercials and game shows, all fervent exhilaration and smooth talk—so if Ecto wasn't sending pictures to Kalero's Stockton base of the beast anymore, that didn't mean the beast wasn't sending word to other people of Kalero. But Kalero operatives now manned and monitored the major ground stations; and he could get no message through to any place higher than eighteen degrees north.

Even so, word spread through the spic zone of the pirate broadcaster with his station ident of a stockinged porno lovely, and his jovial excitement about the progress of the Hispania Cup—and he was enjoyed wherever he mysteriously cropped up.

With Singani on board, the Californians swept all before them in the tournament, marching inexorably toward the Final; and the rock beast, not having encountered soccer while drifting, frozen-pea-sized, through the cosmic gulfs, was entranced. He announced himself to conversion-blitzed villages by screaming, "Goh-o-o-ooaahhlll!!!" like a Brazilian, in his voice of crashing stones.

By other material, on other channels than Globewide Satsport, he was more than entranced; he was overwhelmed. He sat listening to the chaos of communication, the City of Angels beaming up all its gabbling madness in Spanish and English; and there was a third language too, zipping around the circuits of the humming big bird. It came in scrambled and irregular clusters, a million acronym-packed microgobbets of chattering junk, a multimessage mayhem without end of reports, requisitions, instructions, money movements, crackling warfare catechisms. It was the coded gobbledygook of the military and the megacorps, and it was wild; the rock beast thought, even the Suicide Zygotes of Bel-Pourri weren't this crazy.

As far as he could work it out, the military had a problem: half their rockets kept exploding on the launch pads or, alarmingly, right after they'd left them, scattering in the process the desert states and

Pacific atolls with ruptured debris, sheets of flame, spumes of radiation. And they had to hire, as a result, a fair proportion of their network off the corporate birds, the cargo liners of space.

So the garbled blips of war in one place, and readiness for it in the next involved, these Dollarville days—from Hawaii to Subic Bay, from Texas to Tegucigalpa, from the Washington Beltway to Bonn and Grosvenor Square—satellites owned and put in orbit by Hollywood, by Wall Street, by oil and aerospace and agriculture—by the meteorologists of commerce and conflict, the men who talked investment climates, the zecks sitting sweaty-browed in their offices with the need greedily to compete—the shareholders were jumping, the markets braying, and the military paid good; the zecks saw the images wired in from the agencies worldwide, screens pulsing on their desk tops: images and data on all the pies they were stirring with their long and sticky fingers. . . .

The rock beast logged on to a man researching options on meat futures in the burger market. He followed the data.

The data said the children of the Isthmus were starving; that cattle companies were clearing and grazing the land to a quick death by erosion; that hormone-pumped herds of unnatural genetic vigor grew fat, while the landless peasant grew thin.

The data said what piece of Miami was involved, what banks, what shippers, what politicos and *jefes;* it said the business kept cents off the cost of each burger in *el norte.*

And the data said those cents, in the Isthmus, would feed a child; but the data asked, where's the profit in that?

The man researching the market knew, from the data, that this couldn't much longer continue; but he told his client to buy anyhow.

While the party's good, you put off worrying about the hangover.

The rock beast listened to the figures for production and credit, yields and prices, forecasts and projections; he heard procurement authorizations under foreign military sales, and directives in the military assistance programs, and mission statements for joint exercises—lists of helicopter parts, costings, kill rates.

And the forests flamed and died. The blood of the few poor who resisted ran hot onto the ravaged dust. The monoculture estates grew rank with pesticide, herbicide, additive derangement; while up Stateside the burgers were rotting the lining of your gut, and the cartons they came in the lining of your planet.

It ain't no way, thought the rock beast (who'd taken to watching westerns) to run a railroad.

The people in the Heart had cash to join the party—and were on-line to earn, thought Charlie, the most stupendous of hangovers.

He sat looking in motionless silence through his study window at the bright towers of that district, where they work and play night and day; he could hear music from the resident's estate nearby, even now in the small hours, beyond the watchtowers and the walls.

He wondered, as he often did, if that place was the Heart, then where geographic-biologically did that leave Charlie Fish? He was, he guessed, sited somewhere like the lungs; he was at alveolus level, getting second-hand suck on the raw supply where it pumped from the center in rough surges. But he tried to dismiss that picture.

His body was damp, sitting up sleepless in the hot, Heart-illumined dark of early morning. Images of blood and explosion had ruined his nights since he'd been at El Coco; and now, back in Dollarville, he came to see that place, so far away, as just a shredded far capillary in this one big sick body. But he kicked himself out of being morbid; he wondered, with a remorseful grin, where to locate the Sex District in that geography metaphor. . . .

An orange-tinged haze in the sky blanked out all the stars. He'd come back, he remembered, into the worst summer ever. Insects bashed into the screen door that led to the little balcony above his garden. Then he thought, he wasn't rich, he didn't run to air-conditioning; but he was safer here than most, and happier. He had, at least, a garden and a home and work, of sorts. OK, he was alone, in his alveolus—but you can't have everything. He decided in the morning he'd chuck his zip-and-buckle boots away—they were foolish, he didn't want any more adventures—and then he'd sit things out where he was safest: he'd keep his head down, tucked tight beside the barriers of the Heart.

The Heart—it was a fantasy district, a place where the buildings gleamed fanatically stark and imperial with sheets of metal and glass—and where the streets were empty, come nightfall, of all but litter, the wind, a limo with security outriders racing soundlessly by. But what buildings! They were monumentally tall, jostling up together as, together, they leaped skyward like a cluster of gargantuan pins plugged in an overloaded grid. The Heart, thought Charlie, face lit by the turning lights of the place, it was where the world tried to dial into heaven—and where it found it had got a bad line.

Then he remembered there was a thing he'd meant to do for the American girl—just a small thing, but he thought she might appreciate the gesture.

He went to the cupboards where he stored all his maps—Charlie loved maps, he had piles and piles of them, his private index of the world, his library of brown and blue and green, of contour and relief, of infinite stimulus for daydreams about all the places and beauties to be remembered and treasured—and he rummaged among them until he found what he was looking for.

A few blocks along the grid, Chester Gantry writhed in his sleep in the executive suite at the Kalero Center. He would notice in the morning more new coarse hairs, growing now around his navel on his once-smooth stomach. He would think he, who was blond and angelic, now grew simian; he would smile to himself and see in the mirror, with fascination, the first suggestion that his teeth were getting sharper. . . .

Dawn over Dollarville, and already a toxic sun burnt bright through the huge glass roof of the Station.

Everyone came together at the Station—physically, anyhow, as of course spiritually such a thing was inconceivable—and most would much have preferred not to. But the Station was the place through which the city relocated and was, therefore, a place where perforce all kinds and classes of citizen had, waiting for their connections, to mingle one with the other in alarm and dislike. The people of the Heart, of course, were absent—with their private transit systems, their STOLports and helipads for instant easy transfer to the islands and the promontories where the grip of the muck in the air was not yet so fierce; where flowers still grew upright, under sleepless electronic surveillance. But for the rest, if you were going any place and your papers were in order, then you got there through the Station.

There were the service workers, waiters and receptionists and maintenance men; there were parole day-trippers from the manufactories, and militia on raucous leave making for the Sex District; there were the freight and cargo men come in from the terminals to get piss-drunk, and aliens of all skin color come from the quarantine regions to haggle for access at the Data Bureaux—all kinds of souls regular and irregular passed through here. And then Mud Alley backed onto it; but then Mud Alley backed onto everywhere now. It grew fingers creeping out to all quarters; it was no longer so much a zone as a spillage, an infestation because poverty, after all, is like dry rot. You can easily get away with not seeing it—and then one day your house falls down. . . .

Retch Larkins was, he knew, in danger of falling down badly himself if he didn't find the woman he needed. He stood in his uniform, pistol on his belt, his driver Tad with his Uzi at his side, and watched the milling travelers. He had hoped for a while now that the woman he wanted might be found among these people, shining through the murk of the city's lurching commute, and he eyed eagerly all the faces and bodies that passed.

He had a dream. He was sick of being a company cop—and, learning from experience gained from a profitable sideline distributing porn to the airbases, he had gone to the moguls at Network 69; and put forward proposals, treatments, synopses, and budgets for the production of what, in his dream, would be the most perfect pornography ever made.

The schedules on 69 were clogged with striptease game shows, sleazy documentaries in pickup bars, bored models with spotty asses and saggy tits. The ratings were in free-fall; after the initial novelty, people turned back in droves to the nighttime soaps. So what you need, Larkins told the moguls, is to meet the soaps on their own ground. They have the formula—so make a porno-soap, with all the production values. But for such a series, you'd need a Star; a woman all Dollarville could dream of at night. . . .

It wouldn't do, he knew, to tour the Sex District, just pick some half-decent doxy, and get on with it. We were talking quality here. And she was out there somewhere—but proving, as the days went by, more difficult to find than he'd reckoned. He was normally a confident man—and had entered on this project, this bold career change, with no hint of self-doubt, with, indeed, a boundless entrepreneurial enthusiasm—only to find that the things you saw in your head were not, in the real world, quite so easily seen. And now time was pressing. 69 had put up seed money, enough to open an office and a studio in back of it, and to start building sets; they had the proper money waiting, for the day the shooting of the pilot could commence—and they were fretting, because they wanted to know where the star was.

It was happening again. He'd gone down into the throng on the concourse, been excited by the buzz of fear and movement, seen the eddies and whirls of the crowd parting and joining around announcement screens, advert stands, snack bars, and transit gates; seen pickpockets and parasol salesmen, vagabonds and drunks, druggies and God freaks all melting aside, swimming away from the path of his uniform, of Tad with the Uzi clasped loose at his side—and he'd felt, again, the excitement grow pale. He had a drowning sensation in the drab, hunch-shouldered, dirty-clothed flood of all these people, people among whom only the aliens and the crims were colorful, only the silver-fingers and the badge-bedecked pamphlet sellers swimming, eel-like, slippery, and untouchable away, as slippery and untouchable as that perfect strong woman who would look, how could he put it, *ecologically accurate*. . . . But, he abruptly decided, he had to stop coming here. His picture of how she'd be grew blurred, lost shape behind the weight of the faces of the people, their trying-to-be-invisible way of walking, their daily shuffle from shacks and projects in the out-regions on graffito-raddled trolley trains to work, beg, buy, sell. . . . At least, he thought, it proved the essence of his project correct. Because if this was the audience, then the need for a star to lift them up in their evenings, to give them wet dreams of safe sex, was most depressingly obvious.

A scuffle broke out twenty yards through the mass to his left. A gang of white storm-boys had set upon two aliens, a man and a woman. They wrenched at the woman's clothes, one breast was exposed; she shrieked with rage while her man, lashing furiously about him to defend her, gave good account of himself in a gale of fists and booted feet. Larkins nodded to Tad, and they went over.

Spotting their approach, the gang fled. Larkins felt an urge to terminal violence, wished there were not so many people about, wished he could direct Tad to fire the Uzi after the hooligans, blow their legs away from under them in many bloody pieces. . . . The alien couple weren't much hurt; the man stood, wiping at his bruises, helped by the girl who was shaking with anger—but was also resolutely dignified, and, he now saw, quite staggeringly lovely. It crossed his mind that she . . . But it was out of the question, the data work to get her status acceptable would be a nightmare—and there could, anyhow, be no hint that any member of his cast might test positive. Even so, even so he asked if they were OK.

The man was still preoccupied with putting himself together again; but the woman, saying yes with thanks, was reserved to the brink of being surly.

There had been a time, earlier in his career, when Larkins with diligent prejudice would have taken her proud demeanor, her stiffly self-sustaining bearing as sufficient cause for some sturdy harassment—arrest, maybe, or some lingering, invasively physical stop-and-search. But now, with the perspective of a man meaning not much longer to be on the Borough Patrol, he found himself impressed. He pushed his peaked cap back on his head and told her, "I'm sorry there's not more I can do to help. Look, um—what's your name?"

He could see she was surprised he wasn't asking for passes, ID—but then he was beginning to find, these days, the meager and circumscribed accreditations of the aliens indefinably depressing—a pack of restrictions for every privilege.

She answered him, "Miriam. Miriam Patajoli. My man is Acushla."

Larkins's own Christian name was Reg (converted by friends, in the way that nicknames stick, to Retch, in honor of the way his first night's drinking at cadet school had ended) and he'd always dimly resented the blunt Anglo-Saxon of it, the way it was as short and cut off and glamorous as a wooden leg. He now surprised himself—he really was become quite the dreamer—by saying "Acushla," rolling it in his mouth, then asking, "What's it mean?"

"It means," the man said, "pulse of my heart." He grinned. "I know we don't look it, but actually the name's Gaelic."

They all looked at each other. Larkins realized he'd started a conversation that had nowhere to go, with no way he could easily end it; because the woman was, simply, too beautiful to be easily walked away from. She was tall, with dense rich hair, a high forehead and full mouth, thin waist, and long legs; the one firm breast was still, he realized, assertively bare. But it wasn't her body you looked at, the core of the beauty was in the eyes, shining deep pools of brown like melted chocolate. Feeling, quite unlike himself, increasingly helpless, he reverted to his patrol manner and took their address; the sorry sparse code of a barrack in AQ14. But to show he wasn't being heavy, he handed over his number at the Kalero Center. He suggested, if maybe they had a problem again ... it was ridiculous. Bemused, the couple took his card (they were still not deferential) and walked away. Larkins said again, "Acushla," to their departing backs.

"Black Irish," said Tad, who spoke not often, and always to the point. "You can't get much more alien than that." But what he was thinking was, his boss was headed further off the rails every day. He followed him to the jeep, and they set off to clock in at the company's headquarters.

When he was sure the patrolmen were gone, Cairo Jones stepped around from behind a burbling bank of info-screens, and shoved his big ungainly way through the people to the Patajolis. When he got close he hissed, "Hey, Suzie—what did he want? Are they onto us?"

Suzie shook her head, "Nah. Weirdest thing I ever see—the cop was nice to us. He didn't ask no questions. He even gave us his number."

Cairo looked at Larkins's card; he said, "Kalero. I got a drop-off there later, I'll see if I can poke about. That cop, he's been down here too often." Cairo didn't like the notion that they might be getting staked out any more than did the fake-black Patajolis. He said, I'll see you tonight," and walked heavily away.

Jimmy Baines was Dollarville pure, a rising young man, high on the pulse of the Heart. When he got into his office at Vidivici PR, he took the call from the man Gantry at Kalero in his stride. He'd heard they had problems; he'd heard they were flying in a high-up; he wondered what sort of work they might hand him; he said, yes, he'd be at the meeting—then crossed the room and watched the early morning world below his windows.

He was on the thirty-eighth floor and reckoned thirty-eight, for now, was about right—was plenty high enough. He could look down on (and command) a great portion of the chances and thrills then obtaining in Dollarville; but wasn't yet so high that he was disconnected from the action. He could still feel the umbilical links to the towers all around him, still touch the tempests of cash and data exchange coursing around between them—the trade-offs all glued together by a shuttling of zecks and PA's from one vast windy portal to the next, from one hothouse greenery of an atrium to another, from one gut-inverting elevator ride to the next pothole-jolted, liquor-smoothed, TV-watching sortie in the limo to more meetings, more fear-striking visits by helicopter to the manufactories.

Baines reckoned, yes, he was at about the right height. The way he saw it, to have risen any higher when he was still only thirty-two—that would have been inviting rarefication a touch too early. What lay above him would be, he knew, more stressful, less world-related in any graspable sense—it would be more weird.

He'd soon, on the level ladder, be in the forties; and he was gird-ing his loins. It was the management clearing zone up there, from which more fell than could ever hope to pass through and on up. He used the word, "fall," quite literally; as a man of ambition, he'd long considered you might as well go out the window and be jam on the pavement than rise no higher than the forties—and there were many ways to fall.

You might move sideways to a sinecure, with some large and empty title set aside for you like External Relations Director, which meant you spent the rest of your life at lunch. Or you moved out altogether, cashing in your chips and taking what you'd amassed to Retirement County, planning to play more golf, or go rambling, or buy that new racket and work on your game. What a yawn, thought Baines. He knew people who'd cut and run that way, whose wives perhaps would try softly to hint how "sensible" the move had been. Some of them continued to work in a small way, as "consultants" (he tossed them scraps of work and queried their invoices); others opened restaurants, fish farms, "outdoor activity" ventures where you climbed a rock or two. When Baines, rarely, visited them, their too-overt contentment struck him as nervous; he felt as if it were pushed toward him the way a broke street salesman might tout a bad insurance policy.

And then there were the people who really fell, who fell all the way—and who Baines somehow liked best because he guessed their falling was not tainted by hypocrisy, but only by a lack of self-knowledge. They were the drinking types, mostly, who thought they deserved to get more promotion and were appalled, then stunned, then furious when they didn't—furious in a self-corroding way, so the fury gnawed their bellies more injuriously than ever the liquor did their livers. Stalled, they kicked in a frenzy at the broken engines of their careers—then, fallen, they'd crop up later, unexpected and intriguing. He'd see them, maybe, in clothes that had begun to date and get dirty, standing on boxes or chairs in the streets of the Heart (and then later yet at the gates, when access was withdrawn) lecturing on their bugbears over the heads of the work force shunting by. And later yet they'd settle, finally, in the gutters of the Sex District. . . .

Baines wondered if he mightn't prove to be like those men. He was, let's face it, a world-or-bust merchant; he'd have to watch himself, hard and close. Because when you passed on, up into the fifties—you were making levels one to three. And up in strategy land, it all got suddenly—how you say?—more *political* . . . Thousands, tens of thousands, moved, even in their sleep, at the behest of your decisions, and never even knew you existed—until in the seventies you looked down from your huge sheets, your seas and plains of tinted glass, and even the stretch limos had shrunk to insignificant dashes, sliding strips of color in the thumping grid at your feet; the people weren't ants, they were less than ants, they were specks so far below that they vanished altogether beneath the cliff faces of your tower, your little heaven in the sky with its Persian carpets and fine paintings, its workout weights and showers, its malts discreet in the window bar, its secure and instant telecom, worldwide, on private lines to all the other little heavens, to jets and yachts and festivals and estates. . . . Where even pure money was beneath you, and the papers wrote you up as a philosopher of trade.

Baines wondered what it would be like up there, with your view of the big picture determined for good; when you were not yourself important anymore, and only the megacorp mattered, and all that you had was His. . . . With a shiver of fear he wondered, up there, if you'd have any friends. He made ready to mount the heights of Kalero.

The meeting came to order.

"As you know," said Chester Gantry—and Baines was impressed by the small American's lithe intensity, the way he seemed almost to be twitching with force—"we've been sponsoring the Hispania Cup. A goodwill exercise, you might say, for our Latin friends. We have, however, encountered a problem."

The conference room was bright, and sparingly but expensively furnished. Baines had been in the room before, taking briefs for PR programs—their planning, their execution, their distribution. He had not found Kalero, in the past, a forthcoming sort of outfit. On Gantry's right, the three local headmen from marketing, space technical, and personnel all sat in a row, fingers twined in silence on the table before them like, thought Baines, the three monkeys. He knew two of them by sight and one of them well: Bull Mercy, who ran marketing; they'd been at the same college, had lunch often, did a lot of work together. But all three, this morning, looked more close-mouthed than ever. They let Gantry do the talking.

There was, said Gantry, something screwing with the key new link in Kalero's satellite chain. And the corporate solution, he moved on—too hastily, it seemed to Baines—was the sending into orbit of an astronaut to rectify that problem.

It must, thought Jimmy Baines, be quite a problem. And he knew it was for sure, when Gantry then presented the decision to use an allied pilot. Gantry said it was an opportunity for a PR drive around all the colonies, on the theme of cooperation, partnership, hands across the water. . . . Bull said to Jimmy, "What with that and the Hispania, we'll get no end of people thinking we're wonderful. Name of the game, Jim."

The name of the game, thought Jimmy, is your satellite's fucked up, and if you don't get it working, you'll have funded a shitload of airtime that half your audience don't get to see.

"The pilot's name," said personnel, "is Deke Lewis. He's on a base away northeast of town. . . ."

Baines asked, "Does he know he's got the job yet?"

Gantry told him, "Not yet."

And the name of the game, he thought, is you send up an ally 'cause whatever it is, it's too dangerous to risk an American. Nice. He said, with his business mask on, "Fine, that's not important now. But can I say—if I'm going to devise you a campaign here, get a story up and running and the story's on the lines of, say, our brave boy gets the flight of his life to solve, heroically, a problem on the glamorous techbird Ecto VII, well—won't I need to know what that problem is he's solving? I mean, we can't say it's heroic if all he does is adjust three bolts and then come home again. There's people go do that all the time these days—Frogs, Nips, Arabs, Argies, the Russians even put up a Polynesian the other day. . . ."

Gantry said only, "I'm sorry, the problem's classified. It's also irrelevant."

Bull chipped in, "C'mon Jim, it's the exploits that matter. We needn't bore the proles with technology; so long as the pictures look pretty, they won't need too many facts."

Baines took the hint. But after the meeting he got Bull aside and asked him, "So what goes on?"

"Off the record," Bull grinned, "If we were giving our moron friends in the gutter press their headlines, well—let's say we might say, 'Commie Robot Eats Big Bird.'"

"You what?"

"Oh, never mind, Jim, never mind. Just draw us up some proposals, a schedule, a budget. And we'll need some early releases. Can you get a writer on the case?"

"Sure, we'll use Charlie. He should be back by now—he turns things around good and quick. When does Lewis go up?"

"Tomorrow."

"That's quick," said Baines. He realized with a shock just how bad what was happening on the satellite must be—and headed for the elevator. He was turning over in his mind already the possibilities of the Ecto Rescue—the sound bites, the photo ops, the video, the IMAX, the merchandising . . .

Striding preoccupied across the hushed huge atrium, past the flowing fountains and the gross corporate art, he only narrowly avoided being barged aside by a large and lumbering bike boy, creaking in leathers and boots across the marble.

And as he left, Cairo Jones showed at the reception his messenger outfit's clearance; he asked for Chester Gantry. When told he couldn't be seen in person, he said, "His secretary'll do. It's personal delivery. From a Mr. Marcovaloza." They waved him through.

7. MUTATIONS

Gantry stared through the deep-tinted window high in the Kalero offices. He saw, far below, the limos of the Heart, long cream corpuscles plugged in by their boomerang aerials to the telecom DNA, gliding, unhindered by commoner traffic, along the center lanes of wide avenues. The sun, even through the tint, was now a raging disk. He felt its heat on his hands on the sill—and felt the pulse, the big bad last biorhythm surging.... But he'd been sensitive since he could remember, since he was a quiet and earnest kid.

In the little town where he grew up there'd been problems. They'd built a nuke plant, oh, ways down the river; but, long ago, had also buried waste from that plant up the river the other way, and done it sloppily—then kept it quiet when, later, a developer moved in, and had houses going up on the green field site before anyone remembered or realized. And the people who came from Charleston or Huntington to live, peaceful, in the new satellite country settlement found, as years went by, a child here, a child there, coming down with leukemia.

But not Chester.

In the rough outfield of the baseball park one evening, he found an old technician's glove poking from the soil. When he picked it up, it seemed to him to hum, to buzz. He held it close to his face, he breathed it in; it smelt like the air before thunder, tingling, charged, tense with particles. He came to like that feeling. He found other places where that sense and that scent were strong. There was a creek where a pair of old steel drums lay half buried in the muddy bottom. Some summer days, after rain, he'd see the water there grow oily, slick, turning thick and dimly glowing with blue and red veins. He leaned forward, and raised the strange water to his lips. . . . Other kids up and down this street or that lost their hair, their strength, their lives; legal trench warfare began, and went on, and hearings were heard, and committees committed, and opinions opined, and research re-searched (they found, one time, one old lady's shower stall was a hot spot, and another man's porch, and another man's garden shed) but Chester—tiny but perfectly proportioned, fair and very bright-eyed, the midget class wiz—grew healthy. He felt fine.

Out beneath the flagpole at the community's little clapboard school, there was a place where the ground felt especially alive. He felt the force, the rays, running in his muscles, his arteries—and looking back now from where he stood staring out into the stale baked air between the canyon walls in the Heart, he marked his life back to that point, that spot by the school flag. He remembered what he'd learned of how the frontier was won from the red man, and of the new frontier above—of God, family, and freedom in Alabama, Alaska, Arizona, Arkansas, California, Colorado, Connecticut, Delaware . . . he could still recite them all.

He learned in school that they called it half-life, decay. It seemed to him a limp description of the new world force, first fully liberated at the Trinity site whose sandy floor was fused to glass; it seemed to him every particle was more power to the earth's first atomic nation. . . .

He had a good career and at least two good covert wars (the record has gaps in it; there may have been others). In his marine capacity with a previous administration, he learned his trade stoking "pressure," "leverage," right to the limit of all his clandestine capabilities. He acquired along the way the necessary personas—sly, braggadocio, pious, epic—for use at all the meetings in featureless hotel rooms, or for coming on as the hero, when it came time to bullshit Congress. And he learned to lunch with bankers, weaponry merchants, all manner of expeditors in discreetly expensive European back street restaurants. He learned to pass money (oil money, gun money, drug money) invisibly around the cables of traceless account systems. And then he went free lance—the way public servants will, naturally, go private and cash in.

Marcovaloza was a good client of long standing; a firm anti-Commie. Gantry'd sold him systems, methods, networks, instruments, techniques, a data base. Screens in offices in the president's palaces had blinked through the night with new names for the squads, or scrolled through list upon list in the Man's counterinsurgency bunker, out on the edge of the city by the playpen where he fed rebels to his panthers—and it seemed only natural, when he lost his little country of coffee, cotton, cattle, and hardwood swamp (fifty thousand dead, from three million) to advise him, then, on how best to reinvest the contents of the country's coffers that he took with him when he left. A few junk bonds here, some heavy gearing there, and one hostile reverse takeover later, the Man went multinational. He couldn't show himself—there are rules to these games—but he had the properties in Manhattan and the ranches in Texas, the offices in the Free Zone and the airstrips on the cays—and he made himself felt.

And Gantry felt, in the tower, in the air, in the Heart pumping faster and faster, all the world rhythms speeding to their end. . . . He buzzed his secretary, and sent her out to the drug store. He needed antacids, mouthwash, skin cream; thin blood coursed with excitement in his temples.

He moved away from the window to the desk, and opened his briefcase. He took from it the video, and the double wad of Hispania Cup Final flight and stadium tickets. The latter was loose and thick, so he tucked it into the cassette case to keep all the papers and passes together. Then, as he looked away, he felt his hands still moving on the desk top and looked back down.

The muscles up his forearms were crawling, shifting, rippling of their own volition beneath his skin. He felt contractions in his once-almost-luminous but now hairy chest; he put one hand inside his shirt—hardening nails scraped the rough flesh. He felt, beneath his fingertips, the spread of warts and moles, the heaving plexus and pectorals. He was aglow with writhing energy in the glaring hard light of the Dollarville sun; his face worked and twisted, sharp-toothed, thrilled. . . . He turned, realizing the door to the reception area was still open, and walked quickly away into the office's private rest room. Then, locked in, he waited for the fit to pass, surging, exultant—with searing delight he barfed yellow bile, holding his bristling face in his hands. The waste basket by the basin was over-flowing already with disposed-of disposable razors. . . .

Cairo arrived, bearing Marcovaloza's invitation to Gantry—there was to be a dinner in Dickburg that evening. He found the front desk unattended and the office door ajar. He pushed it open and went in. There was no sound from the washroom. He stepped up to the desk and set the envelope down on it, then stared in amazement at the priceless wad of all-access Hispania ticketry poking from the edge of the tape box by the briefcase. If he paused, it was barely for a second. His arm jumped out and he gathered up the cassette case, the tickets and all in one go, in one slab-of-meat hand. He stuffed it all hastily in his shoulder satchel, then quickly made his exit.

A short time later Gantry, shaved, with his body back in control and his breathing low, unlocked the rest room door and went back into the office.

Cairo was in an elevator headed down, heart leaping with excitement at his treasure-trove find—he could fly to the Isthmus; he could watch soccer's Latin greats—he could get out of Dollarville.

High above, Gantry thought, He shall come . . . and he wondered if someone might first catch him before He did come, see him in his bulging, particle-energy fits that were now so strong, as the beat of things accelerated toward that day—and what, then, would they think of Chester Gantry, God's American soldier? He saw on his desk the embossed envelope from the owner of Kalero—and saw beside it that the tickets were gone, and the Ecto video with them. Still beady with spasm-sweat, he dialed, immediately, the tower's security.

Retch Larkins's face appeared in black and white on the desktop monitor. He was wearing, Gantry saw, an outlandishly customized uniform—white, navy-style, with bold gold epaulettes—but Gantry'd heard, this man Larkins who ran security here, he was getting uppity and unreliable. He said to him, "There's a messenger, a bike rider"—he read the name on the delivery docket attached to the dinner invitation—"works for Sharply Sharply Couriers, he has a video cassette and some documents, company property, stolen. He must be leaving the building about now—get after him, retrieve that material. Go—do what's necessary."

He cut the connection, and the picture shut down. And he had a different twinge, now, of pleasure; pleasure at the knowledge that when he told people to do "what's necessary" that meant, he'd given license to kill.

Cairo, clicking up through the gears, sped off the slipways across the forecourt in front of the atrium. In the basement carport, Tad and Larkins gunned their jeep up the ramp, and gave chase with their sirens gone *a-whah, a-whah-ah-ooohhn.* . . .

Charlie, who'd at last got to sleep in the small hours, woke to the sound of sirens away in the Heart—but felt, here in his home, untroubled. No war zone shit here—the situation status was, he thought, Condition Calm; alerts Amber (freeze) and Red (flee) were no longer the order of the day. Well—comforting illusions were, by then, common enough Dollarville coin.

He wondered if he should wake the American girl; but left her, when he came down to find her sleeping sound amid the clutter of the living room floor. He went through, instead, to the kitchen; found himself falling easily back into the comfort of routine. He wore, like every morning, his kikoi—and he took, like every morning, a one-eye check over the switch panel, to see the house was still secure. Then he thought, like every morning, of his bladder, of Florida grapefruit, of herbal tea and antibug tabs and, yes—now he was back—of work. He'd have to get some in. He'd go see Jimmy Baines, and find out what Frontline Ricochet had to say for themselves now.

The first time Charlie saw Jimmy Baines, one mealtime at college—he also, like Bull Mercy, had been at the City Tech—he'd not have guessed that the guy was ambition-intense. He was, on the contrary, as unstiff as you could get, light-stepping in flopping moccasins past the refectory tables. He was good-looking like a film star, not quite real; he had wide shoulders held straight, and a strong tanned chest of which the most part was arrogantly, casually on display between the open buttons of a working man's shirt. He walked like he knew you were looking at him.

And late one evening in Baines's room they drank—with, in Charlie's case, that laid-back bravado young men have when they talk of who they are, and what they'll be—coffee and whiskey, and then more whiskey. Charlie told a ludicrous story of how, poor and free and "on the road" (as he put it), he'd slept on the beach a few nights at Cannes (or was it Nice?) and got to know, and then to sleep with, a ravishing Brazilian girl, a fellow traveler mahogany-skinned, rich of hair and full of breast.

Well—there wasn't, back then, the inhibitory business of showing potential partners your neg card; and it might have been true. Tale spinning, Charlie added the nice detail of how he and the girl washed their hair together at dawn under one of the fresh-water showers installed on the beach for bathers, to wash off the salt from their swimming. Baines rather liked that touch. But Charlie was, in fact, not only a word merchant (learning the art of mendacity on a corporate scholarship from an ad firm) but, also, a virgin.

Baines didn't bother saying whether he was or not. He only said, he meant to make a million.

And he set about doing so while Charlie, a few years later, set about getting fired. He told friends he'd gone free lance—but what he'd actually gone and done was join a demonstration, back when the rumors spread (unconfirmed) that Pretoria'd gone tactical. And he got his photograph taken; and his adfirm told him they couldn't have politically motivated people writing ads, *now could they?* . . . Charlie thought, now, thinking of Mel in the next room, it could be a thing in your blood or a notion in your head, but wherever it was they found it—and then they dumped on you.

Baines told him he was an asshole; and began to feed him a stream, albeit an unsteady one, of work.

So if you go in a store, and there's a video telling you about that lawn mower you'd really, really like to own—or if you visit some conference or exhibition and there's a wall-load of screens and computer-run tape-slide, babbling about what pension to get, what car to buy, what bank to borrow from until you, too, are another private mini-Mexico, another walking debt bomb—or if a salesman comes around to your house or your office and asks you, "You VHS? Or Beta?" then shows you his tape about the design you want, the image you love, the speed you need, the state-of-the-art, the leading edge, the desktop of the decade, the microwave of the month, or any other complacent corporate garble about our-strength-is-our-people, fast-forward-to-the-future—well, just remember, pay attention—because with Traderstown before him and the pumping Heart behind, his income rocky and his head kept down, it might be Charlie Fish who wrote that shit.

He finished his tea; from the Heart, closer now, came more sirens. The American girl slept on, undisturbed. And he guessed, erroneously, that she must sleep long, injured that way.

He didn't want to wake her, and left the map he'd dug out for her amid the mess on the kitchen table. He sat, instead, remembering Suzie; she'd been a heavy sleeper too, after staying out at all hours up to nefarious little bits of no good; you had to bounce on the bed, yodelling mezzoforte, to wake her. And he remembered, when he'd met her one evening, newly jobless, how she'd seethed. She'd said, "God's sake, Charlie, you can't even turn an *honest* buck, can you? Don't you know what inflation's at now? Don't you know three figures in a row when you see them? What you going to do, you idiot, you *idiot*—I mean Jesus, what did you *say* to them?"

He told her, "I said, I hoped their mucus turns to ashes and their shit into shrapnel."

He shook his head to clear the memory, and quickly went upstairs to dress. He left Mel a note saying he'd not be long, then ran fingers in a quick riffle through the vouchers in his wallet. They said his plastic was still good for a few last thousands yet—though one day, he still managed bravely to think, there'd be yen on his balance; one day they'd key in his codes and smile up from the screens, new-age-processed-clerkishly beautiful, to say, "In yen, sir? That'll do nicely." We all dream.

There was a siren near, and louder. He reached the door in the hallway, stopped, and checked himself over. He was always a checker, Charlie, checking he had what he needed in order about his person because it was, after all, a disorderly world. He was smart (but not executive) in clean jeans, ironed shirt, a livid tie in swimming-pool blue and pheasant copper, and—he couldn't, after all, bear to part with them yet—those gray zip-and-buckle boots that said (lying), This Man is an Adventurer. . . .

If the truth be told, the state of the streets these days, Charlie Fish gets scared just stepping out the door. Outside, he knew, the smoke-steam-traffic of Dollarville was rising to meet the yellow sun. He shuddered; he felt some chemical imbalance, some atmospheric-celestial disturbance, some turbulence he'd do well to avoid—but didn't he always?

His fingers ticked digits into the panel to unbolt the front door. The miniscreen blipped, READY TO UNLOCK—SELECT ENTER, OR CANCEL. He pressed Enter, and the door told him it was open. He stepped out and hit the street, and saw Cairo Jones die. *Parp-parp, a-whah-whah-ah-ooohhn* went the sirens in his soul, Condition Red Immediate.

In the Dickensian den of low tenement facades around the market yard, the garbage truck had come on one of its infrequent and irregular calls; it had just commenced the grinding ritual of a multipoint turn, rocking between the stall-loads of vegetable and electrical detritus as Charlie opened his door. He saw the rusty yellow monster, its only clean aspect the emblazoned borough and corporate logos on its side, go *clang-jolt* forward into a crate of watermelon. Burst purple flesh, seed-packed, dribbled down the truck's radiator; the trader whose stock was smashed whipped past the flapping hood, and started yelling in the driver's window, banging his fist on the dented door. The driver shrugged, window wound up, face hidden in the shadow of visor and breath mask. Charlie stood, just ready to pull his door shut behind him—and heard the motorbike come.

It was a sudden shriek of engine over the low rumble of the juddering truck, the high angry shouting of the trader. Charlie's head spun left, looking back up his side street to where it met the main road by the big gates into the Heart; he saw the bike tear around the corner, jolted and bucking where it had cannoned over the speed ramp by the security cabins. It veered, then straightened up toward him. He heard gears clicking, the engine catching, accelerating, and with the rider hunching down it came faster and faster. A jeep streaked around the corner behind it, siren howling. A man in uniform—flat peaked hat like a navy officer's—held one hand above him on the roll bar. The bike was up to Charlie's house already; it dipped to turn the angle into the yard, and went straight into the back of the garbage truck, which was reversing there directly into its path.

The truck registered nothing; its churning backward progress wasn't even momentarily disturbed. The bike simply stopped, lost all momentum, all velocity, crumpled to debris in the blink of an eye. There was just the one bad, ugly metal bang, and an instant howl as the engine cut. Charlie watched as if in slo-mo, in the coming of that same terrible, cavernous silence that he'd already heard just a few days back in the war zone, as all the pieces of machine went spinning and flying away; he saw the rider's shoulder bag hurl off into the air in a tumbling arc (and realized it was coming his way); he saw the body of the rider then, understood the physics of impact; saw it part from the bike and fly straight on, a flesh missile, into the crunching-down jaws of the waste muncher, great chewing blocks of rough-toothed metal chomping into the pond of cartons and papers, cans and wrappers. He saw the neck break, saw the head snap to an impossible angle on the shoulder as the trajectory stopped dead, the body seeming to pause, horizontal, at this moment of terminal energy release—then it fell into the rubbish, floppy as a trash bag.

Charlie stared, fixed, at bits of bike ringingly whirling to rest on the cobbles; then looked up, stepped forward, caught the strap of the shoulder bag as it sailed earthward in front of him—it felt light, not much in it—and stayed motionless for one stupid long instant before backing hastily through his still open door. The jeep pulled up as he sneaked a last glimpse through the crack; he saw the guy with the officer's hat swinging out, walking forward to inspect the body slowly vanishing into the truck's still-working innards. Charlie edged the door shut; then stooped to peer through the grilled mailbox—thinking, as if it were any normal day, that he should really get rid of it now all his mail came electronic. Who knows, he thought, peering, what some stranger might pour in the slot. . . .

The truck's engine was turned off. The uniformed man pulled the corpse back by one foot; he seemed to turn the body a bit, looking beneath it, then dropped it. He took a piece of old curtain rod off the waste and poked with it into the wobbling surface, looking for something. Charlie felt the bag in his hands. Then the cop stood back and wrenched the lids off the panniers on the back of the ruined bike. Nothing there either. He directed his driver to look around the yard; he asked the melon trader if he'd seen anything, but—Charlie sighed with relief—from his gestures he plainly hadn't.

The last thing Charlie needed was patrol in his house, with dope on the kitchen table and a blood risk asleep on the living room floor. Then he saw, echoing again, the snap of the neck in the engine-loud silence; his breath rushed out of him, he felt briefly sick.

Mel on her crutches behind him asked, "What the hell is going on?"

She'd be tall, thought Larkins, tall and blonde—his mind wasn't really on his work. He studied blankly the crusty boots in the bloodied garbage, not seeing them; seeing instead the pictures in his head, of silk skin on silk bedding, maids, nurses, wide wet . . .

He said to Tad, "He must have dropped it someplace. We'll go back. Go easy, keep your eyes peeled." He stepped back to the jeep. It had on its low doors, like all city management vehicles, its sponsor's logo; this one showed the world, ringed with its necklace of satellites.

Slowly the jeep moved away, tacking up the uneven road toward the gates of the Heart. The truck followed behind, the men in the cab arguing what they should report back at depot, and to whom. Did Cairo now qualify as refuse? The aggrieved trader stood watching as they went, maroon melon flesh drying around his shoes.

Once the jeep was out of vision, Charlie rose and retreated past Mel into the living room, the bag held out before him in both hands. She waited for an answer to her question—but he'd not really heard it, and was only now beginning again to register his surroundings. The silence slowed its booming in his ears; the plaster walls took shape, the ratty old armchair, the pictures he'd taken in happier times—the world nervously, carefully, settled back into place about him. But the body still flew, the head still snapped aside . . . he looked down.

There were two snaps; he pulled them open and took out the contents. The ticket wads didn't interest him—the last thing he wanted was to be back in the spic zone watching soccer—so he tossed them aside, more interested in the videotape. It had on it that Kalero logo, the world with its necklace, and a weighty security restriction.

He slid it in the slot of his VCR, picked up the remote, and turned things on. He pressed Play. The screen hissed, showed white snow, turned the frame over and over on itself a few times, then settled down to a time code, and the stark, flaring light of orbit.

The traders gathered outside around the wreckage of the bike.

Inside, Charlie stared at the rock beast. The image was a blurred black blob, moving jerkily about on the tip of the satellite's solar wing; but seeing it Charlie remembered, in every detail, the tale Mr. Squalatush had told him, the crazy old man in his hole by the river with his video of God—who wasn't, he thought, so crazy after all. He reran the tape, stunned; he whispered to himself, "There's your techspirit, old man, your god who talks on television. . . ."

Mel asked him what on earth he was talking about.

Hurriedly Charlie told her, "Not *on* earth, *off* it—listen, sit tight, I got to see a man about an alien." Because what the hell else could it be?

Baines would know how to handle this; there were dollars galore for the man who broke this story, and yen—Jesus, the Nips would pay an arm and a leg and a gold kimono too. Charlie was jump-started out of shock, now, into electric awe and action. He headed out fast, mindful this time to leave by the back way.

Mel followed him, and, again, asked urgently what was happening. He stopped, waving the tape in front of him with a manic inability to articulate; then he gabbled, brain rattling with the possibilities, "Listen, there's a space creature on this tape, *I'm gonna make world history.*" He turned on his heel and sped panting away through the kitchen door.

Mystified, Mel clumped behind him into the garden.

The garden amazed her. It was small, and what wasn't protected was in a fearful state, laid waste by the terrible summer, the pollutant mesh generating spavined weirdness in the pots and beds and window boxes.

But what was protected, was protected fanatically. She saw an array of sealed wood-and-polythene structures with sprinklers, dripfeeds, gas bottles, zippered vents; her flashing eyes took in a feast of flora. The guy, she thought, was a herbalist already.

There was coriander, basil, tarragon, and dill; but then she saw bloodroot and skunk cabbage, evening primrose and valerian, sticky willy and echinacea and meraa—she saw, with disbelief, *datura stramonium.*

She wondered, had he popped a seed for breakfast, to make the kindly man of the previous evening now so thoroughly unhinged?

Then she caught him, as he wrestled loose the last cranky bolts on his garden gate. He turned and said, seeing her stare around the rickety herb tents, "Hey, what you looking at? Man's gotta do something, when the work don't come in. Look, stay here, OK? Talk to the plants, amuse yourself. Me, I got some business just now."

And he was on his way, wrenching the gate open to get out through the jerry-built back wall. She saw through the opening an alleyway, and on the far side of it the dull glint of sheets of steel. She called, "No, hey wait, Charlie Fish—*are you crazy?*"

She swung frantically after him on her strong big arms—and damn near made, as she came through the gate behind him, what might easily have proved to be a fatal mistake.

Charlie'd built the back wall with his neighbors—on the one side Sweet Doreen, who ran doxies in the District; and on the other, his good buddy Les the Flower Man.

The Flower Man's yard was a sheathed and airtight jumble of sheds and forcing pots, a crowded artificial nave of prepollutant purity. He supplied offices in the Heart with bouquets, at unbelievable prices. Charlie's own eco-systems were the result of his considerable expertise.

The wall, a bodge job of brickwork ten foot high, was rather less expert. It was, in fact, a sadly shambolic imitation of the Heart's more forbidding outer barrier of steel and concrete—the barrier that towered six feet away on the far side of the shadowed alley.

Charlie's side was topped with a ramshackle tangle of cast-off wire and splintered glass, half-inched from the fringes of the Heart's frenzied construction sites. But the barrier opposite was lined, by contrast, with a squeaky-clean, razor-sharp sequence of blades and lenses; nor did the installations of the Heart stop there.

Four foot six of the alley, on Charlie's side, was safe. Eighteen inches out from the other side, however, you could see, if you looked down at the cobbles, a regularly spaced string of laser eyes set in the stones, spraying up into the air an invisible sensor. Step into that and all sorts of stuff broke loose, cameras swung around, red lights winked demented on consoles in watch houses, lights crashed blindingly on amid an organ-toned cacophony of hooting, *bloom-bloom, bloom-bloom;* all of which was good reason why Charlie, when drunk, made a point of coming home by the front door.

It was a seventy-thirty gamble you'd get away with it—he'd calculated those odds from the way things had gone since the system went in—and thirty percent wasn't a risk he much fancied. Because if you couldn't get away what you risked at best was snarling dogs leaping suddenly down the alley; while at worst it was patrolmen, peeved at being disturbed from the computer games in their lodges, just stepping idly out—and letting rip from the hip.

The barrier scared away from in back of their houses all but the most feckless of the criminal fraternity. Their trespasses noisily illumined the night, and Charlie'd jerk up in bed at the alarms and pyrotechnics as another scofflaw bought it. But it scared Charlie too.

Mel came through the gate, picking up one crutch as she leaned on the other, swinging it toward the Heart wall towering opposite.

Charlie stared in disbelief at the way the girl was so blithe, so resolute—then he lunged to grab her with fierce haste around both arms and her chest, arresting the movement of the crutch in midair bare seconds before it pierced the invisible screen of the sensors.

There was a moment where they stood still together, and he silently pointed to the unblinking eyes in the cobbles; then he hauled her back into the garden, his skin prickling in the heat glare. His heart had all over again gone instantly *thumpa-thump, thumpa-thump*. Breathless and still holding her, he told her what she'd narrowly missed; and he said, not unkindly, "You Americans, you never look about you, do you, you just pile on in. But will you stay here, OK, will you stay in my house and stay safe for me now, until I'm back? Because you don't, yet, know Dollarville from dogshit."

"I have heard tell"—she grinned at him—"that the two do smell much the same."

It was nice, holding her, it was cool beneath the maniac sky—but by now she was stable again. He let go and made off for the Heart.

Behind him, she leaned against the gate; she stared at the mutant yellow grass, and wondered how the crops were making out back home.

8. UMBRELLAS

"Ours is one struggle—integrate!"

The billboard showed a campesino armed and ready. "If the Yanqui intervenes . . ."

"*Nuestra dispocion de combate es de triunfo—es de victoria—jamas nos venceran!*"

Mr. Squalatush looked about him in the square. Another billboard announced, "*Nuestra guerra es guerra de libertadores para matar la guerra de los opresores!*" The livid painting of the GI showed a mad-grinning skull beneath the leaf-netted helmet, a bone face of lustful leer, of hollow-eyed craziness. It was screwed and clipped onto the twisted rusting girders of a bombed-out hall, now open to the sky, in whose center a brave little flowerbed had since been dug, a single shabby palm at its center.

That damage, guessed Mr. Squalatush—and all the bullet holes still pocking the walls all about him between the stenciled slogans ("*Muerte al especulacion!*")—would be damage left over from the overthrow of the feudal dynasty of the Marcovalozas. That was years ago now—but the damage stayed, with no money left afterward to make it good. Certainly, thought Mr. Squalatush, it could not have been wrought subsequently by the parted dictator's Congress-funded mercenaries—they'd never yet dared to go too near to any town.

"*Patria libre o morir . . .*"

He'd walked several days to get here, and it was the biggest town he'd ever seen; the population must have been fifteen thousand at least. A young boy rode by on a mule, wearing a cowboy hat; a stall sold papaya juice, and a hand-cart vendor called out the flavors of his ice cream. Mr. Squalatush yearned to buy some; he was filthy with dust, parched, and desperately hungry.

On the far side of the square, a fat pink pig slept between two poles from which hung a Victoria Cerveza sign, advertising the tin-roofed Restaurante Gallo de Oro. He'd have given limbs to eat there. He slumped down on a bench by a wall; in front of him, dug into the earth, was a small, flaking-painted cement pond, in whose shallow water basked two turtles, and a rather meager crocodile.

The old man's paunched gut ached with its emptiness; his sore head swam at the strangeness of things. He'd seen a fun run, school children bearing flags of the revolution trotting behind their leader, who held high a flaming torch; and seen, on a low dais outside a weird museum down the road, a bizarre tank barely bigger than the ice cream cart—"*Ridiculo tanque,*" explained the placard, "*que el dictador facista Italiano Benito Mussolini obsequio . . .*"

Mr. Squalatush stared at the sky around the ring of volcanoes to the east and southeast toward the lakes, then dropped his head forward in his hands, his body burning with fatigue.

A pinched, gruff, high little voice above him said, "That's the strangest thing I ever saw."

Mr. Squalatush looked up and around, and saw a dwarf sitting on the top of the wall behind him. The dwarf wore a rhinestone-studded turban and a bright orange oriental jacket with rich red embroidery, fitted at the waist and padded in the shoulders; he wore baggy harem pants, also orange, and slippers whose pointed toes curled up backward with a baby tinkling bell on each tip. He said, "You could make money, old man, with that head you got there."

"I need," Mr. Squalatush told him, "to eat and drink."

The dwarf jumped down and, stubby hands on his hips, said, "You come with me."

He waddled away past the church, and Mr. Squalatush followed, stumbling unsteadily. Behind the church was a broad open space of dusty earth, with rusty cars and trucks parked here and there across it. To one side, a minibus made heroic efforts to take on board a vast gang of silently shoving people; the roof was full already, with women and boys and bags and sacks, and squawking chickens tied to wrists.

The dwarf hurried the old man along; then pointed out on the far corner of the lot a battered old delivery van, the fading words Alka-Seltzer still visible beneath a roughly painted barrage of bright stars and crescent moons. Sitting at a card table beside it were a giant, a beautiful young girl, a magician, and an enormously fat lady in gypsy gear. They whacked scuffed cards down onto the tabletop with wordless vigor.

Arriving, the dwarf said, "Umberto, look here what I found."

The magician was of middle height, with a gleaming Clark Gable mustache, white shirt and black trousers, and black hair slicked back. He stood and came over to Mr. Squalatush; he put one hand on his shoulder to hold him still, and walked around him three times looking at the pattern of continents mapped out on his bald dome, on his cheeks, and around his neck.

He said, "The man has the world on his head."

"Quetzals," said the dwarf, "lempiras, pesos, cordobas—wherever we go the man's head is a gold mine. Let's bring him with us. We can feed him—yes?—and still do well."

The magician nodded; the young girl brought Mr. Squalatush bread, fruit, and water. He sat in the back of the truck among tents, weights and iron bars for the giant, the conjuror's crates and cabinets, and the sorry choice of tatty sparkly costumes on the wardrobe rod. The others went back to their cards; the dwarf watched him eat. And when he was finished he asked the dwarf, "What do I do?"

"Just sit in a chair, I should think. Maybe Maria will make you a costume. And then you let people look—or perhaps, Umberto may give you a little speech to say first. Could you handle that? Could you put on a performance?"

"For sure, I can tell tales—but for money? Where?"

"Anywhere, old man. But just now we're going north," said the dwarf, "to the big city up there. To the Hispania Cup Final. Many people, good business."

Mr. Squalatush gaped in a rush of excitement. "Can we—can we see the match?"

"You mean," the dwarf laughed, "can we get in the stadium? What d'you think we are, rich?"

When Dandy Royle next visited the settlement, he found it empty except for the women and children. In the mercenary compound, two of the hated admin men from Tegucigalpa and Miami had stayed on a few days, with a skeleton guard for the weapons and rations left behind—but they'd all cleared off, when news of the drubbing dished out at El Coco filtered back in garbled and panicky radio calls. But then that was, as far as Dandy saw it, no part of his business. He put his feet up and watched Hitachi, and smoked a joint and drank a beer.

He hoped—as he was hoping all around his wide circuit of the company's far-flung ground stations in that sparse and wet region—to see again some sign of the crazy pirate who'd bust in on Ecto's wavelength. He had, of course, reported that first sighting—but had had no notion of its possible significance. He merely tacked a note on the end of his latest tech-section update; it said, "PS, hey—who's the wacky pirate down here? Someone butted in on our signal last night. Got a voice like he's choking on gravel—must smoke too many of these filthy local cancer sticks. Any info?"

There was none, officially—and the sightings, from what he did hear, were too scattered and random for him to have much chance of catching another one himself, or to know how many of them were nothing more than rumor. Because, if rumor was true, they were cropping up as far south as Potrero Grande, and north up to Chuntuqui; from Buena Vista and Cabayal on one coast, to Monkey River and Monkey Point on the other. And that, thought Dandy, is impossible; no one down here had equipment could do that.

He was pondering these matters when, begrimed and tattered and furiously mean-eyed, *Jefe* Scarskull got back with just four ragged men in tow. They grabbed rations and ate and cleaned themselves up, then came, with evident menace, to where Dandy was lying in his hammock. On Hitachi, morons were winning millions by spelling four-letter words. Scarskull turned it off. "You," he said, "Yank nigger. Drive us to town, now."

Now Dandy wasn't keen on getting talked to that way—but he was less keen on getting shot; and this man, he knew, right then, would shoot anyone or anything. There was more (or less) to Scarskull, than a proper horror of Communists—the guy was, simply, an out-and-out psychopath. Trained, word had it, under Marcovaloza himself. Dandy offered him a beer and said, "Sure, let's go."

They didn't speak much on the journey. Scarskull growled occasionally about the hearts and minds leash; he was, he said, held back too tight to do his job right. Listening, Dandy had to conclude that the *jefe* only measured his success by the body count. It seemed he didn't care who got saved, so long as anyone who didn't got killed.

When they got to town, Scarskull stepped up from the baked mud of the street onto the duckboard verandah of the mission store, and greeted with a nod the Lebanese Phalangist who ran the franchise. Then he walked straight through. Xavier Morales was waiting for him.

"You've been brave," said Morales, rising smoothly to greet the *jefe,* "and you've fought well." He went three steps forward and took him by the shoulders. He said, "And we shall fight on until we beat them. Will you accept a new mission?"

"Every mission they organize is a fuck-up. Too many of my men are dying—"

Morales cut in, "We've had setbacks—and this has been a bad one—but this mission can change all that. You do it alone—you needn't risk your boys—and Marcovaloza himself has organized it, the Americans are not involved. He sends his personal hope that you'll accept. He says, we have no better man."

"Then what is it?"

And when he'd heard what it was, he smiled. It was clever and nasty and it was terrorism, naked terrorism—and that, of course, was the sport he was best at.

"The pusillanimous Congress," said Morales, "will sing a different song after this." He handed Scarskull a sheaf of papers and cards and said, "Here are your passes and your Communist ID. There are new weapons and rations and medicines in my truck out the back. Take what you need and send your boys back to camp with the rest. Tell them, Marcovaloza sent this material himself. Tell them, our leader keeps his promises, whatever Washington may do."

"I just hope enough of them get back," said the *jefe*, "to appreciate that."

Outside, he selected grenades, an Uzi, two hand pistols, ammunition, and a handful of Semtex—then he checked through the papers. With these passes, he thought, he could go anywhere in the whole stadium.

Waiting in his own truck in the street, Dandy watched the other mercenaries backing out in a new pickup, loaded down with crates and cases, and heading off back to the forward base at the settlement. Then Scarskull came around the side of the store, and dropped his new weapons on the front seat beside his old ones. Dandy looked blithely at the gathering arsenal, then up at the *jefe*. He asked, "So we going somewheres?"

"We're going," said Marcovaloza's favorite man, "north to the big city. We're going to watch us some soccer."

Dandy groaned. "That's one hell of a drive."

"This'll keep you going." Scarskull, who had now climbed in the cab beside all his gunnery, opened a small Jiffy bag, and took from it a clear sack of white powder. He opened it, stuck his nose in deep, and snorted up a great gust of Medellin Pure. Passing Dandy the bag he then said, leaning back and luxuriously inhaling, "Who said the Man don't look after his own?"

Along the alley on Charlie's side of the Heart's main gates there was a smaller entrance portal, manned by guards whom he'd taken assiduous care to cultivate.

To see him stroll toward it with his big blond charm, his easy dissembling, you'd not know, right now, how seriously nervous and excitable a man can get when he's been shot at, and seen a man die on his doorstep, and then discovered we're being visited by an alien. Nor would you see how, locking his garden gate behind him, he felt again that bad suspicion, that shuddering intimation that any minute soon would come the outbreak of the terminal fear. You'd not guess the way he hunches up inside from the fire in the belly of each plane overhead that might be, this time, not another bunch of souls on commercial or military transit, but the bomber, the incoming missile sent to fry us. Nor would the guards, who thought they'd got to know him, guess any of this either.

There were several of them in that category of oafs, to his great good fortune, who continued (despite all the evidence) to believe that the production game was glamorous. They imagined that because Charlie was a writer, he must make money, and disport himself among carefree and intriguing people—when in fact, if they called him up to write another page in the text of our times, another PR paean to the CAD/CAM machinery of corporate endeavor, if they wanted that sales message to flow—then they called him up the same way they called a plumber if the pipes were blocked. He was a tradesman and lived in Traderstown; he didn't even, for the Heart, carry automatic access anymore.

Still, when he wanted to get in, a quick call to Vidivici from the gatehouse did usually suffice. He spoke with Baines's PA, Reynalda. "Hi, Charlie! No, he's on his way back from a meeting right now—

with Kalero. Uh-huh, and let me tell you, that's one active account just now. You want a day pass? No problem—and listen, big boy, me and Maurice got a party tomorrow, we'll have the Hispania Final on big screen, so if I told you when and where, do you think you could remember?"

Reynalda was, from where Charlie stood, a major cog in the getting-things-done department—she hustled his checks through, and kept him posted on any work opportunities that might pass across Baines's desk—and he invested a lot of time in keeping her sweet. She sent the day pass in minutes down the wire with a confirmation fax for the guards, who acquiesced without demur; they talked, in the interim, of what Charlie was up to these days. What kind of program was he making now? they asked. He told them, "A training program on how to handle aliens." And they laughed, thinking, of course, he meant people with funny-colored skin.

And he stepped through into the first streets of the Heart.

The resident's estate was parked snug in the shadows that fell where the outer blocks of office first leaped up from the overloading core. The people here went into their homes from garages that locked shut and sealed fast behind them. They had town mansions with air-conditioned gardens, plush piles of apartments with atmo-sealed conservatory balconies perched at vertiginous angles all around the sides of the buildings, multilayered extrusions of glass and plastic and steel like Christmas baubles on the tree—except, where the fairy should have been, there were aerials, dishes, helipads, and a maniac chaos of 3-D and diamond-screen poster sites, running ads for new kitchens and holidays, old liquors and news, for in-car sound and telecom. You didn't mess with homes like these.

And there were signs that said so. Private, Dogs Night and Day, Vigilant Surveillance—all manner of electronics from screens on the doors to panic buttons by the bed. Slip on the wrong side of systems like these one dark night and boy, you had the men out their dinner parties and around the streets in Suzukis, Toyotas, jeeps from Korea, rifles on the passenger seat—wives and PA's left glittering behind them making small talk with shiny teeth over peach ice cream under canopies of spun sugar, all glistening in candlelight—while the men, smelling of fine, peppery red wine, went a-barreling down the bright-lit and silent pot-holed tarmac of their patch past double gates and chrome grills, past untouchably magnificent flower displays moored artfully on those airtight ledges and balconies where their wives came out to watch the sport. You'd need company, big weaponry—you'd need inside data to make any kind of headway against those people.

They were crazy people. They hugged tight their lucre in the ventricles of power, while the veins beyond clogged, the walls of the arteries stacked up with insolvent debris, with fatty ooze, while tumors trembled beneath the surface of the far regions. Or was it, like Charlie also thought, really in the Heart that the biggest malformation now waited ready to burst out in stroke and fire and seizure, leaving millions of shards of data-fused glass glinting unintelligibly over the shadows of the people on the pavement. . . .

He rounded a corner at the end of the estate, and drew up at a security screen. Behind it he heard noise growing louder, right-turning into the cavernous avenue beyond as he lightly showed passes and the patrolmen, distracted, glanced and nodded OK, straining instead to see what was coming.

Charlie stepped out into the work force lining the barriers along the path of a sudden blaring parade, a march past of flags and marines and outriders and camera vans and crawling limos full of dignitaries among legions of high-stepping miniskirted majorettes twirling poles, parping on trumpets, squeaking on pipes and pattering on drums; and amid them next came the floats on their flatbeds and Charlie thought, shit—*Disneyland* . . .

It was the Reagan Tomb Tour. It would take an age to go by.

Mel studied Charlie's plant life. You could, she knew, cure ailments aplenty with the collection he had here. Skunk cabbage, *Simplocarpus foetidus,* that would soothe asthma—and she judged that the Dollarville air would, indeed, stir up trauma without warning in anyone's chest. Or, if you had trouble sleeping, the pink-flowered valerian would help; but Mel noticed, also, other plants less likely to help him. Evening primrose, *Oenothera Biennis*—the best use of that was to help with PMS. It occurred to her then, for the first time, that the guy would have a girlfriend—she thought about that and decided if there was a girl, she was probably pretty lucky.

She smiled when she saw that he was growing golden seal—it was probably a nice little earner. It erased from your urine all traces of any other drug you may have taken; she could imagine well-paying yuppies, trooping into druid Fish's parlor whenever the government drug tests came around. She bent down to pluck a small clump of the Somali speed weed, meraa, feeling kind of drug-peckish herself. She got a few stems chewing nicely around her gums, thinking, gotta look lively now—and also picked herself a few datura seeds; you never know, she thought, when you might feel like getting high.

She went back inside and started leafing through directories to see what people she might call—and was interrupted by the breathy roaring of a truck outside, a clatter of dismounting boots on the cobbles, short shouts of command, a noise of hammering on doors and questions being fired. She heaved herself up and swung across to the front door. She had the feeling, somehow, that it would be better to be waiting ready when they came; better to be there in the doorway and see them coming, and for them to see you, than to give them that frightening advantage of being there already, weaponed-up, and the moment you'd keyed in the codes and the bolts snapped back, pouncing right through in your face. She gathered up her risk card from the hall table as she went.

Charlie'd warned her about the blood raids, but there were, when she opened the door, no syringe men in sight, just patrol regulars and, in a pool of fuel and oil, the smashed carcass of the motorbike in the entrance to the yard. Then she saw a sergeant approaching, and judged from his stride—imperative, arrogant, of course, but not edgy, not brimming with hostility, not immediately prone to violence—that the patrolmen were quite happy to be working here. But they'd know that around here, on the Heart edge of Traderstown, the people would mostly (obsequiously, nervously) be glad the patrol was around to keep them safe from the bad quadrants beyond. The people here, they knew, would not have them labeled outright as the enemy; would not be sullen and agawp and setting booby traps.

Then Mel saw another thing, which she hated—though she guessed she'd have to learn how to milk it now, for every ounce of goodwill it was worth—and that was the effect on men of the combination of her beauty and her disability. Charlie, she realized with quick surprise, had not looked at her this way—and she wasn't, she thought, teeth clenching meraa, just some fucking gimp to be gawped at.

Looking up at her where she stood, three steps above him off the pavement in the doorway, the sergeant seemed to slow up and lose rhythm from his cocky advance; because he saw first the graceful long neck, the wide shoulders, the bright deep eyes, the flat belly below the cut-off T-shirt—and then, eyeing her with admiration, saw next, made obvious below the flapping wrap of her kikoi, the out-of-kilter twisting of her too-thin calves and ankles.

It made the man, coming to a stop before her, uncharacteristically polite. He was ill-at-ease, not knowing where to put his eyes; and then even more so with the sudden surprise, for once in his life, of instinctively attempting, unschooled, to be a gentleman.

So it was quite possibly the first and the last time he'd ever say it, but he said, "Officer Sinclair, miss, and I'm sorry to disturb you." Mel felt sick with loathing—though he was trying to be nice, that patrolman sneer still played raw below the surface—but she smiled, as he waved behind him with his muscled arm and continued, "We're making inquiries about that accident there."

At other doors down the side street, patrolmen gestured at the folded-up stack of scrap on the cobbles. Knots of stall holders stood telling their versions of the event to other members of the squad. Flies buzzed in the flat hard heat over the burst and baked watermelon; the purple split flesh was now dried out to white. At the end of the street, the permanent backup of vehicles coughed and snarled and fumed gasses, waiting to get into the Heart's clearance port. The sun high above the street, blazing off the buildings—all the patrolmen wore shades—was now insane; Mel felt her body gasping in the glare.

She said, "You're not disturbing me." She noticed that her accent seemed to complete the man's faintly leering uncertainty—she guessed he'd not mess with her, nor knew anything of Charlie laying hands on what they sought. But of course she was disturbed and was, she realized, going to have to get used to being disturbed. Even as she thought it, two more men from the squad came now, sheepish, to stand by their leader; sideways, they sneaked quick little glances in her direction. Their driver too, she noted, was studying her from under his antiflare green visor in the cab of the truck.

She said, "I'm afraid I can't help you. I sleep"—she made a gesture at her crutches, just faint enough to stir a bit of shame in them—"I sleep a great deal, I get tired. I've not been up too long, and I've no idea what happened." And they were backing off now, working to make their private and unfamiliar sense that they'd intruded look like a public satisfaction that their duty was done. They moved away and reasserted their authority over the easier meat of the stall traders.

She watched them go, then backed away herself into the hallway. With the door shut behind her, she lay back against the wall and breathed a few deep breaths to get calmer again. She should never have chewed the meraa; she felt glazed, staring-eyed—then, falling across the room with relief that the patrol were gone, she made for the cool pink haven of this good man's homely kitchen.

And she saw now for the first time on the kitchen table—she couldn't believe what a sweet, thoughtful thing he'd done—that he'd got out a new map from the store of which she knew he was so proud. She dropped her head on her chest, half smiling; she sat down and opened it up to look at it, fingering the folds with a heart full of memories, wondering at how he'd reached for such a naive and simple gesture.

A message said, "Official State Highway Map—prepared for free distribution—not intended for private promotional use." The state was white, gridded with roads and splattered with blue lakes; Minnesota, Iowa, Illinois, and Michigan were set in yellow around the borders. She let her face fall down upon the paper, and it rustled against her hair on the tabletop. She ran fingers before her eyes over this, her rural heartland of America, with its roster of resonant names—Chequamegon, Tomahawk, Spirit, Stetsonville; she saw Iron County, Rusk, Eau Claire—until the tears ran down her cheeks and soaked into the dying forests, and the dessicated farmland. The map said, "Welcome to Wisconsin."

It was thousands of miles away.

It was the length of the avenue as far as Charlie could see; it was a chaos of noise and color. He was jammed in the crowd of all the people spilled out of offices to check it out. He cursed himself—he'd seen the promotion on the news, he should have remembered this was happening. Floats rumbled by with sets from all the movies, actors lurching about like Pluto under blown-up plastic look-alike head masks in all the costumes, in uniforms for *This Is the Army,* *Hellcats of The Navy,* *The Last Outpost,* in baseball togs for *The Winning Team,* in the cowboy kit for *Law and Order* ... Charlie stared agape in disbelief at this honoring of the great dead man, this all-quadrant festival tour now come to his town, this capital of this most faithful island colony.

The air above filled suddenly with a strident, throaty shrieking, and the compacted space between the towers pulsed and boomed and reverberated as a flyby of fighters raced, gushing red-white-blue smoke, bare inches over the tower tops; Charlie, always jumpy at planes, ducked instinctively and turned—then started trying to push away in the opposite direction to the parade. He jostled through analysts and investors, PA's and publicists, a stink of perspiration through scent rising in the heat from the baking sidewalks. The crowd was a sea of intercoms and clipboards and underarm stains and running makeup all leaning, straining to see, then crying out with laughter when the set came by where Grenada got liberated. Don't you love it on the streets of the Heart?

And there was further delay when the Tomb Tour was gone. He came upon a block with a different milling crowd where, capitalizing on the tour, the Heart was having one of its cast-off fiestas—charity galas where the monied made piles of all manner of domestic paraphernalia in the street, chucking out the old to ring in the new as the consumption fever grew—and gleeful group C's, D's, even lucked-out E's with special access dispensation went sauntering among the treasures, freebie hunting. Even B's went too, dressing down, pretending there was nothing among the 'tronics and the wood and the *Waschmaschinen* that they, who had to act like they were thriving upward, could possibly use. Charlie edged and barged and jostled past panting, grinning men with trophies of furniture and household equipment, bedding and lights and micros and pot plants, their fronds and leaves and ferns waving hectically around above the heads of the crowd. Then he felt the nimble fingers lifting the videotape from his jacket pocket.

He spun around, reaching one big arm out to collar the thief while the other hand clicked his little Mace can up off his belt, sprayed it in the man's face as he yanked him back toward him—then he grabbed back the tape as the man's hands went to his eyes. He was gagging, retching, and as he went down Charlie found himself yelling, "Get the fuck—just get the fuck—Jesus get the fuck, *get these scumbags right out of my face* ..." And people eddied away from him, eyeing the man choking and weeping on the ground. Charlie turned in his anger on the spot; every goddam place you went was spilling out with fuck-ups and wickedness *trying all the time to do you over*. ...

He clipped the Mace back on his belt. You don't, in Dollarville, ever walk out unassisted. ... He pushed his grim way forward.

And he thought, if that thing on Ecto VII was an alien—and if Charlie was in his shoes (do aliens wear shoes? zip-and-buckle boots?) then, for sure, he'd clear off pronto to some faraway and altogether more pacific kind of planet. Because this one was the rack.

But not a bit of it. The rock beast, now over two foot long, and looking like a cross between a cocker spaniel and a coffee table carved of gneiss and zinc, was having the meal of his life. And—as it happens—right now he was following some Oklahoman antispic White America signal, on which the preacher claimed that Chiriqui, "the ghost," tooted lucky lines of cocaine off a mirror bearing an image of the Virgin Mary before every game. "And the Good Lord knows these degenerate brown subhuman silver-nose papists *are* not fit, and *will never* be fit, to be citizens of these Our Lord's United States. . . ."

There's just, thought the rock beast, no pleasing some people.

Grief told his favorite girl Suzie, all the rich brown skin pigment of her Patajoli guise now showered off, that the rain would come tonight.

There wasn't much that old man Grief couldn't fix. He'd been underground for years now, and they'd never caught up with him; he had a wide range of immaculately forged IDs, and a chain of dodgy operations making money around every canton of the city. And his inside track? He'd become, with resolute application, the hacker to beat all hackers—and had a web of bribed spies feeding him new codes and passes every day. And he was logged in, right this minute, to the military's weather analysis.

Now for sure, the public knew too that the weather was due to break and some blessed rain fall at last; they just hadn't been told about the content of that rain. But the military'd been watching the buildup for some days, and had flown through it out at sea taking measurements. No one was quite sure how bad it might be; no one quite knew how to make the problem public; and high fingers were crossed—authority hoping, as usual, that whatever happened would just happen and then pass.

Grief, however, was not a man to let go an opportunity. He knew that consignments of one-piece lightweight acid-resistant designer jumpsuits were being turned out already, for the monied of the Heart; and it had not been a complex matter, to hack into the Cargoport Transit network, and isolate a load of one thousand antipollutant synth-stuff umbrellas. A spot of sleight of hand in the data—a docket altered here, a destination swapped there, a reduction in the load figures to make those one thousand umbrellas vanish—and then he rerouted them to a holding store at the Station. Next: send in Suzie, his chameleon lieutenant, with some counterfeit Cargoport Patrol IDs, to get a key to the store from the Station staff. Then, the minute the rain fell, wham, in go the gang of twenty-five salesmen with their handcarts for forty umbrellas each and whoosh, scatter them out around the seething concourse to sell, sell, sell.

Grief cut out of the military's weather, and turned smiling in his swivel chair to Suzie and her sidekick Acushla—alias Marvin and Renee, or Ramon and Consuela, or Henry and Annabel, depending on the scam of the day. They wore, now, their Cargoport uniforms, and looked, he thought, splendidly mean.

They would handle the operation. Some of the salesmen would almost certainly be mobbed—but if Suzie and Acushla could keep that down to only, say, five of the twenty-five, they'd be laughing. They'd sell at one hundred dollars an umbrella—way, way below the market rate—but they'd got them for nothing, hadn't they? And Grief had always rather thought of himself as a kind of with-profit Robin Hood. His salesmen would get 20 percent of whatever they hung onto—generous, for what would surely be a lot less than ten minutes work each, making fast on the move through the eager, stinging-faced throng. And the ones that got ripped off would get two hundred bucks ex gratia. Everyone, thought Grief, comes out good on this deal.

"Well," he said, "we got a few hours yet. Fancy a game of pool?"

"What about Larkins, the cop?" asked the now gleaming blonde Suzie. "He's been down there the last three mornings, right since we started planning this thing out."

But Grief told her, "I've been all around his files. Whatever he's up to, it's not to do with us. Did you hear from Cairo yet?"

"Nah. Right, heads or tails? You break."

9. MENTITIA KHAN-CARTO

Larkins parked in the patrol depot by the Area Victim Colony, and swapped banter with a few of the duty squad who sat gambling in the shade of the sentry cabin, shirts open. Through the fencing he watched the plague people play tennis on dusty earth over a hardboard net anchored down with old cement blocks; others read books on the barrack-hut verandahs. He took a deep breath and strode out into the sun. The tarmac was cooked soft enough for vehicles to leave tracks in it. He strode along the sidewalk, the road glare dizzying even through his shades; the huge peeling billboards shouted down not only their messages of Enterprise and Jesus, but also great blasting blocks of pure glossy heat reflected, intensified from out of the sky. On the sides of a few taller buildings, the colors in the big diamond-screen adshows were washed out almost entirely to a gasping gray-white; the names of pharmaceuticals and soft drinks dimly flickered, bleached in the heat murk.

Around the corner stood the ticket office for the Sex District. It was the quietest time of day; the action would not begin again for real until dusk. Larkins waved his ID at the counter, then passed through and plunged, gratefully, into the cooler—or at least tepid—air, the many-scented sheathing of mote-laden fug that hung in the district's narrow streets.

He walked the winding, flagstoned twists and kinks of alleyway, coming now and then on a little church in a small, cobbled, circular plaza, or a thin rank of brown-leaved trees dying of thirst in an empty square; and crossed dainty bridges over rank strips of canal. The little cinemas were mostly shut, as were all the clubs. Gashed and fetid garbage bags lay in piles outside the grilled-up take-out bars, spilling little stains of mutton, poultry, salad, and fries onto the paving. A bar or two was open, in whose deep red wombish interiors a solitary early drinker here and there could dimly be seen, propped earnestly staring at half pints of lagers. A sign said, "Boys! Pint of Lager $29!"

He passed, from time to time, the odd deal going on in the shadowed recess of a basement doorway, or behind the bars of otherwise empty cafés. Seeing him go by in his admiral's hat, those scoring and those selling would subtly move apart, and study their surroundings with a forged degree of calm; then rejoin when he was past, as if they could only pull away from each other so far, and must then passively be reconnected by the elastic of their transaction.

"What you got?"

"Got Afghan, Leb, Thaisticks, Colombian . . ."

Larkins didn't feel like busting anybody. He felt like busting his own head. He needed a star.

He'd dropped Tad off and come straight here; he'd set other coppers on the business of the American's wretched tape. His own problem was too important.

He wandered, eyes down and blank, past the big front display windows of the doxy shops, most of them dark and curtained now, waiting for business to come in with the night. Then he arrived at Map Portal Mews.

The cinema on the corner was closed, the door beneath its sorry ply-and-red felt yard's worth of overhang sleepily shut. The boxes of the Super 8 shorts in the week's show were pinned, knocked about and with their colors faded, in a dusty glass case on the brickwork by the door. A stencil sign said,

$45

UNCENSORED ORIENTAL, DANISH, AMERICAN
ALL-NEW PROGRAM WEEKLY

and a note was added by hand,

Big Boys & Eager Girls

Larkins stopped and looked up at the mechanical positions on the boxes of the films. The program promised Teenage Discovery, Three-Way Women, Fisticuffs, Anal Memories, Love Bizarre—it was schlock. But he'd show them how.

He stepped past the theater to the next door in the mews. On the wall was his new Map Portal sign, freshly mounted. It showed a gateway opening onto a tiled floor, on which a map of the world ran away in surreal perspective—and it appeared also on the letterheads and compliment slips of his new company: Worldmap Productions. And why?—because he was, in his series, going to make an image of the world. . . .

He felt better, now he was here. He went into reception, and greeted with a nod his office-minder Zara. She'd been a Kalero secretary, getting by OK until she went with her boss, a level four, to a conference in Tokyo on the Debris Dilemma. (New satellites kept getting kicked off-base by rogue old ones that had fallen awry of their original orbits: Was the loss rate from these mishaps acceptable? Or was it cheaper in the long run to send up a spring-cleaning team? And if so, who paid?) And she'd slept, in the course of the week's game of musical hotel bedrooms (pick your partner, show your card) with a smooth individual from the big Indian outfit SubContSpace, who'd gotten her to tell him the odd datum re Kalero's new bird Ecto VII—causing minor downturns on the profit graph, and herself to be unemployable. But Larkins picked her up and said if his project came good, there'd be salary again, and a better one too—so would she mind the shop while he got it under way? "So long," he said, "as you don't interfere with my actors."

"If I read the script right," she said, "they'll be too tired for that."

Besides, the only person she was eager to bed right now was Larkins himself, who was an ugly brute but had compelling, animistic eyes and also, of late, with his project pulling out of harbor, a steadily more energetic and appealing dress sense. He looked, she thought, not so much a mid-rank security man anymore, but, through constant fine-tuning and adaptation of the original uniform, more like he was about to go off and retake the Pacific. He had indeed told her, "There's ratings out there, and I'm going to conquer them."

Though he'd be in the wars, if he didn't find a star. He went through to the backyard, where two men, Lev and Blok, were at work on the set for the first scene. A plastic lawn had been laid and was impossibly green; and a grave was dug toward the back of it where the yard ended at worn, black-painted old iron railings, fencing off the heavy rear wall of an ancient municipal toilet—the look of whose grime-sullied stonework would serve, for the purposes of his more and more unpleasantly tight budget, to indicate that the scene was in a churchyard. The sight of this—his being obliged to make like a toilet was a church—gave him one of the sharp flashes of anger with which he was now increasingly afflicted: If they wanted Quality, they should pay for it. But then the sight of there being progress at all restored his—not equanimity—but, at least, equilibrium.

The builders at the grave were making a minimausoleum, a crypt at the center of a family plot—a paint-and-polystyrene construction from which the plot of the whole series would kick off. It was called *Carto*. The crypt was the resting place of the founder of the dynasty, Magnus Carto, and the present funeral was for his daughter's husband, the unfaithful and spendthrift Jenkel Khan-Carto, who (with his racy lifestyle) had seduced the daughter when she was glamorous fifteen. Larkins couldn't wait for the flashbacks; he'd show them Teenage Discovery.

But Mentitia—the star, the new head of the family—was a mature woman now, and planned ruthlessly to grasp back to herself the reins of the family empire.

After working for Kalero, Larkins knew plenty about empire. There'd be timber, cattle, coffee, cotton, gold, hotels, arms, oil, an airline, and a drug ring to run—and Mentitia meant to run them. You would see that she did, in her steely eyes, in the bleak cut of her suit, as she stood in rod-backed and empty lack of mourning at the graveside; there was something about her, something different. . . .

Well—the way Larkins saw it, the tomb of Magnus Carto was where the spirit of America lay—our too impatient master—with Jenkel Khan-Carto as the recalcitrantly exotic world that had driven the big old man to his end—and Mentitia, for whom he needed a star? She was the hard bitch that was left now they were gone. . . .

Not that Larkins had put it that way when he pitched the project to the moguls at 69. What he'd sold them was instead, of course, the drama of who won and lost power in and around the lavish Carto household—its extended and vicious family, its partners and its bankers and its lawyers and its doctors, its tools in news and politics, its staff in the businesses and its servants downstairs; and what he'd sold them was the sex-suspense, and the sex, that the drama would involve—like who would fuck whom as the conflicts, the rivalries, the takeovers, and the money matches unfolded? And how? He'd give them Fisticuffs . . .

Larkins watched Lev and Blok erecting the false tomb; he envisioned the throng of his cast at the grave of the feckless old world. The scene, the way he saw it, would have a funk-horror tinge: the wind getting up, long shadows, cobwebs, an unspoken menace that ghouls and the undead with rotted skull faces might shortly rise again from the earth; the light would be deep, dark blue, and orange beneath dense, overgrowing trees, a smoldering, end-of-summer-before-the-rain sort of light; and the skin of the people gathering for the burial would be ablaze, their eyes dry and horny at the prospect of the night now to come.

There'd be Jenkel's mistress Erasa, his boy-son, Baxter, by her, and his elder son, Isolo, by Mentitia, between Mentitia and whom the hatred would be ferocious. There'd be Jenkel's associate Lunik, the nervous banker Crestney, and the unassailably dashing lady lawyer Martha Saturn; there'd be Mentitia's half-sister Tijuana with her lousy teeth, and her witch spic mother who owed Crestney unpayable billions. . . .

Tad appeared at Larkin's shoulder with a videotape in his hand. He said, "I think you better watch this, chief."

For a brief and uninterested moment, Larkins thought his driver might have somehow retrieved the American's tape—then he saw from the label that what Tad held was standard patrol issue.

"That American," said Tad, "he's real pissed at you for not getting his gear back. So when I found out where it is, well—I thought maybe you'd want to go get it yourself."

And keep in, thought Larkins with some bitterness, with the boss—but not for much longer. They'd be laughing on the other side of their faces when they were glued lusting to the edge of their seats, desperate to know the fate of Mentitia.

Mel stood before the mirror which leaned haphazardly against the wall in the disarray of Charlie's study. There were maps all over the floor, the desk, the walls; she saw herself in the glass surrounded by desert and ocean, taiga and tundra, jungles and cities—except, of course, she knew the world wasn't really that way anymore, its systems were as broken as her legs. And then the lines, too, that marked where one nation began and the next one ended, these too were now inaccurate on, as they say, the ground. For what were most nations, these Dollarville days, but plantations for *el norte?*—megacorp fiefdoms through which they moved, under arms, extracting minerals and foodstuffs. . . . She put it from her mind and turned on the TV. In Atlanta, it told her, an Isthmus vet had gone ape with an M-16 in a burger bar, killing thirty-seven people. He was later found at his mother's grave, digging like a dog. Mel turned it off again. She couldn't worry about the state of the world anymore, just getting back down the stairs would take her quarter of an hour.

Across town, Charlie was trying to wrestle in his head with imagining precisely that kind of problem. He sat in a coffee shop thinking of the girl in his house and the things she had to deal with—because she was, basically, the best thing he could think of to think about, as he tried to regain his self-possession before continuing through the Heart. She had, he thought, a lovely voice, a delightful accent; he replayed in his head the way "out" or "house" would be gently lengthened and rounded into "oh-ut," or "hoh-us." And when she laughed, it was like a stream on a hillside, clean water found, by happy accident, during a long ascent in the sun. Perhaps, if he made some money with this story here, he could help her sort something out; he pushed off into the heat again, wishing he had the cash to run a car.

And Reynalda told Jimmy Baines, when he got back to Vidivici, that Charlie Fish was on his way. "Fine," he said, "I just found him a new job." He went into his office thinking, what's the betting the poor idiot got his ass shot off on the last one? He knew no one who was more often up to the neck shit-deep in trouble; from college onward, it was fecklessness and mishap all the way.

Jimmy feared, by the time he'd made it to the towering spacious sixties and beyond, Charlie'd be so shabby and broke they'd not even let him in the atrium anymore.

Every patrol jeep carried an on-board video, the camera mounted on the hood, the recorder tucked away in the dash on the passenger's side. Tad had switched it on automatically in the low-ceilinged carport when they set off after Cairo; he now played the chase back to Larkins.

As they gunned up the ramp toward the light, Cairo, hulked on his machine, shot right to left across the screen over the Kalero Center's front paving. The jeep spun out off the access ramp, the towers opposite rearing by, the angle of the camera manically listing as Tad accelerated through the turn. Straightening, the bike slid back into the frame, flying off the curb ahead of them, then crashing out between two waiting limos, chauffeurs agape, onto the avenue.

From here, there was a sequence of mad speed down the canyons beneath the megacorps, the image bashing up and down across potholes, knots of the work force spinning by at street corners where the jeep leaned hectically through the right-angle turns of the grid's roads. The bike was more often in vision than not, but was steadily getting away from them amid the stately traffic; while on the rudimentary soundtrack could be heard the powering engine and banshee sirens and the steady *whoosh-whoosh* of their passing each limo that, serenely, pulled aside from their path. You could catch, too, little snatches of grumbling advice from Larkins, and hunched curses from Tad at the wheel.

The exit gates leaped into view, as they rushed out into sudden and glaring full light from the shadows of the buildings of the Heart; they were in the clearance area, a flat pan with white-marked route ways snaking through the channels past security cabins. The bike went wide to the right for the pedestrian shutters, where a single pair of speed ramps lay beyond flimsy wooden hurdles, and a few thin ranks of fluorescent plastic cones.

Larkins watched the bike cannon through scattering people and cones sent flying, and then lurch up airward off the ramps. It dropped, losing speed, ungainly, back wheel slithering out from under it to the left, the bike tipping down the other way. The rider wobbled, then held it together; and the bike, sliding, followed the leaning of his body around and away in a steep turn right, out of picture. Larkins heard himself tell Tad where the bike had gone as they slowed abruptly, jammed angrily past a snack-food delivery van, then immediately and smoothly accelerated again. "Right," said Larkins, "slow up and go right, the side street there."

"Fucker," said Tad through clenched teeth on the tape.

"Now," said Tad to Larkins, "stop the tape."

In freeze-frame they rounded the corner onto the cobbles. Up ahead the bike, frame by frame, dipped to turn into the yard; the back of the garbage-truck emerged; Cairo parted from his crumpling machine; his shoulder bag flew up and away off his flung-back right arm, a scrap of motion above his back.

"Go back now," said Tad, "and look here." Standing at the screen, he pointed to the right-hand edge of the frame where the doors of the terraced row stood shut one after the other in the fanatic yellow sun. Rewound, the bike, image by shuddering image, again passed down the street. "There," said Tad.

At the end of the row, Charlie Fish stepped out of his door. The bike again hit the truck, and the shoulder bag again flew away from the man who was twenty-four frames a second from death. "Now see," said Tad, his fingertip following the skimpy blur of the bag arcing through the air; and Charlie moved forward to catch it, just barely in-screen. He looked stupidly about him one second; then retreated quickly, with the bag in his hands.

"I ran him up out the data," said Tad. "Group B, lousy credit, dodgy politics. Name's Fish."

"Right," said Larkins. "Let's go see what he tastes like when he's grilled."

In a heat haze of humming engines, the fighter wing taxied one by one to the take-off lines. Beyond them lay pill-shaped, partly grass-roofed low hangars, squat concrete bunkers, layer upon layer of intangibly shimmering perimeter fence; and then a mirage of marshy flatland growing malodorously, gaseously dry in the sullen hot weight of afternoon. One by one, each roar of power grew, each afterburn erupted out ferociously pink-white-turquoise, and each plane lifted, heavy with shell pods and missiles under sharp stub wings, away into the murk of the horizon line. At the end of the runway a dashing sign exhorted from its concrete stand, *Right People. Right Mission. Right Now.*

Deke Lewis watched them go from the dark red and blue neon belly of the base's bar. He sank his incisors into the flesh of a lime wedge, sucked on the citric rush through clenched teeth, then hit down, in one go, another shot glass of tequila. The barman, knowing his man, brought more. His T-shirt, Deke bleakly registered, was a Sex District advert for Dollarville doxy; but then, the barman was the base's pimp, and its black market quartermaster too. When Deke had first gone in the bar, he'd tried to sell him in quick succession cocaine, a case of bourbon, and a girl; this last, with a special offer of two tickets to some dreary rock band thrown in. Deke said, "What the fuck is this, Tangiers? Shut your mouth and give me the tequila."

In a world full of problems, Deke Lewis ("Right Now") felt he had his full share. Coming on base to find he was grounded from the day's flight, well, that was nothing new. They made it plain enough that he was only there at all to be the squadron's token local pilot; he did PR sorties and space training programs for the cameras, sure—but actually to go out and work in their planes day by day, that was considered a privilege and not too frequently granted—if they were a man short, maybe, or if local politicos were passing through, OK, tell the minister here how much you appreciate the teamwork, Lewis—but otherwise, hell, he could go loiter weightless in the centrifuge for days and they'd not miss him.

It was a regular drag; but Deke had problems on his mind more immediate than that. He had woken up that morning to find on the e-mail that his wife was petitioning for divorce.

The first thing he couldn't believe, hadn't ever believed, was that she really would leave him for that terminally vacuous geek, that monster of tucked wrinkles and makeup, that *actor* . . . a guy named Steadfast, who used to go massacring assorted aliens by hand, blade, rocket grenade, and flamethrower in low-budget action videos—but who was now run to flab and passed his days, instead, living on his residuals, and massacring whisky sours in the bars of golf clubs between the opening of hypermarts, the endorsement of products, and the conning of gullible women. "If you want action," Deke had proclaimed, mystified, at his wife in their last argument, "well for chrissake I'm a fuckin' fighter pilot—a marshmallow's got more balls than that tire-gut. . . ."

But the second thing he couldn't believe was the size of the alimony she planned to hit him for. Did she think he was an astronaut, to ask for money that big?

Nothing was going right. He couldn't even leave the base; he'd been told he had to hang around for orders on some new project— and what tomfool bloody circus act would they dump on him now? Photo calls, posters, newsfeed, "In Readiness as One," jocular allied beer drinking for the propaganda trough—or worse, Jesus, another profile for *Newsweek* on the antirebel strafing runs in the mountains up north. . . .

Hands in pockets, kicking litter like a kid around the trash can with frustration, he'd stepped out of the adjutant's office, stared at the other men gone to mount their planes, climbed in his convertible, turned on the engine, switched on the CD—and even that was bloody broken. He leaned down to rummage among the wires, check connections and switches, but got nowhere. He could fly a fighter, and here he was defeated by an in-car poxing stereo. He leaned back to grasp his head in both hands, howled with inarticulate rage, and drove intemperately fast to the bar through the loading pans, past the trolley-loads of smart weapons and detonators being programed for end use by the company-seconded technicians.

The bar TV was on Network 69; it was ad time. The camera hung in close to a large, square, unappealingly stupid Anglo-Saxon face. The face said, "Hi, I'm Steve." The camera began to track down Steve's body; he was wearing nothing, it seemed, until the camera came upon a pair of drab polyester briefs. Steve said, as if describing a piece of livestock, "Six-four, two-twenty pounds, very well hung— nine and a half inches—neg card on request; I cater for straight, gay, bi, or group"—the camera by now had returned to Steve's ox-head face—"so call this number."

"No way," said the barman, "will a soul call that man till he's got some new underpants. I mean"—he turned to Deke—"he could have made an effort: a mylar jock, a sequinned cock ring, anything. But those briefs; I'll bet"—he leaned over to Deke conspiratorially— "they're stained. . . ."

Deke sat up and away, not wanting the conspiracy to mutate into more offers for sale of purloined and illegal goods. He said brusquely, "It's cack, that channel. Change it."

As if to prove it, 69 now inadvertently gave Steve double his airtime by playing him out again. "Hi, I'm Steve. Six-four . . ."

Deke groaned, gestured for tequila—then, "Hi," said a voice behind him, "I'm Chester Gantry. Five-six, a hundred-forty pounds, and have I got a number for you." Deke turned to find a small blond zeck with his hand outstretched. The man, thought Deke, needed a shave. He was going on, "Flight Lieutenant Lewis," as he briefly displayed in a leather flip-wallet some alarmingly senior IDs, "we'd like for you to go into space."

Well, thought Deke, it'd pay the bitch wife off. But the zeck, looking at him, made him somehow feel cold in his blood; he sobered up rapidly and went off to get briefed.

Mel lay wondering why the Data Bureaux bothered listing their numbers; they were, all of them, permanently engaged. She gave up and lay back in the armchair; she gazed around the room. Above the fireplace was a map of Africa; she could have pointed out to you where she'd worked, if she'd had the energy or inclination to stand up. She wondered how her rhino were getting on now. The poachers would be there—sawing horns off the magnificent heads, shipping them north tucked in truck loads of wood to San'a via Khartoum and Djibouti. In the country where she'd worked there'd been, fifteen years ago, near on twenty thousand black rhino. There were, now, rather less than two hundred; it was, she thought, a decline of nuclear dimension. . . .

But would this be the rest of her life—immobilized with sad memories? She couldn't allow it. She forced herself to think of better things—of the Mara the way she'd seen it one evening in August, the enormous monochrome yellow of the grasslands rolling away in rich shadow beneath livid mauve cloud, the skyline a pulsing band of vermilion. Suddenly the doorbell went and the talkbox crackled. "Patrol. Open the door."

Buzzy with meraa, she jumped forward in the chair, grabbing for her crutches. Larkins spoke again, saying, "I said open the fuckin' door. I haven't got all day." His voice, disembodied on the little speaker, was thin and frightening. She made it into the hall, rearranging her kikoi as she went—then, after checking his ID in the viewport (never, Charlie'd told her, be too careful in Dollarville) she opened up.

She began, "There were other officers here already—"

He stood sideways on; he said, turning his head to look as the door opened, "I want to see a Mr.—God—Jesus . . ."

He strode through the door, taking the handle from her and slamming it shut behind him, leaving Tad, not for the first time, bemused in his wake on the sidewalk. He grinned at her madly; he had what he wanted: she was perfect, the woman for the image, beauty badly messed with. He said in triumph, "Mentitia—you're *ecologically perfect. . . .*"

Mel stared in horror and consternation at the uniformed lunatic who was, now, pointing a gun at her and demanding that she undress.

He was thinking, of course, of course—*the bitch is a cripple.*

Deke toyed with the model of Ecto VII which Gantry had handed him across a low table in a secured room in the company's weapons directorate; a squat bank of flat-roofed labs and offices from which the base's ordnance depot was managed. "I have," he snorted, "to go and mend one of these? I can't even fix my car CD."

"When you mend your kid's bicycle," Gantry told him, "your brain directs your hand and your hand holds the wrench, right?"

"Spanner," Deke corrected him.

"No matter. My point is, when we go to fix a satellite, Mission

Control is the brain. The shuttle is the hand. And the astronaut, basically, is the wrench. Or spanner. You get told every move you need to make."

Deke thought, as spanners go, I suppose you could say I'm adjustable.

"Now I'm afraid," said Gantry, "we have very little time to consider how you feel one way or the other, Flight Lieutenant. We have a problem, and you happen to have been trained in the business of getting to where that problem can be solved. Obviously, if you accept, you know the kind of bonuses an astronaut can pull. Equally obviously, if you don't . . ."

The man, thought Deke, had ants in his pants; he was intense with weird energy, pacing the room. "You think," he said, "that I wouldn't accept? But why me?"

"Because you're available. And the PR," he said, "is awesome. Now listen. We have a tape to show you the size and location of this debris on Ecto, but there's been, I hate to say it, a small problem with that: it's been stolen—and your patrol trying to get it back's been about as much use as a girl at tight end—"

"Hey"—Deke shrugged—"you trained them."

The phone burred softly on the table between them. The American gathered it up in one move and said, "Gantry."

Tad had put an all-points watch out on Charlie. The call was from Dollarville, from the listening room at the Kalero Center. A pleased supervisor had tracked down word of the man Fish off the bug in the phone of a Vidivici middle-rank who worked for Kalero. (And it was, of course, standard practice by then to put a watch on every person to whom you contracted any work—a whole fraternity of technicians and detectives roamed the Heart on a plethora of forged IDs, continually shutting down old mikes, installing new ones, catching each other at it and swapping secrets over drinks afterward; every megacorp was entwined with every other in a humming, clogging web of wavelengths and wires. . . .) "The guy's called Baines, he's a five at Vidivici PR. We just traced a log of a contact from his

PA today; she sent a fax to a Traderstown entry gate, gave Fish a Heart day pass. He's on foot in there now on his way to see Baines. Is that any use?"

"Absolutely." Gantry cut the connection. He'd heard already about the jeep-tape evidence—Tad had filed the information, and it had funneled its way upward to reach him as he was setting off from the heliport to the base. It was time, he thought, to chew the ear off the laggard Larkins. He redialed, and the signal went out on the cellnet.

Larkins clipped his cordless off his hip with a jerk of irritation, and snapped, "Yes, what is it?" He couldn't take his eyes off this American girl. She had tried to belt him with her crutches the second he lowered the gun; she had fire and fury in her eyes—she was perfect.

"It's Gantry," said Gantry. "And did you get me back my tape yet?"

Larkins had forgotten about it altogether. "Oh that," he said, "no."

"Well what the fuck are you playing at? You are supposed right now to be repossessing company property—"

"Yeah, well, I just took possession of a property of my own," Larkins said, with sudden self-confidence, as if waking anew to his surroundings. "So you can go find your own bloody tape. I resign."

Gantry took a deep breath, waved at Deke to stay put, and said, "OK, Larkins, let me hit you with some information here. Has it ever occurred to you to ask who owns your little Network 69?"

Larkin's jaw dropped.

"Did you think, Larkins, you were the only guy in the world hoping to cash in on the fact that half the people's too scared to get laid anymore? Kalero, Larkins, owns 35 percent of your precious 69— and if you don't go do what I tell you right now, you won't be shooting one single frame of your goddam *Dallas*-with-erections. You will, instead, be pensionless and unemployable, you'll be E, you'll be shit on the sidewalk. So listen. Fish is meeting a man called Baines at Vidivici in the Heart. Go there. Find them. Kill Fish. And retrieve me my tape."

Mel heard every crackling word; and Deke stared at the twitching American. He thought, I'm going into orbit for this man?

Larkins gulped and said, "Sure. Right now. I'm on my way." He handcuffed Mel to the bar around the fireplace grate, and told her he'd see her later. Then, running out to the jeep, he told Tad where to go; and put a call through to Lev and Blok, the men who were building him Carto's tomb by the old municipal toilets. He told them what to do, and where to go.

Mel saw where she lay, with frantic relief, the terrace's home-made, house-to-house alarm bell—another bodged-up contrivance from the paranoid firm of Fish & Flower Man. He'd told her he'd never used it, it'd be bound, he laughed, to fry you in a surge of misguided electricity; well, now was the time to find out. She wriggled and wormed her wrists behind her a foot or so along the bar; then took a breath and heaved her body, grimacing, up from the waist to lean back against the fireplace. The alarm, a plastic touch pad, was set on the wall about the level of her forehead; she strained to rock far enough to reach it, and missed; strained again, until her head was millimeters short—and made the final push. The panel depressed into its socket.

Les was out.

But Sweet Doreen on the other side heard the tone sound around her house, where she was making up for the evening's work; she grabbed her keys and burst around into Charlie's living room in her silk dressing gown with a pistol, for all the world like Gordon Steadfast in *Commiekill*, that old base favorite—not like a fifty-year-old madam at all.

"The phone," Mel croaked, "get me the phone."

Doreen flew across the room in a whirling of silk, snatched up the mobile, then came to a halt on skinny knees at Mel's side. "Dial," Mel told her, "Vidivici. Get the level five switchboard. Ask for Baines."

The atrium was several floor's worth of hanging garden, high over seas of pink and gray marble. Charlie traversed its hushed and luxurious expanses, coming finally to the island on which receptionists, like castaways, watched the company's people sailing by. He asked for Jimmy Baines, and a girl called up. "He's engaged," she told him. "If you'd wait a moment, please, I'll try again shortly."

"Sure." He wandered off to examine the irrigation systems. It was, in the atrium, blissfully air-conditioned. He sat down to wait.

Mel wrestled with impotent fear and rage against the handcuffs. She said to herself, Charlie, Charlie—while Sweet Doreen collapsed on the floor beside her, exhausted from futile labor over the cuffs with a hacksaw.

By her head beneath the chair where Charlie'd tossed them down, she saw the Hispania ticket wads.

Mel stared at the ceiling saying, "I've got to get away, I've got to get away."

Sweet Doreen couldn't believe what she was looking at. She studied the thick sheafs giving access authorization to every part of the Cup Final, and then said, almost laughing, "Well—you could always take a break in the sunny spic zone."

"You what?"

"Look at these, Jesus—even a level three'd pay black market, to get access like this."

The possibilities in the tickets slowly dawned through Mel's alarm. Could she get to the Isthmus? Could she make it north from there? What kind of wetback ever made it with a pair of broken legs?

But how could she, first, get rid of these handcuffs?

· · ·

Baines, putting the phone down from Mel's frantic call, was told by Reynalda that Charlie was in the atrium. He sprinted for the elevator.

Charlie, looking up, saw Larkins come through the tower's vast glass portal; he recognized the man's uniform. He felt the weight of the tape in his pocket—and he'd been too close to death too often just lately not to sense now when it was coming for him again. He tried inelegantly and unsuccessfully to vanish among the atrium's palms and ferns; the patrolman drew nearer, hand on his holster.

Dandy Royle dropped Scarskull at a cheap hotel in the big city; then sat in his pickup, staring out around the traffic. There were twelve lanes of it, snarling and bumping over the unmended earthquake cracks, spilling acrid fumes. His eyes stung; he'd heard tell, in this town, just to breathe was the equivalent of smoking sixty cigs a day. He watched an old van jolting and coughing its way past in the jam, the words Alka-Seltzer still just visible beneath its fairground livery of moons and stars. Posters showing the California Squad stared down from all sides.

Gantry told Deke, "You leave for Florida in two hours"—then retreated to the washroom. His cheeks were trembling in an ecstatic leer; his eyes were bloodshot, the irises shrunk to yellow slits. Outside, the fighters roared into the dusk.

Baines shot into the atrium through the elevator doors the minute they began opening, and saw the body on the floor. The man gagging and retching on the marble wore a white uniform; Charlie stood over him still holding the Mace can, looking stupid and frozen, security men closing. Baines got to him first, and waved them off. He whispered, "Let's get you out of here," then hustled him away into the streets of the pumping Heart.

When Lev and Blok took Larkins's call, they grumbled like hell. Who said the production game was glamorous? Larkins had promised them work as bed athletes in his glossy drama; and so far they'd barely got as far as a hard-on. They spent all their time building cacky little sets, or kidnapping tarts to play maids, nurses, extras—and now he was telling them to go pick up another one. Still, as Lev said, "We might as well go get it. I mean, we're going to fuck it in the end."

All over Dollarville the glare eased, as the first clouds of the end of summer came over the sun.

Part 3

HE SHALL COME

It's a funny old game.

—JUST ABOUT EVERY ENGLISH SOCCER MANAGER
IN THE HISTORY OF THE SPORT

10. DICKBURG

Night was coming down quicker now than in previous days; Charlie Fish ran beneath a darkening shadow of big gray clouds.

As he pushed himself on his mind was numb, clocking over and over how a girl he barely knew had called to warn of his danger when in danger herself. His eyes still watered from the spray overspilling when he'd Maced Retch Larkins; and behind the stinging sockets the ghastly image replayed, again and again, of the gun rising from its holster toward him . . . he kept his feet going as the dark sank down, praying he'd find Melinda Isenhope safe.

He jogged through the emptying streets, seeing through every towering facade the arching webs of the monitors, hung on spider-leg extensions, flickering over the chrome and goldfish-pond foyers of the Heart—the screens scrolled, relentless, through sheet after sheet of teletext data.

Glass-sheltered, ad-splattered limo ranks jostled with the last few besuited zecks, making eagerly away to the night's entertainments. Fashion videos showed models twirling on catwalks in the windows of boutiques; glossy snack bars ran glowing promos of happy, baseball-jacket-and-bobby-socks youth, guzzling burgers and soft drinks on the hoods of fifties cars, chewing gum in American streets. Everyone on television was happy; unless, of course, they were in other countries far away. . . .

Stumbling with breathless haste and aching legs, Charlie pulled up by a crew of workmen dismantling a sidewalk exhibition stand from the route of the Reagan Tomb Tour. They'd tuned a bank of monitors to the war-movie babel of the news channels. Charlie stared—it was your chaos ABC: Angola, Burundi, Chile, there was earthquake, massacre, tempest, and typhoon, locusts in swarms of unimaginable magnitude; on the shores of many nations, beached sea mammals wheezed and gasped; in farm valleys soaked in chemicals, and away where the reactors hummed, genetic disorder sneaked from child to child. . . .

One of the workmen stood beside him, and watched the flashing of images on the three-by-three videowall. He said, plainly uninterested, "Drama, eh?"

The last limos purred by, heading now for the restaurants and cocktail bars, the plush dens with armed guards at their doors. Charlie saw a wildlife slot; the story was a 95 percent decline in the rhino population of the Central African Republic—but did that place still exist? Where were its borders? He heard a report that a biologist once saw a bottle of horn tonic in the office of a government minister. It was labeled, For Extra Strength. With his breath back now (but his eyes were still wide and sore, his instincts all jangled with fear and incomprehension) Charlie said to the workman, "I got to run."

He trotted on toward Traderstown, holding the weight of Larkins's gun in his jacket pocket. Baines had made him take it—but what, he wondered, in fuck's name could he do with a gun? He'd never held one before in his life—but then, the world never set out to kill him before.

Behind him, the workman watched footage from the plains of north Germany; he saw the throaty roaring engines of tanks firing up, lurching forward through the mud across fields and windy heath; he cut the power and started packing up the screens. With his mates he talked a little of Singani's prediction, that California would win the Cup by three clear goals; but mostly, they didn't speak too much, and worked quickly and quietly. It would be curfew soon.

At the perimeter gate leading through to his back alley, Charlie handed back his day pass to the single guard left there on evening duty. The guard routinely fed the data to the machine, but then looked up and said, "Shit, sorry, Charlie, I got to arrest you—there's an all-points watch on your head. What the fuck you been up to, man?"

"Nothing," Charlie groaned. "I done nothing." But he thought, fingering the gun, he'd be doing something soon if any bastard got in his way now. Mel needed help. Baines had told him what she'd said, that she was handcuffed to his hearth—and no one, but no one, treated people that way in his house.

He tried to put out of his mind what he'd been trying not to think of for twenty-four hours—that Mel looked so much like Suzie—and he succeeded in doing so easily as the guard stood up from his terminal, and came heavily toward him.

The world didn't allow memories, anymore, of old hopes, old dreams, old girlfriends. There was nothing left in Dollarville but the terminal. . . .

Chester Gantry showed passes to the sentries, and stepped into the hangar. It was many football fields in size. He waited for the monster doors to wheel shut behind him in an electric humming of motors; then he stood, gleaming, as it grew dimmer in the echoing metal space. He stepped forward when the doors where shut, and he was alone.

Soft lamps high amid tall scaffolds and hydraulics, on wire-fenced walkways and overhead conveyor slings, cast a slim, gassy radiance. He passed the angled, low-slung shapes of the fighter bombers in poised, eager ranks; missiles of impeccably sleek and purposeful design hung ready beneath the tight, sharp, sexy little triangle wings.

He came to an enclosure whose grilled walls had built into them lifting shafts, oiled pulley systems, weapon carts on little tram lines—all silent now; while in a marshalling area where the track folded out into a mesh of loading bays, an array of those carts stood waiting to deliver Leaper, Midget, Vixen, Gatebreaker—finned javelins and clubs, nuke-tipped, smart fast big death in little rockets, Kalero's finest, the fanciest bangs your bucks could buy. Chester Gantry squatted amid the waiting weaponry, he put his arms around the tip of a cool dark Fencebender, stroked, caressing, the smooth cone—felt the nugget of plutonium just a-ticking away inside. . . .

The bleeper on his belt alerted him from his warm, doom-pregnant reverie. He snapped the talkbox open; the voice that came through was Jimmy Baines.

He said, "Baines here, Mr. Gantry, Vidivici PR. I have your tape, and the man Fish is dead."

It was a protective lie to take the heat off Charlie while Baines tried, meantime, to fathom what was happening; Larkins, recovering from the Mace, had told him nothing he could use.

The patrolman lay wheezing on the office sofa, his eyes still streaming, and his throat as he breathed was a rasping chain of soreness. Listening to the call he thought, if Gantry thought Fish was dead, than his back was covered and the job was over. His head filled with other images altogether, of garter belt and nipple, of gorged erections and Mentitia. . . .

Baines ignored him; the disk drive in his brain was busy whirring through the options.

He was a company man. No matter that it was thinly substantiated, he could live with the provocative corporate line that Ecto VII was being sabotaged—that was just business. But when inadvertent possession of the scanty evidence for that line became, suddenly, a death penalty offense—that was seriously off balance.

He asked, "Why, Mr. Gantry, did we need Fish dead?"

Gantry chuckled, sitting himself down on the broad cool back of a Siloman. "Serious measures, Mr. Baines, for serious times."

Gantry operated on the basis of experience—Indochina, the Isthmus—and experience said the level of fear must be maintained. Who actually died didn't matter as long as terror overall could work its steady debilitation; as long as there were bodies in the street, from time to time mutilated, it signified nothing who'd once breathed in them. It only mattered that the corporation could go about its business, unhindered by alternative organizations—or by unwanted news stories displacing any stories it might have planted itself.

He said, "We can't afford information, Mr. Baines, to go out in any form we haven't vetted first ourselves; in your profession you surely know that. So show the tape to no one, and bring it to me tomorrow. Now, I take it Larkins is with you? Uh-huh—tell him we don't need him anymore."

We don't, he thought, need anyone anymore, only Scarskull and Lewis—and he could feel, now, the momentum was unstoppable, the elements of fire and anarchy all in place. He Shall Come . . .

Gantry set off for Dickburg.

"You heard him," said Baines, "you're retired—so scram."

Larkins lurched up off the sofa; he asked, "Why did you tell him Fish was dead?"

"So you can lift the all-points watch on him." He invited the ex-patrolman, with a gesture, to sit at his desk. "You can use," he told him, "my terminal here."

"Why should I do that?"

"Because if you don't," Baines bluffed, "then I turn you over to Gantry for fucking up. Just do it."

Larkins keyed in the codes, only eager now to leave, and get the Worldmap cameras rolling.

And while the micro winked and chattered, Jimmy Baines looked out across the Heart. He was baffled by the brusque opacity of the American's instructions; these were serious times indeed.

Outside the huge windows, he saw the sky grow tumultuous; great bundles of cloud swirled around the tower tops, heavy and drooping; sunset made the colors bilious, mauve and orange and smoggy brown.

Larkins at the keyboard faded back into the warpworld of Carto. For too long, he'd been beating up on people for these smooth and arrogant men; but now the time was come when, entrepreneurial, he'd beat up on them for himself—and there wasn't no one going to get in his way. The boys at 69 would get a screen test they'd not believe. They would love it to death.

INTERIOR. HOTEL ROOM. NIGHT.

ISOLO serves MARTHA SATURN champagne. SATURN wears a short skirt and lacy stockings; she grooms her glossy raven-black hair. She sips champagne with ruby lips; she shows her cleavage.

> SATURN
>
> I've not seen you since Jenkel's funeral. I hope you've been busy.

> ISOLO
>
> My bitch mother won't let me run anything. With father I had respect—now I am a clerk.

> SATURN
>
> And you'd like, perhaps, that we cooperate in some way? I would love to cooperate with Isolo Khan-Carto. . . .

She runs a bright-nailed hand up slowly between her thighs.

> ISOLO
>
> You know Mentitia has new lawyers?

SATURN

Come here, boy. We'll win your business back.

She strokes the front of his trousers, expertly unzips, and extracts his cock in her hand.

SATURN

Let's cooperate.

One hand's in her panties; the other tugs his cock toward her mouth. The law sucks money deep down an eager wet throat. . . .

Larkins, pants bulging, stepped from the elevator into the silent atrium thinking, Lev could play Isolo. He had that mean and stupid, that vengeful air. . . .

But when Larkins had lain spluttering on the marble, Baines had taped into the band on the inside of his cap an electronic follow tag, lightweight and wafer thin.

Puffed up with anticipation, the ex-cop jumped in his jeep on the tower forecourt—while Baines ran in the basement to his coupé, hitting the infrared remote switch to click open the central locking as he went. He climbed in, and tuned to the signal in Larkins's hat; then, keeping always a corner or two behind, he followed him on the road to the Sex District.

And Jimmy Baines knew, helping Charlie was hardly likely to advance his career; but he figured, if he forgot his friends now, then one day they'd vanish—and he'd have nothing to do but look down from the high smoked windows, life's best pleasure all withered away.

Charlie pulled the gun. He told the guard, "No movement. Hands still. Now—back off. Slow, now—open the gate."

"Charlie—look, listen, man—"

"Just open the fuckin' gate." The guard fumbled with the keys, and the door slid squeaking open. Charlie gestured him to back through it and turn around. "Go right, keep ahead of me, keep moving." They stepped away down the alley; behind them the open gate yawned, unmanned, into the glowing lights and faint music of the resident's estate. In the guards' rest hut, other duty men, unaware, played Deathrace in Hyperspace on the security micro.

In the empty gatepost, Larkins's message came through down the wire, wiping Charlie's name from the list; the data screen sat blank—but it was too late for that.

They came to Charlie's back gate; without warning he stepped swiftly forward, and clubbed the guard hard as he could in the back of the head with the pistol butt. He caught him as he fell, grunting, and lay him down away from the laser sensors. He paused—how d'you knock a man out? He kicked him in the ear with the tip of his pointed boot for good measure; then rattled open the locks with trembling hands, stepped into his garden, and sealed himself in. Overhead, the sky was a filthy murk, patchily lit with sickly, reflected Heart light. A drop or two of rain fell, but then stopped; the clouds, as yet, were only teasing.

Charlie went quickly into the house, fingers unsteady over the buttons as he keyed in the entry numbers, the bolts shooting back with oiled, electronic rapidity—then he ran through the dark kitchen, banged with his fist at the switch to turn on lights in the living room—and saw Sweet Doreen dead on the floor by the hearth, the pool of blood around her waist from the bullet wounds in her belly now a clotting, dull-glistening stain on the dark wood. The body of the elegant old tart in her silk lay like a flame of lily on a dirty pond. He stared around at the photographs that watched down on her from better days, of grassland and farms and blue ocean, of Suzie and himself gone hop-picking when they were younger, and a working holiday out of town had seemed like a fine idea ... little gashes in the silk showed her madam's weary flesh slit open by the bullets, drying—Charlie felt sick.

Out in the alley the guard moaned, slowly coming around. The weight of the arm across his face was intolerable on his thick-throbbing head. He flung it off, and it flopped ragged as a doll's limb onto the cobbles. The fingers fell inches short of the laser eyes.

Charlie steeled himself and stepped forward, and saw that in Sweet Doreen's left hand was a sheaf of tickets. A pencil had rolled away from her dying last effort and stopped, stuck in the edge of the congealing blood. He leaned down, teeth clenched, face turned away, and picked the wad of papers from her chill scrawny fingers. Jagged and faint, the pencil had managed to scrawl, over marketing announcements about Kalero and the Cup, one word: Worldmap.

Flicking quickly through the permits and passes, he realized only now the significance of what he'd earlier thrown aside—tickets out of Dollarville. He thought, boy, the good, the bad, the very, very ugly—it was all of it landing in his lap today.

But the tickets were no good if he didn't find Mel. He hurried to switch on the TV, and went tracking the name Worldmap in the data-base directories.

Outside, the pulsing-brained guard rolled over, coughing. His fingers slid forward and crossed the sensor line. Lights leaped on, klaxons and horns burst into cacophonous song. The guards in the rest hut cursed at being disturbed (the one playing just now was in the eighth dimension, totting up exhilarating death among the Banshees of Zeta Three-Zero on his way to a stunning top score)—and they lunged angrily out into the night to find the gatepost empty, and open.

Charlie jumped, nerves quivering in the sudden blaring on-and-off of the turning lights through his back window. He spun back to the screen, manic, sweating, to hunt down a listing. There was nothing under companies, it wasn't residential, security, transit, Heart—the name wasn't anywhere. The screen whipped past list after list.

The guards spilled out into the alley; they saw a body turning on the cobbles in the harsh flash-and-shadow of the whirling beams. They let rip.

Seventy-thirty, thought Charlie, fingers frantic on the keys as the shooting rang out. Some people, he thought, are just born unlucky.

The guards ran to the body, looked down at the uniform in the blood, and scratched their heads. One said, "Oh shit."

It's an over-eager world.

They started banging on Charlie's back gate. He stared at the screen thinking, Think, man, think—what did he know, what had she told Baines? A crazy man had come and ordered her to undress. He checked the adult listings and landed in a bank of teletext porn ads, Ivan Goes Riding, Isthmus Pussy, Mine's a Big 'Un, Hard and Homemade. He stopped short, and read this last one. It was a 69 preview, *Coming Soon from Worldmap Productions*. He mouthed the words of the trailer with bewildered distaste—it told him, TURN THE PAGE FOR AUDIENCE INPUT. He did, and found he could call up this Worldmap, he could tell them his sexual preferences—Jesus. The man who'd kidnapped Mel was researching what positions and combinations, what sucking and fucking the country most wanted to see. . . .

He stuffed the tickets in his pocket, memorized the address off the screen, and rushed for the front door—only to see from the steps two guards, turning at a run into the end of the street. He dived back into the house, a kaleidoscope of lights and sirens and rifle butts and boots all hammering at this home where he'd planned to live in peace. The teletext threw a wan light over the body on the floor. He turned it off and sprinted up the stairs to the attic.

In the dark he hauled himself, arms searing at the effort, off a chair through the skylight, and shut it behind him; then, crouching, he ran across the row's flat roofs, weaving past fire escapes and canopied pot plants, hopping over low dividing walls that marked the boundaries of each house's sunning area—not, in Dollarville, that anyone dared tan anymore. . . .

There was construction work going on at the end of the row. A rubbish chute hung down the side of the last building, swooping over the sidewalk to land in a dumpster. The dumpster was full of rubble from the conversion of the loft here, and the chute was held steady in a line by a taut rope down its center. Feet first, Charlie pushed himself in and slid down the rope. When he came out the bottom there were no guards in sight. They were all down the other end of the street, wondering who the old lady was that was dead, in her silk and her finery. Charlie rolled out the dumpster, brushed off the dust, and peered around the corner back up his road.

And it was the last time he'd ever again see the little house of which he was, like all decent and ordinary people, so shyly and ridiculously proud, and for which he'd had such definite good dreams—before he met a man who told him about gods in space, and a girl who brought back his past, and a motorbike crashed ... like he thought, some people just get born unlucky.

He crossed to the taxi stand, where a few cabs still waited optimistically for last fares from the Heart; he told the driver where to take him.

The guards in his front room wondered why a pair of handcuffs, untenanted, hung from the bar on the floor around the hearth.

Gantry rode the Huey, his hand inside his shirt feeling the rug of warts and moles and coarse new hair. He looked up, flashing-eyed, to the second pilot who turned back to tell him they'd be down in Dickburg soon. He leaned forward and saw, through the canopy, the lights of the compound ahead, a bleak patch of glare isolated in a ring of abandoned farms. The watchtowers and barbed perimeters came hard-edged into focus as they set down in a gushing whirl of dust on the pad. A jeep waited to take him to Marcovaloza's place.

And Dickburg? Dollarville had become, these days, the garbage dump in more ways than one. It wasn't only the world's nuke waste they shipped here for reprocessing, their PCBs and their dioxin—but also, now, their political rubbish too, to be tucked safe away behind the screen of the Special Relationship. All the trash whose span of usefulness was past got put away here, in the compound the streetsmart called Dickburg—shorthand for Dictator City.

They had generous security. They lived restricted, as if we were ashamed of them; and yet preserved, in a surreal and frozen splendor, as if we looked on them with guilty and idolatrous reverence, the way we looked at wildlife. Men and women from all manner of poor islands and continents, they lived, with their loot and their families and their uniforms and their shades, in a constant state of scheming and plotting. There were mediaevals from Peshawar, Hispanic anti-Communist crusaders, poppy barons from the Golden Triangle all spinning out their byzantine days on the artificial grass of the luxurious miniature golf course, at private poolsides, or in stiff, proud little circles at the bar of the compound's country club.

Gantry's jeep bundled past the glossy branch offices of the major banks, art dealers, and designer stores around the compound's main square, and away down a spanking-clean tarmac avenue of colonial-style mock mansions, each set behind walls and cameras and magnificent clear Perspex garden domes, each full to bursting with eruptions of rhododendron and frangipani. Then they pulled up at the gates of Marcovaloza's place, and were passed on through with self-important, engine-revving haste. Dogs barked madly in kennels the size of cowsheds as they went by; gun-toting plainclothesmen from the Man's private militia stood watchful with walkie-talkies as the jeep rounded the gravel forecourt and stopped. Gantry got out.

"Madam's upstairs," smiled Marcovaloza, his shaking hand held out from where he stood at the top of the front steps; behind him shone a chandeliered hallway, spectacularly vulgar with statues and mirrors. "She's deciding," he smiled, "what shoes to wear for our little dinner tonight. She'll be down, well—I better not say shortly. Come in and have a drink."

They took their malts in back of the house, on a white screened porch so long you could have moored a frigate alongside it. Built-in barbecue equipment, a dancing area, a ready-set table for twelve, and a full-size bar all ran expansively along its length. Gantry looked out across the rolling green plastic fibers of the garden to the antiaircraft gun by the pool; he said, "We have an astronaut, sir, on his way to Miami right now."

"Fine," said the sly old man. They were about the same height: a gray-haired daddy dwarf and his radioactive child. "That's fine; it'd be a great shame if Ecto VII wasn't functional. After all we wouldn't, would we, want anything to impede the world's view of *Jefe* Scarskull?"

"I take it he's in place?"

"And so are his victims. I had Morales go to brief him—we'll give your chickenheart politicians a reason to back us properly." He chuckled, then paused, then he laughed out loud. It was going to be an interesting soccer game.

Gantry excused himself and went to the bathroom. He had the strangest and most lusty feeling that he was beginning, just beginning, to grow horns.

11. THE STINGING RAIN

The rock beast patters, a clanking space dog, on his ornate little lion's paw pads of carved stone around the wings and the cylinders of Ecto VII. His digestive system is a miniature blast furnace; his breath and his wind are rich with fiery reactions. Around his neck, he's grown a starburst ruff of six-inch black igneous lances; there shimmers between them a diaphanous web, veined and matt-marbled with feldspars and hornblende. He looks like an Elizabethan Jack Russell. And he's bored.

Rock beasts, by nature, are gourmands. It was, indeed, this very quality that had determined things when, eons ago on a Fat Hot world, the species first gathered in myriad conclave and decided, as one, "The food here stinks." And so they voyaged into the void in quest of a better diet—with, as they parted at the start of the great adventure, much genial spitting of acid in each other's faces; that being, of course, a rock beast display of respect and affection.

And it was the instinct to gourmandize that now made the beast restless on Ecto. Menu-wise, see, there's only so much satellite a creature can eat—a creature likes a change, right? Why, down below him, they had oil rigs and skyscrapers, cars and trains and planes, reactors and turbines and dams and grids, all manner of tastebud sensations he'd gotten eager-keen to go gobble down his chops. . . .

He was on the brink of deciding it was time to hop off—time to make an entry through that atmosphere there, time to fall in fire from the sky like the preachers were promising—he'd hate to let them down—but it was right about then that he heard, by chance, new signals whipping up from the Florida launch pad. Kalero was precharting the trajectory of the rocket that would bring him Deke Lewis. They were sending him up a visitor? It would, he realized, be only courteous to wait.

It would also be a good thing, he thought, to get a one-on-one briefing before sallying down to the surface. There were, let's face it, some unreasonable aspects to those people down there; he'd not want to rub them the wrong way. . . .

Pensively, he gnawed on a link rod down the back arm of one of the bigger signal masts and found he was tuned in to the good citizens of Eagle Pass and Piedras Negras; but only barely for an instant before some bastard, yet again, jammed the beam.

If they didn't want to talk to him, how come they were sending up some person to greet him? He shook his little head. This was, in his opinion, some really fuck-headed species; the things they were capable of made him *anxious*. . . .

In Dickburg, it was a third round of stiff drinks before dinner. Madam had still not decided the question of the shoes, and, awaiting her arrival, several tyrants (retired) were teetering with liquored bombast already.

On the porch in the clouded evening, a flunky handed Gantry the message of new damage to Ecto, and of how another zone of coverage was gone down. Gantry growled; and the old dictator frowned beside him. What, he thought, was the point of staging this thing for Congress, if the screen then blanked out?

And meanwhile in houses, flats, shacks, and bars on either side of the multifenced line, a fair few people in Eagle Pass and Piedras Negras did, in fact, briefly note their TV's going weird. And a strange voice said, "Hi there, how ya doin'? Now look, I wanna tell you some stuff . . ."—*Click*. But they none of them paid it too much mind; they were too fussed, just then, about the latest round of car bombs.

A few drunks, maybe, slurred at their barmen—Hey, Jack, an alien transmission—and then a few barmen, maybe, told their drunks the latest tales of how ol' Jed, or ol' Jose, got kidnapped by small green men, why, truly now, it was just the other night—heard tell, they took him to Hawaii and had him teach them how to tap dance; he'll be in *National Enquirer,* just you wait. . . .

Overworked Kalero techs wrestled to jerry-build new ground stations, to get backups up and running; the Hispania Cup crescendo continued.

On a bench across the park from the stadium, Mr. Squalatush sat with a big hat hiding his valuable head. Earnestly he learned the lines that Umberto had written for him; it was a good story, and had a deal of truth to it. "I am," he would say to each paying group of freak seekers, "a miracle come before you—a prophetic admonition fashioned in flesh by Mother Nature and sent to you now. . . ."

The president flew out of Andrews Air Force Base, his advisers making ready to score some truly juicy TV backdrops at the imminent triumph of the California Squad. His wife's advisers flew with him too. The stars, they told him, were in a turmoil unprecedented. . . .

Grief was late to meet Suzie at the Station. En route he'd stopped in at Milla's, his club on the corner of Crack Street by the rail yards off Mud Alley—and found he had to deal first with a public order problem. The ecstasy supply was running dry—and without the drug to fuel the dance beneath the pyrotechnic rig, the pulsing electro-beat was turning the kids' nerves a little dangerously jangled.

The threat level was such that he determined, in the end, to have the staff at the metal-grilled bar dispense free toots of coke with every round they pushed out through the double-doored serving hatches—it was more like a bank than a bar. And he thought, one day, juggling all his business, he'd slip up—or, he smiled, maybe not. He was beginning to feel, surviving rich in the bilges of black market Dollarville, both invincible and invisible; a ghost in the system. . . .

He gestured to his guards, and stepped out the back door into a maze of mire and hovel. Burned-out tenements lined the split-surfaced, piss-stinking empty avenue where the crack lads lived in a warren of miniature forts; and where the last cells of plague people hid, injecting, wasting, sleeping among rats. . . . Grief walked away to the rail yard gates, and the night guards on his payroll let him through.

He stepped light and careful on his toes across the tracks and the truck ruts, a man at each of his antiacid sheathed shoulders. The rain still held off; the air was dense, muggy, almost dripping—to walk was to sweat.

From the flickering dark all about came shouts, wordless boozed-out yells, the smashing of a bottle—it was Vagrant Park in here, come nightfall, a hobo-debris zone. A huddle of men and women in ripped and filthy shirts and holed sweaters squatted, skin open to the hot night, white-eyeing him from mud-stained faces around a crackling of smoky flames. Grief felt a huge fatigue. This wasn't the city he'd been young in.

They rounded a corner, the black bulk of the back of the Station looming now ahead of them—and came on a slouching gang, clubs swinging, advancing behind a vanguard of dogs held straining on leashes from bare-muscled arms. Grief stopped, his men on either side of him.

Everyone stopped.

There was a shaking in the air, a rattling susurration of fear in the structure of the Station buildings across the yard. All heads went up as three fighter planes went racing low in a scream of noise across the city, so fast they were gone before you'd heard their angry roaring rip through the air. Instinctively Grief thought, Is it now?

Is it now? thought Fish, hunching shrunk-testicled in the back of his cab just a few blocks distant . . . well no it isn't. Not yet.

The gang looked back down toward Grief. There were eight or nine of them. They saw, and heard, in the echoing wake of the overflight, the deliberate snapping off of the safety catches on the machine-guns Grief's men always wore wherever he went. They stepped aside, and Grief passed through.

Nice, thought Grief, it was nice every time; yet how much nicer it would be not to have to live this way at all—to be back in better days now lost. . . . The gang shuffled respectfully away, their dogs uncertainly snarling.

He left his guards on the depot doorway, nodded to Acushla out on the concourse, and passed down corridors to the storeroom where Suzie waited with their umbrellas. Stepping in, he caught her looking at an old photo of Charlie Fish.

Grief knew that story, and he asked her quietly if she was OK; was she getting regrets?

Briefly surprised at his mood, she looked at him a moment, then shrugged, tucking the picture away in a uniform pocket. She said, "Nah." She thought, sure, the guy was kind—but it was that teleworking thing, it fucked him up. He ended up opening maps more often than he ever did the door, he got old, got scared—"Nah," said Suzie. "I mean, I ain't the kind of girl that was made to be married, right? And you got to keep busy. Did it rain yet?"

"No."

He went to look from the door across the thinning concourse and thought, you got to keep busy. But till when? And for what?

INTERIOR. SOLARIUM. ARTIFICIAL LIGHT.

ERASA, blonde and tanned, lies naked on a sun bed. She is masturbating. The door opens. Enter CRESTNEY. He is middle-aged, hectic, obsequious. ERASA studies him, amused.

CRESTNEY

Mentitia . . .

ERASA

I know. She's moving Khan-Carto's business to new banks.
You're going belly-up, Crestney.

CRESTNEY

And has she taken from you?

ERASA

Oh, plenty—plenty . . .

CRESTNEY

So what can we do?

ERASA

Come here.

She lowers herself to the plush carpet floor, spreading her legs wide,
parting her labia with hungry fingers.

ERASA

I'm horny, Crestney. Come here. Get down.

The banker laps, kneeling, snuffling, at money's hot wide wet hon-
eypot. . . . ERASA comes.

ERASA

We'll get the bitch. We'll have her. All of us.

The way Larkins saw it, it was a morality tale. All those aggrieved
by the new America—this hard dry beautiful crippled bitch—would

gang up and rape her. . . . He turned off the road toward the Sex District car gate. A block behind, Baines waited to follow him in.

Charlie was in already—not that that was any comfort. They could, for all he knew, have held Mel for hours; they could have done anything.

The cabbie wanted to know if he was Saved. He said, "You wouldn't need no Sex District, if you was Saved. Jesus, man, would be all your desire."

Charlie told him, "Just put a cork in it."

He watched in a daze the narrow streets winding by, humming with thieves and soldiers and bar girls and tourists and pimps. Every other window was a red-velvet-curtained showcase; the skin of the beckoning women in their lingerie glowed, otherworldly, under ultraviolet strip lights. Big back-lit blocks of plastic color crudely illuminated the busy lanes, wide yellow-red-orange signs saying Videos, Books, Erotic Bed Show, Double Act Live. The world, thought Charlie, fucking itself to death—since, let's face it, a neg card was easy enough to come by, on the District black market . . .

The driver turned on the radio to drown out catcalls, murmurs, tapping fingernails on his window. Sudden and loud from the cab speakers, a voice exhorted all people to turn with faith to Revelations, and promised soon the tremendous advent of the City of God. "Turn it off," said Charlie.

But the driver insisted, "You *got* to know Jesus. 'Cause there ain't *nothing* that's certain in this world—"

"What's certain," said Charlie, showing his gun, "is you're dead if you don't shut it and drive faster."

The driver accelerated—Jesus, it seemed, couldn't help him out here—and they nudged forward quicker, past the sea of winking lights, the Topless-a-Go-Go, the Naked Encounter, past Randy Mandy from Manila in the Saigon XXX. And Charlie's face was a clenched mask. Kidnapped for the sex biz before she'd been in town twenty hours. He shuddered; he tried not to think of unnatural acts, of bestial scenes, of the mad cop pimping her on Channel 69 as a fuck with a difference. They'd drug her, fill her full of junk and make her animal—it happened all the time—he read the papers, he knew. . . .

The Worldmap studio was set up ready for the finale of the *Carto* pilot. Isolo and Martha Saturn, Erasa and Crestney, Baxter and Tijuana and Tijuana's mother and Lunik, all would enter together, spectral in evening wear in a dim-lit midnight scene. The setting? Mentitia's office, high in the sky. A quick exterior shot of some tower in the Heart would suffice to establish that; while in the office, the blinds would be drawn down; we'd be sealed in the power seat. From somewhere below there'd come faint chatter and tinkling music, the sounds of the annual family bash—but here it would be silent. The family would gather, and take climactic revenge.

Mel sat shivering at the big desk. She was cold, bruised, and aching from the manhandling she'd had—but their talk was worse than their physical roughness. In sweatily anticipatory detail, Lev-Isolo and Blok-Baxter had several times outlined what the script had in store for her, on the desktop's leather expanse. "Audience got to want to know, see—does Mentitia survive? So then they watch the series, right?" And this was Lev's last coherent comment.

He stood now pointing at her, the other hand going up to the side of his head. He said, "What the fuck, here—" His eyes widened, narrowed, widened; he shut them hard, opened them, looked about him; his mouth was dry, his heart racing, his erection had shriveled. He said, "What's happening to my head?"

They hadn't drugged her. She had drugged them.

It was easy. They shoved her on the set for what Blok, giggling, said would be a "creative meeting." They poured themselves drinks; then—when Lev went to take a piss, and while Blok's back was turned as he tried (and failed) to raise Larkins on the phone—she quickly crushed a datura seed between thumb and forefinger into each man's glass on the desk before her. She then sat, enduring the lubriciousness, and in a while the datura went to work.

Lev fell over.

He had some trouble locating his hands in the deep pile of the carpet. It seemed to be growing, wavy white tendrils seen in elephantine detail. He gasped. The walls were surging floods of color, curving around him with fish-eye intensity. All motor neuron activity was gone haywire; like a beached fish he flopped out an arm, knocking a bag of props over. In fearsome slow motion, whips and dildos spilled down on his head; each seemed the size of a building, falling from the other side of the clouds. He wailed and flailed in an avalanche of leviathan sex aids.

Blok was on his hands and knees, chortling.

Mel swung off the set, and out into the dark reception area. The front of the ground floor was all window. She approached it. She saw, in the street, a furtive figure sliding toward the cinema next door; light from its entrance spilled a phosphorescent slick, a red sheen on the cobbles and in through the glass—then there came a hammering on a door behind her.

Looking around, Mel saw a woman mouthing, eyes wide, through a small, reinforced glass window in the wooden door. Going closer she heard her say, "The keys, get us out of here, get the keys." Mel looked around her; then crossed back past the settee and the pot plants into the studio. She ached in every corner of her body; her head hummed with the need to escape—but to where? Images of Charlie dead recurred, a naggingly desolate cycle of loss. She found Lev on his back, trembling, staring fluttery-lidded at the ceiling, mumbling. Blok was slumped, dribbling and grinning, at the set's bar. He had out whiskey and a glass, but couldn't get the one into the other. He tried positioning the neck of the bottle over phantom, replicating glasses and poured whiskey, with eager concentration, onto the tabletop. Mel told him, "Hey, Blok, I'll pour your drink if you give me the office keys. Deal?"

He gawped at her. It took some time to get through, but he managed to work it out in the end. She left him tossing liquor on his shirtfront, the inside of his head a hysteric kaleidoscope.

In the reception area, she opened the door. The woman on the other side stepped back—she had stunning floods of black hair—and called up a bare flight of stairs, "Come on, let's go." First a deep-tanned blonde, then two Hispanic women, one teenage, one obese and late thirties, and then others, five more in all, came tumbling down from where they'd waited at the top of the stairs. One was barely out of childhood; two, at least, had the glazed dazed eyes and wandering feet of gone junkies. They helped each other out hastily through the door. Mel watched them ducking past, bewildered. One wore a nurse's uniform, cut short right to the stocking tops, another a shiny black maid's miniskirt and white apron. Mel reached to take the arm of the first woman and asked, "What the hell's going on?"

"The dormitory where they kept us," she said, "above the studio—there's a camera position cut in the floor over the desk—for overhead fuck shots, right? And we saw you spike those drinks, that was neat. But come on, let's clear out." Mel gave her the keys—the woman could fumble through them quicker than she could, propped on her crutches—then the front door was open, and they spilled out blinking into the street. As they emerged, a cab was pulling up outside the cinema.

Mel saw Charlie stepping out, throwing money at the driver. The cab pulled away as, for an instant, they stared at each other—then he was rushing toward her. And then, he pulled his gun from his pocket. Behind her, there came the sudden angry snarl of a jeep's engine as it rounded the corner, and the screech of brakes as Larkins pulled up.

He saw his cast scattering into the night. He saw *Carto* evaporating. He saw the man Fish run past Mentitia, as he was jumping out onto the sidewalk, raising a gun, halting, arms out in front—his own damn gun—Charlie fired. The bullet took Larkins like a mis-thrown heavyweight punch, cannoning against the top of his left shoulder, spinning him backward and down. Where his head hit the pavement, he registered the heels and ankles of the women he'd been collecting flashing by. The pain was phenomenal—he was losing everything. Looking up, he saw Mel had stumped across to look down on him. Her face was blank, frighteningly beautiful. She told him, "In one way only, it's a shame you didn't get to do what you wanted. I'm blood risk, see—and polluting men like you would be everything you deserve." He blinked up at her. His America, his ruin.

The sound of an expensive car purred up beside them where they stood with the first small clusters of silent onlookers—popped out, at the sound of the gunshot, like bugs from the district's busy rooms all about, and now gathering to stare. There was the slim whine of the car's electric window opening; Baines poked out his head above an elbow laid casually through the open window. He said, "Can I take you folks someplace?"

And Charlie told him, "To the Station, James."

But even as they were stepping into the back of the car, Larkins with grim determination was wrestling himself up to his feet, clutching with his right hand at the wound. He stumbled into his offices. He found Lev and Blok, whimpering and slobbering—with furious, clumsy haste, he barged into his own room, clattering with padlocks until he'd pulled, wincing, the pump-action shotgun from his gun rack—because no one, but no one, gave him this sort of shit and got away with it. He burst panting back out into the street; an instant eddy of gasping people backed away from him. They stood, hands over mouths, watching him teeter bloodily before them, shotgun wedged on his hip in his right hand. "You," he picked out one man and lurched toward him, waving the barrel in his face, "drive the jeep, move, now, Christ." He gasped, his voice hoarse and wild; he fell in the backseat, spitting out directions.

He could not, he thought, be many minutes behind them.

Mel leaned against Charlie on the back seat. He was shivering, no matter the humid sweltery heat. She told him, "Talk about something. Anything."

The city night streaked by outside, Baines veering through thin traffic. They were out of the District, making across the shut-down back end of Traderstown. On the pavements lay cabbage leaves and onion skins, booze tins and coke beakers, unspooled cassettes and discarded micro-parts. Charlie said quietly, "I never shot a man before." He shook his head. "I'm just an ordinary guy." And suddenly, he thought, he's mixed up in people dying every way that he turns—and is that the way the world is? Is that what you see, when you leave your house and take a look? Jesus ... and what's more: "Baines," he said. "Ecto VII—there's an alien on it."

But Baines's answer was thumpingly categorical. "Bullshit, Charlie. It's a Soviet robot."

"What?"

"Look really, Charlie, an alien—this is Dollarville, the real world, this ain't sci-fi. Where'd you get an idea like that?"

"From a little old guy ..." He was, he realized, intensely disappointed. He let his head fall back on the seat, lights flashing past on his face between the stretches of dark. It could not, he thought, be that prosaic.

"I watched the tape," said Baines. "It's just some sabotage effort."

"But it communicates ..."

Mel put a hand on his shoulder. "Relax, OK? We're getting out. And thank you, Charlie—thanks to both of you for coming after me."

Charlie turned slowly to look at her. How'd he gotten into this?

She said, "What's the best time you ever had?"

He stared at her.

"C'mon, what is it? I told you mine—fireflies, cornfields. What's yours?"

Slowly he appreciated the effort she was making.

Outside the rain began, a steady drizzle. They were pulling up at the Station. All around on the big steps and wide approaches people were stopping, looking up, and then down at their hands, their forearms; putting hands to their faces, wincing, cursing, running for shelter.

They sat in the car.

He said, "I knew a girl once, she looked a lot like you. We went hop-picking one year, when we were young." And as he talked, he remembered—how there were dawn starts and long hard days, and long warm evenings afterward in the country bars, at the tail end of summer. You'd stand on the trailer, yanking and heaving the big bushy plants off the wires over your head. The stems and leaves of the plants came bedecked with tiny prickles, each with its trace of faint sharp juice. And as you worked, sweating and pulling, your wrists, your neck, your face all grew spattered with patchworks, criss-crossing patterns of mildly inflamed red scratches—scratches straight and true, in their minute thin way, as Roman roads or Nazca lines. He remembered it because you didn't, he told her, have to go hop-picking now to achieve that effect.

You had only to stand in the poison rain, and let the droplets run stinging down your cheeks and your hands. . . .

He stepped out, feeling summer's end collapse on his flesh from out the sky. They say, in Dollarville, it never rains but it sores. . . . "Hurry," he told her; then he said, "Here, I'll carry you," as she struggled out the car.

The intemperate clouds flashed with lightning; scurrying people made for cover. Charlie took her weight in his big arms and jogged away up the steps toward the lights, wheezing snatched thanks and good-bye to Jimmy Baines. He was thinking, I haven't got a toothbrush.

Jimmy called after him, "Don't forget me, Charlie." He turned the car and pulled away. In his mind he was seeing all the unprotected plants of the city now dying into winter. Their last faint stabs at growth would turn splayed and awry in pots and window boxes, in borders and parks; colors would break down into pale, singed variegation, leaves would split, and misshapen seeds fall out of the acid soil—thalidomide petals would turn brown on the crumbling earth.... In his side mirror he saw Charlie, a lone figure striding in the rain up the big steps to the Station's vast stone portals, carrying a stranger to safety.

He knew at that moment he'd not see them again.

And in a street nearby, Retch Larkins turned his face to the sky. As the jeep crashed down the avenues, he released a long, wounded-animal yell of rage and pain. The rain ran down his face, and the night now glistened with its pollution.

Dollarville's rough?—try Miami ...

Deke's body clock told him it was getting late; but he'd flown backward to early evening, and felt more alive than he had done for months. Even the fact that the cassette stereo in his rental car seemed to be broken, didn't faze him; tech-jinxed or not, he was here, and it was out of the blue certain that, imminently, he'd be riding the Big One, getting strapped atop King Candle and fired against the g's into orbit. And he couldn't sleep with a buzz that keen now landed so sudden in his lap—though it wasn't just for that that he now propped up a barrio bar in his air force casuals, watching spic cable TV on the wall set across the room; because he also had a little mission of his own. He wanted, before they had him on his way to the launch base, to try someplace to score some grass. Deke Lewis, see— he had this long-held private ambition since the first time ever he was weightless: to be the first man stoned in space....

Just being in Miami was a high wild enough. He could feel the tang of war there, more sharp and immediate than any base he'd ever been to; the drawing in, the battening down, the black marketeering, the Anarchy Bands of Isthmus vets, dealers, race vigilantes, and victim killers all roaming the spaces of the night. Machine pistols cracked out here and there around the streets and underpasses where the gangs fought it out; the choking traffic on the freeways above tuned in to hear what firefights to avoid, voices on the radio crying out in excitement and warning and prophecy against a background of sirens near and far in intermittent, wailing chorus. Driving around downtown was to be perpetually half blinded by the neon pyromania; on key avenues and intersections the National Guard were dug in at command posts, taunted by whores from the hot, rubble-specked sidewalks. And all the waitresses where Deke now sat, with come-on eyes and spangly short skirts, looked like they too would take money for pleasure, life being short, and the dollar weak. It was thrilling, animal; Deke savored his fourth margarita, and the pulsing brass of the salsa band, and the leaping shards of light through the darkness from the old-fashioned mirror ball turning slowly over the sticky parquet dance floor. He eyed the scrawny brown men in their ragged pants and T-shirts, playing pool around the faded felt and worn cushions of the battered old tables, and he thought, c'mon, guys—sell me some herb.

On the wall set they were running the Hispania buildup. The California Squad were interviewed training, swimming, weight lifting, having breakfast, lunch, supper, shopping with their wives, going to church; their wives were interviewed, and their children and their parents and their grandparents, in the luxury condos that their permits had brought them. They all said how good things were in America. . . . Deke jumped as a skinny guy materialized beside him and said close in his ear, "Hey, airman. We gonna win, for sure.".

Deke turned, and asked, "You support California?"

"Sure, man—god's country, right? Listen, you want some grass? Coke? Girls?" He was urban campesino, beer-drunk, uprooted, shifty-eyed, pretending hard to be American because his own country probably barely had a name anymore—just debts and, no doubt, a lousy soccer team.

"Grass," said Deke.

The room went suddenly insane. People dived to the floor as the bandits burst in, firing from the hip. Deke flew off his stool and rolled across the bar to drop down behind it, bottles smashing and spraying liquor and glass down his back where he crouched. The hand of the salesman, shot where he stood, fell flung back in death over the edge of the bar, dripping a trail of blood through curled fingers onto the floor by Deke's feet. In a tinkling silence as the shooting stopped, he heard booted feet advance, coming closer to the bar. The only other sound as the debris settled was a whimpering of dancers and diners and waitresses, a wounded quiet moan here and there, the oblivious happy chatter of TV. He looked up at the stock-still and white-faced barman, frozen miraculously unscathed; he saw a fist reach out to grab him by the collar, heard a voice say, "The money. Now." Nodding aquiver, hands held up defensive in clammy soft bunches before his chest, the barman backed off to obey. Then, leaning over in his wake as he went, Deke saw coming the owner of the voice, a pock-smeared face, slick-haired and unshaven. It cracked into a grin; said, "Eh, gringo"—and beckoned him to his feet. Slowly, carefully, raising hands, Deke stood.

The bandit moved along the bar top to study him closer. Behind his silhouetted head, Deke saw the colors of the TV across the room make meaningless patterns on the darkness. There was a hushed babble of excitable commentary; he heard, in the death-still room, that Chiriqui could do the 100 in 9.95. He thought, of all the bars in the world, he had to walk into this one. . . . The tip of the bandit's automatic nudged up across the bar and under his chin. Deke was ready to whisper, hey, let's be reasonable, guys, I'm supposed to be going into space tomorrow. . . .

The rock beast strolled on clacking flint heels through the lethargy of vacuum to the central girder from which Ecto's outer segments unfurled. He was sniffing out new kicks, hunting down bigger signals; with a tinny rustling of pebbly vertebrae, he dropped his fierce-collared and gaudy neck, and landed his tungsten teeth down hard into a cylinder of high-grade alloy packed, he discovered to his delight, with a fat core of the very finest glass-and-silicon transponder links.

Deke thought he was sure now to die. But even as he could feel, without seeing, that the gangster was slowly, with a mad malicious pleasure, just beginning now to squeeze his finger on the trigger— Deke felt his head held up taut, the muscles of his neck pulled stringy with shocked fear; he had an awful, full sound-and-picture vision of the explosion of his brain toward the ceiling—so then, at that moment, behind the grinning face darkened in shadow before his own, the television halo grew suddenly bolder and whiter. The set began to buzz and hum—and, at first still holding him by his shirtfront, the bandit with his widening eyes as the room grew bright now turned away, and let him go. Deke stepped back, eyes darting over the body of the dealer, as a white sparking haze turned over and over on the screen, and then formed up into the beast's stockinged call sign.

"Well wow," said the beast, in his ether-amplified growl, consonants like the crash of quarried stone, "does this taste good now, this big city transponder here, doesn't this taste fine. Who'm I talking to there? 'Cause listen up, you big city people, I'm a-comin' in fire mighty soon. . . ." *Click.*

The screen went dead as the techs on duty got the station shut down—but not before people of all creeds and colors, from Leisure City to Juno Beach, in hovels and shacks down Alligator Alley and the Tamiami Trail, in every kind of dwelling from mobile to mansion round Dade and Broward and Palm Beach and Martin counties, all joined, in some bewilderment, the growing numbers of those who, briefly, had heard an alien say hi.

The dead dope dealer lay amid the broken and tipped-over glasses. Nimble-fingered, Deke lifted the man's grass from his bloodied top pocket, then plunged away through the bar's back door and out through storerooms to his car in the lot. The bandit looked back from the blanked-out screen to find him gone; he vaulted the bar top and gave chase. But Deke was already screeching off down the anxious avenues; he found to his satisfaction that the car's music now worked again. As shots rang out behind him he got the bass pump-pumping; the horns surged, and the guitar sang *chang-a-chuh-chang* to feed his adrenaline. Torched buildings and battered shop fronts raced by; he veered around the potholes, trying to get safe onto the freeways, to get out and head north up on I-95. He wanted the wind and the road racing by, because he was alive—and because, tomorrow, he'd be out of his gourd in outer space. . . .

"Go go go," cried Grief, clapping his hands, laughing out loud at the sight of his volley of vendors fanning out among the crowds; already it was plain the operation would be over in minutes.

Charlie's eyes scoured the info-board. Red blips of data sprinted sparkling along the stripsigns giving headlines, destinations, share movements (down, down); he saw, mingled with the latest on the civil war in Kazakhstan, that the next departure for the airport was imminent. He hurried, breathing hard now, still carrying Mel, running at a slow, deliberate, and determined pace, his legs full of the effort, and his exposed skin prickling everywhere.

"Umbrellas, umbrellas, take the sting out of the weather for just one hundred dollars," yelled some guy in his ear as he passed.

Larkins stumbled into the station, half his white shirt now red. He gazed frantically about him. The crowd was gathered into knots of grasping, yelling people around each salesman and his trolley. He pushed forward, his face a mesh of inflammation, people backing agape from his wound and the gun.

Suzie abruptly nudged Grief, saying, "Shit, it's the copper." Grief looked hurriedly around, saw one of his bodyguards, and waved him quickly to come with them. They ran across the blaring concourse, knocking the packed bodies aside.

Charlie had Mel fumbling in his jacket pockets for the Kalero transit passes. He stood, hustling edgily forward in the line at their platform gate. The computer clerk all but touched his forelock at the quality of their credit and said, "That'll do nicely, Mr. Fish. First class at the front of the train." Seeing Mel in his arms he added, "And have a nice honeymoon."

Several paces ahead of Suzie, Grief and his guard burst out of the crowd. Larkins was ten yards from the platform gate; screaming people dived away all around him as he raised the shotgun. Charlie turned back at the noise. Grief yelled, "Stop!" Larkins spun around, saw the weaponed-up guard arriving right close to him, and fired.

At short range, the shot exploded the man's face. Without pause, like a robot, Larkins pumped the action and fired again; the second shot hit Grief full in the gut. It buckled him in two and cannoned him backward into Suzie, knocking her over as he fell. Her own gun spun away from her hand through the litter. In the echoing silence after the crash of the shots as his body fell off hers, it seemed he whispered to her, "Ah well—no one's invincible." He died smiling.

She looked up, pushing herself away from him, but Larkins reeled close over her, the gun pointed in her eyes.

And she'd forgotten, changing that morning from black to white, to take out her chocolate contact lenses; Larkins knew, immediately, those deep and fathomless eyes. "Well," he hissed, "little Miz Pata-joli ain't so black after all."

He saw Charlie backing, peering, down the platform beyond the fences, Mentitia in his arms. And they saw Larkins, wild-eyed and sweating, grunting at Suzie to stand up, forget the gun, walk away before him. As she stood, Charlie saw who she was.

Dollarville. It always likes to give you one hefty final kick in the teeth before you leave.

Speakers called the last passengers on board. The train fired up its engines.

Suzie watched Grief's blood spilling out among the cans and the cartons. She was thinking, pretty calmly, Acushla'd soon sort out this copper. He was in a bad way—he nudged her in the back with the gun barrel, breath phlegmy and crackling, saying, "Move it, move it." The crowd ebbed away from their path.

But Acushla was a hundred yards of concourse away, fighting off four members of a rival umbrella gang. He heard the shot but saw nothing, and could do nothing.

Larkins was thinking, one hard bitch will do, in the end, just as good as another.

Mel and Charlie stared through the back window of the train as it pulled away; the scene receded and vanished into the blackness of tunnels. "I saw her picture," said Mel, "on your wall."

Charlie said, to himself more than Mel, "Suzie can handle herself." What was she to him anyhow?

Just a few years of his life. Sometimes he felt like he could remember every minute.

But what can you do? About anything?

On the in-carriage monitors, news screens carried unconfirmed reports of a nuclear incident on the Korean DMZ; and announced the movement south across the spic line of new divisions of American military. The nominal reason given in his press conference by the chief of staff was security for the Hispania Cup—they'd make base around Soccer City—but everyone knew why they were really there. Wall Street wanted its money back; and the president would be waving his big stick on their behalf, just the moment the sportfest was done.

Charlie and Mel made their way up the train for a drink in first class. A big drink. Several. Wouldn't you?

By the time Madam had made her final decision on the footwear front, one old dictator was sound asleep. A second, at table, fell snorting face first into his rabbit and sweetbread terrine, while a third delivered tirades to any who would listen on the limp-wristedness of Congress—but they all knew that story. Marcovaloza himself railed at the injustice of their suspension of aid to his men. So they'd shot up a few tourists, so what? They were fighting a Holy War here (growls of agreement) and if El Coco had been, he'd admit it himself, not the most successful of engagements—why, were they not taking on here the massed forces of international Communism? And did his men not, therefore, need more aid, not less? But Congress would see soon enough, he muttered ominously, reaching for more brandy, that there was no limit to what the devils of Marxist-Leninism were capable of. They sat hissing into their liquor while Madam's children came charmingly to entertain them, performing their party piece—a rendition, *with feeling,* of "We Are the World."

The message came through to Chester Gantry that signals to Miami, now, had been interfered with. He made excuses and went to the phone to plant stories in the company media. The Kalero channels, Satsport, 69, and several others, would get dutifully frenetic about "enemy plots"—more strongly than ever would come the cry for "firm action." The president would be harassed, and denounce worldwide conspiracies. From his plane en route to Soccer City he'd announce, in the name of the free world and Christ Our Savior, that he was putting the forces on full readiness.

So it's only a few last pushes down that road we've been traveling, since the first sign of His Coming on the White Sands range. . . .

Gantry saw himself gleaming in the mirrors in the hallway, eyes flaring with fire. He felt strong as a lion; his voice was hoarse with expectation as he whispered down the phone.

12. OMEGA

It was a public holiday in the Heart, so that everyone could party and enjoy the Cup Final. At Maurice's place, Reynalda nodded a brief hi to Jimmy Baines as he arrived, bearing liquor; she was on the phone, ordering pizzas the size of wagon wheels for delivery to the door. All around the resident's estate, tables groaned under mountains of nibbles and dips, and fridges overflowed with cold beer; while in the ad breaks, when airtime was still cheap with hours yet to go before the kickoff, charities grabbed their shot at the viewers, and appealed for money for the people of Sudan or Mozambique, or whatever other place just then seemed especially irretrievable; not, of course, that half the viewers knew too well anymore where those indistinguishable places might be—but sentimentalists among them might still reach for their check books before grabbing another sandwich, or getting another beer. . . .

In the empty Kalero building, Gantry sat alone, watching through the tall windows the steaming sun that alternated unsteadily with gusts of gray and windy rain; the streets far below between the glass and steel canyons were mostly deserted. The little blip of a reveler's car zipped by now and then, trailing festive banners: Go, California! And on the television he watched Ephraim Evangel, who had bigger chunks of Globewide airtime than any poor charity.

"The time is near—He who is firstborn of the dead and the ruler of kings on earth is coming with the clouds, and all the tribes, I say all the tribes of the earth will wail on account of Him."

Which generated, for Ephraim, bigger pledges by far than Sudan or Mozambique . . .

Mel nudged Charlie awake and pointed down from the airplane window. "We're coming in." As they dropped toward the runway, he noted the banks of antiaircraft guns along the borders of the tarmac. The plane bumped down, and he thought, Oh, no—here we go, here we go. . . .

Whisked on their stolen data through VIP ingress by fawning officials in the seething terminal, they might have felt, on an ordinary day, underdressed in the face of such treatment—but not today, with all manner of louche open-collar personalities flying in all around them from every continent for the final—pop stars, TV types, corporate sponsors and PR men, old footballers turned commentators—and all in all so much smooth-shining Beverley Hills and Madison Avenue come to town, that the airport runners had one hell of a time finding them a taxi. Charlie told Mel, grumbling after a lousy night's sleep on the flight, "I never thought, when I got rich, it'd be like this."

Waiting, he read the local papers, in which insurgent activity against "loyal forces" was admitted from Puerto Rico to Panama, from Sonora to Tamaulipas. The president said the Russians were behind it, and had, it seemed, on the high seas, started taking out their freighters. He claimed, giving justifications under nebulous international law, to be interdicting arms shipments.

The Russians said, "What arms shipments?"—but nobody heard them. . . .

On their way into town through smog and barrio, the route was lined with festival flags and bunting, and massed ranks of slogan-busy billboards from the tournament's many sponsors. "The Hispania Cup—brought to you on Globewide Satsport by Kalero, we're all the world needs." The route was lined, too, with tanks and armored vehicles.

Ducking between the traffic on exit ramps off the freeways, shanty folk sold flowers and oranges, counterfeit cup programs and souvenirs. Their driver had to warn off a gang of boys with his baseball bat when they threatened, unsolicited, to wash the windshield.

Ahead, Charlie saw the clutch of leaping towers downtown, the international hotels purveying that indeterminate worldwide blandness that disabled you from knowing, once inside, whether you were in Jakarta or Cairo, Bombay or Buenos Aires—and he wondered, wherever you went, did you ever leave Dollarville?

Deke arrived in orbit, and slowly regained full consciousness after the flattening near-blackout of lift-off. He stared in exhausted joy at planet Earth, the dazzling blue-brown-green curves of it beneath him, whirled around and adorned like a beautiful woman with veils of gleaming cloud. He saw too, across vast distances, other pieces of her glinting necklace, shuttle docks and spies and relays and robolabs . . . the Stockton Plateau tried to raise him.

He ignored them, the vision was too much. He took, instead, slow deep breaths, and waited for his balls to stop aching from the weight of the g's.

"This is Kalero Control, over." *Click.*

Deke rolled from his seat, and drifted slowly back to his kit case in the compartment behind the cockpit. Beyond that again was the payload bay, and the extravehicular work pod. He'd have, he knew, to go run a check through its systems, before he arrived at Ecto VII—but first things first.

"This is Kalero Control, over." *Click.*

In his kit case, Deke had ten space pens. A raised eyebrow at the small parts store had greeted his request for that many, when he presented his inventory. "What you gonna write up there, boy, your memoirs?" But he'd told them, he was keeping a diary for the PR department.

And he'd then carefully replaced each one-piece, pressure-sealed ink tube with a neatly rolled joint.

"This is Kalero Control, do you read me, over." *Click.*

Deke had noted, spending prelaunch time in the simulators, two cameras in each forward compartment. They were not presently switched on; energy for image transmission was expended only in emergency or at prime time.

So he now floated from one camera to the next, covering each lens with a small square of material and an elastic band. He always was a high-tech guy, that Deke Lewis. . . .

"This is Kalero Control, Lewis, are you OK there, over?" *Click.*

Deke sat back down in the cockpit, strapped himself in, and lit up. He said, grinning, "Yup, never better."

Meep-meep, meep-meep. Lights winked and blinked on control center consoles.

"Kalero Control, Lewis, we have a smoke warning signal here, please evaluate, over." *Click.*

"No problem, guys, no—ha—no problem at all." He winced, and sucked in his breath. The grass had a real good kick on it.

The void above him was of a blackness impenetrably perfect, bejewelled with wild stars; and then it faded to a halo of ravishing white brightness around the rim of the earth below.

Meep-meep, meep-meep.

"Lewis, this is Rutger Mengel, mission command. Our telemetry suggests your whole cockpit's on fire. We're turning on the cameras. Please describe your situation, over." *Click.*

"Describe my situation," mused Deke, "now that's a tough one. . . ."

"We have total camera malfunction, Lewis, over." *Click.*

"Yeah well," said Deke, "you would have. But listen now, ah—to describe my situation here, what can I say?—what can I tell you? This is something else—I mean, you could really get bit by the God bug up here. . . ."

"His face shall shine brighter than the sun in full strength but be not, I say be not afraid, for we are Saved in these great United States—for He saith to us in the Book, he who conquers and keeps My works until the end, I will give him power over the nations—and he shall rule them with a rod of iron, as when earthen pots are broken, broken in pieces ..."

People huddled around the TV Word, as vague news began to fly around the networks. The Soviets, said reliable sources, were sabotaging our satellites. Spokesmen were outraged, and spoke darkly of space piracy. Gantry smiled.

Scarskull, in his grubby hotel room near the stadium, oiled and cleaned his guns one last thorough time.

In a larger and smarter hotel, Charlie investigated absentmindedly the quality of the fixtures and fittings, the contents of the minibar, the movies on the in-house film channel. Mel told him to turn to the soccer.

But she fast found the nationalism, the PR patriotism in which the team's success was now wrapped, enraging—this, the country that had turned its back on her, now appropriating not just the one sport it didn't have, and this tournament, but a whole team too to play in it; the triumphalist interviews rolled on.

Charlie called room service, and asked for a toothbrush; then went back to pacing and poking around. Propped on her bed, she watched him. He seemed possessed by a jittery, enervated curiosity, not like him at all. He'd seemed a calm man, at first—she told him, "Sit down," and he did. She asked, "What's the matter, Charlie Fish?"

He collected himself and told her, "Oh, nothing—it's just, you know, here we are, in a fancy hotel room—and our lives are in ruins. And I hate bloody football."

He realized, as he said it, that he was not anymore such a nice guy as once he had been.

But she said, "That's too bad—because we're going to this game whether you like it or not." She was firm; she told him, "We got access better than most journalists get—and I want your help to use it."

She had thought, studying the stadium layouts in their documentation, of a way to make foolish this frantic pride of America—because if no revenge was great enough, then at least some would be better than none at all.

Charlie shrugged, and fell silent. She seemed alive, while all he felt was adrift, unanchored in a world gone crazy; he felt there was nothing now left to defend.

He remembered how once he had things all in place: a home, a girlfriend—the simple hopes of the average Joe; but what chance simple hopes in a world of sickness, of fouled waters and corrupted air, split through with the angry shouting of leaders amid a rattling of warheads—trying to drown out the rage and hunger of the people on their doorsteps by blaming the people in the house across the road, until the insidious lies infect us, make us complicit, and drive us all, finally, mad . . . .

Lev and Blok recovered slowly from awesome, stunned-head hangovers. Larkins's wound was dressed, but his eyes were bright with fever. Suzie was tied down in a chair, gagged at the desk in the Worldmap studio. Larkins, shirt still bloody, knelt beside her. He felt her breasts between the ropes. His gaze was intense, his stubble thick and dirty; his hand shook against her skin.

This woman—she was dark in the morning, then white at night—he suspected he was going crazy and, also, that he'd been generally fucked about with by the world at large.

But he'd show them. He'd made decisions about the script. He was gonna heavy it up a bit; gonna get him some material more in tune with the times. . . .

Her cloth-stuffed mouth was dry—but all mouths will be dry, when the world reaches its terminal passion. . . .

"And out came another horse, a horse bright red, and its rider, saith John, took peace from the earth until men slew one another, and see how it is prophesied in Revelation of the red horse of Communism—so hear, I say hear, He Shall Come. . . ."

Congressmen gathered in the Capitol for a complimentary, invitation-only screening of the big game. Elmer Rayban (marketing) moved softly among them, murmuring of vital interests, and of the trouble his brave men—the moral equivalent, after all, of the founding fathers—were now having in winning back lost markets for America, since their funding was withdrawn. "I'm sorry to have to say, gentlemen, we have no choice but to favor prompt and firm action in the face of these provocations. Why, all through the Isthmus, we have men in place, and all they want for is your support. . . ."

Your guns—and a few helicopters, maybe. And some air support, some napalm, some serious bombing, some big-stick stuff—because for sure, Marcovaloza wanted his mercenaries to win him his country back from Communism; but being the mercenary type himself, he figured on the whole that the Yanqui could pay for it. Hadn't they always?

You just had to prod them now and then, that's all, steer 'em to the right sort of notions. . . .

Mel had been steered by her anger (and by a big, innate streak of mischief) to a subversive little notion of her own. She explained it to Charlie, en route to the stadium in the hotel limo. He thought it was completely batshit and said so; but then he himself, by now, was so spiritually AWOL, he couldn't be bothered to argue—and besides, hadn't he told her he hated football? He also now told her, "You'll upset a lot of people."

And she said, "For sure, that's the point. Think of it, if you like, as herbal warfare."

In the smooth hush of their fast-lane transit through the city, she studied his expressionless face. He seemed whittled by events to a nothing person, not blank, but unintelligible—a thin collage of scraps of memory. Did he care about anything?

"You come in the room," said Larkins to Lev and Blok, "and she's tied up here waiting. You knock her about a bit, then you put her on the desk top. . . ."

"When he opened the sixth seal I looked, and behold, there was a great earthquake; and the sun became black as sackcloth, the full moon became like blood, and the stars of the sky fell to the earth. . . ."

The approach road to the stadium had five lanes, access into which was determined by the grade of your tickets—from A for the limos, to E on foot. It was transit bureaucracy gone crazy and worked, of course, abominably—one of those things about security, that the more of it you have, the less of it you get. Not that it specially mattered, as tickets were priced in dollars; and anyone holding dollars hereabouts was almost certainly a loyalist. . . . Still, there were uniforms everywhere. Charlie and Mel rode lane A, struck silent with amazement.

The stadium was enormous, taking 144,000. Spilling out of corrals and walkways and buses and monorails in all directions, people raced and pushed and stumbled around in cheerful bands. There were fenced-off tents and marquees for the dispensing of corporate largesse, and then minstrels, magicians, mariachis, fire-eaters, food and juice and ice stalls. They passed, peering through tinted glass, a stand on which a wrestling priest challenged anyone prepared, first, to make a donation to his orphans—a kind of loopy last outpost of good humor in a crowd interested more, let's face it, in the getting of money than the giving.

The festive throngs pushed forward—oblivious cogs in the media bonanza, collaborators in the business of making airwave whoopee—to distract a few billion viewers from their problems. Or, if Scarskull had his way, to focus them.

He strode through the crowd in spotless captain's uniform, a pistol in his holster, an Uzi on his shoulder; he had grenades, Semtex, ammunition, and another pistol already waiting in one of the security staff locker rooms. He'd paid a visit in early morning when it was quieter, but he liked it better now—more targets. . . .

The car pulled around to a drop-off point in the deep shadow of the stadium's towering side; Charlie, getting out, turned to help Mel up onto her crutches. Fenced off, far across from the car and the railings and the guards and the celebrities, on scraggy stretches of grass and mud, the curious milled about among the fairground sideshows. Charlie saw a man in bright costume crying, "Come, see, the unexplained miracle, Mr. Roman Alberto Squalatush, the man with the map of the world on his head, a unique and prophetic peccadillo of nature . . ."

Charlie started forward, and was politely turned the other way by the guards saying, "No, sir, this way, if you please, just follow your lady friend . . ."

Umberto the magician called from the steps of his now canopied Alka-Seltzer van, "Come, see, he serves as warning to us all. . . ."

Mel, stumping off ahead with a frowning certainty of purpose into the carpeted warren of corridors beneath the VIP boxes, turned and hissed at him as he hastened to catch her, "Charlie, behave, for chrissake. Our accreditation's with the biggest sponsor here, we're supposed to be the people who paid for all this—so will you please look like you're glad about that?"

He squeezed her out a sickly grin; he said, "But listen, Mel, outside—there's this guy—"

"Screw outside," she snapped. "Just follow me."

"What"—he groaned—"to the changing rooms? Now?" Then he shrugged and thought, well, he could talk to the old guy later. Let's face it, he wasn't going anywhere—and anyway, Mel's idea was, he admitted, rather growing on him. . . .

Scientists and technicians stood in hectic conference around Rutger Mengel. They were having trouble with Deke Lewis, who, giggling, slowly wrestled his way into his spacesuit. Outside, Ecto VII was just a short hop in the work pod from the shuttle.

The rock beast eyed the craft appreciatively; hanging stationary nearby, he wondered what it tasted like, and waited contentedly to meet a human.

But which human was he going to meet first?

There was another craft now, coming his way around the rim of the world. The Russians, see—they'd sent the president this furious message saying they were innocent and were sabotaging nothing, and they'd send a man around from Mir to investigate and assist. . . .

But the president wasn't taking any calls anymore—except, that is, the odd update from the military—and he listened instead to his old pal Ephraim Evangel, howling on the TV in his hotel room that "*a third of the earth was burned up, and a third of the trees, and all green grass—but the Saved will come out of the great tribulation in robes washed white in the blood of the lamb.* . . ."

In Germany and Korea, the battlefield warheads were primed.

There came a knock at the door. An aide quietly told him, "It's time to leave for the stadium, Mr. President."

"Repeat, Lewis, describe your situation, over." *Click*.

Deke floated through the gleaming metal silence toward the work pod in the bay. He said, "Well, my wife up and left me, I know that—and I'm in space, no question, spaced out in space. Hey, Stockton—this pod thing here, does it have a sound system?"

Mr. Squalatush did his last show before kickoff. He appeared before his silent little audience in the dim tent, wearing a cobbled-together patchwork of Zorro pants, a conquistador's white ruffled shirt and quilted gilet, a gaucho's cape and, on his head, shading his face, a king-size sombrero.

He told, with as much flourish as he could muster, of the mighty mass of Asia, the wracked wastes of slave Africa, and withered old dame Europe, her hands out begging for a dollar; he told of the proud and blustery cockerel's head of North America, and of the scorpion's sting in the tail of the South. And he told how when all is denuded and dessicated, and the last souls scratch through the poison chill of a permanent winter, how he, Roman Squalatush, would be nature's last pointed memento—a map of pollution, a mark of our sins of greed and bad husbandry. . . . He whipped off the hat and slipped forward to a roped patch of light; people pressed forward to peer, and to finger. . . .

Umberto counted takings in many currencies, stunned at the level of trade; but then, in time of disturbance, people grab at any old miracle, myth, sign, prophecy, or charlatan. . . .

"A third of the waters became wormwood, and many died of the bitter water . . ."

The small knot of people around Mr. Squalatush drifted away, whispering among themselves. He felt his head was like a fruit, tested with kneading thumbs by picky housewives at the market stall. Then he saw, as the others left, one figure staying back. His teeth were a white grin of light in the shadow; and Dandy Royle told him, "One wild show you got there, old guy—but listen, you wanna come see the game? I got me a spare ticket."

The old man's jaw dropped with simple pleasure. He turned to his boss, eyes bright with hope.

Umberto said, "Sure, go, go—you earned it."

"This," said Mel, "should be easy."

The California Squad stood lined up in the Kalero hospitality room, tersely polite as they were presented, like gladiators or members of some exotic tribe, to their paymasters and assorted high-class liggers, a whole raft of local business and government types. Charlie and Mel drank champagne at the back, and eyeballed a PR guy at the corporation's literature desk.

Charlie greeted him with a firm handshake, saying, "Fish, Dollarville." He had a dangling Kalero name tag to that effect on his lapel. He had adopted, like an automaton, the hale and confident demeanor of the partying businessman, remembered from countless ghastly celebrations with lawn mower salesmen and video producers, those wretched forced merriments with Baines at Vidivici—no more of that for Charlie. Just this one last performance.

He was doing what Mel asked because there was, simply, no one else anymore that he could do things for.

The camera turned. "Get her clothes off," said Larkins. "Rip her naked." Her mouth was bloody, staining the gag. "Do it," said Larkins, "with objects first."

"Let me introduce," said Charlie, "Mel Isenhope here"—the PR man was charmed, her smile was gracious, modest, dazzling—"the winner of our promotional competition," Charlie improvised, "supporting sport for the disabled—you may have heard."

He hadn't—who the hell gave a shit what happened in Dollarville? But he'd have hated, what with pride and good manners, to admit it. "Of course," he beamed, "it's a great pleasure, Miss Isenhope."

She murmured, more smiles, "Call me Mel."

"And how are you liking it here?"

She looked around the jostle of liquored faces, a roomful of flushed and arrogant boors sucking proxy manliness from the sportsmen they owned, and whose success they lived off, like screeching gulls.

She told him, "It's terrific, absolutely wonderful—but look, may I ask one great favor, is it possible—for my son back home"—she thought, that sounds good—"he'd be just thrilled to have a picture of me with Singani. You see, he still can't believe that his mother's really here—he's only seven."

The PR man was effusively sure that such a thing could be arranged. A photographer was gathered from among the zecks and celebs shaking hands with the players. Then Mel said sweetly, "Would you mind—I find the crush a little difficult, people knocking into me; perhaps it'd be easier if we just quickly stepped aside a minute. We could go," she said, "in the locker room there. Before the players warm up."

Singani was extracted from the line of footballers, and they stepped through into the team's empty changing room.

On a table in the far corner stood iced jugs of mineral water, Coke, OJ. Mel sat herself down on a bench by the door at the near end, Singani providing practiced smiles beside her. Behind the photographer's back, Charlie sauntered away; then, behind his own back while, apparently, paternally looking on at the happy winner being pictured with the Michoacán maestro, he crushed a datura seed between his fingertips, into each of as many jugs as he prudently could.

"There," said Mel, once they were back in the bean-feast, "I said it would be easy."

Most of the people, by now, were in the stadium.

The great stands and sweeping terraces were a riot of colored smoke bombs, banners, hats, mad drummers, and trumpeters. Old Glory hung from every stanchion, and a military band marched up and down on the field far below amid weaving flocks of photographers, cheerleaders, escapees from Disneyland. Vast electronic scoreboards flashed with loud and bright freedom slogans. Cameras beamed aerial shots worldwide from blimps of the seething annulus of the stadium and its waiting green center, a crater of ostentation set in the vast smoggy sprawl of a city where tens of thousands lived on rubbish dumps. . . . Other cameras in the girders of the roofing scanned the honking, hooting, foghorning thousands—and yet other cameras looked up between the rank upon rank of field-side signs and policemen, to take close-ups of pretty girls in the crowd.

Reynalda, idly toying with a stick of celery in an avocado dip, watched at the party in Dollarville the final moments tick away before kickoff. She complained to Jimmy Baines, "That precious Charlie Fish. What's he up to that's so special that he couldn't come to my party?"

"I'm sure," said Baines, "he's enjoying himself someplace."

In scanning rooms in several quadrants of the command-and-control network, the Russian craft approaching Ecto VII was tracked with growing cries of mistrust. Messages whipped in ever noisier confusion around the overloading ether.

"And I saw a star fallen from heaven to earth, and he was given the key of the shaft of the bottomless pit; he opened the shaft of the bottomless pit, and from the shaft rose smoke like the smoke of a great furnace, and the sun and the air were darkened with the smoke from the shaft. . . ."

The work pod was a transparent sphere of plastics and ceramics, veined with a red, yellow, and sky blue filigree of wiring running from the core computers behind Deke's seat, and from the consoles on either side of him, away to robot arms and instrumentation on the skin outside.

Beneath his feet, the bay doors fell slowly open. Hydraulics released and withdrew; the pod dropped away into space. The world opened like a flower below him as his width of view expanded until, free from the bay, he could see glowing up from the world's every

corner an onrush of radiant color so bright it seemed he could physically feel it, a storm of holy wind. . . .

A man, thought Deke, could sit here forever, turning with the
earth through day and night in the perfect silence of heaven. . . .

"Kalero Control, smooth release, over." *Click.*

"Will you shut the fuck up and let a man enjoy the view?" These
people, he thought, they had no consideration.

He tried to remember what he was up to up here.

"Lewis, we're going to nudge it on retros four and eight, do you
copy, over." *Click.*

"Hey, man, do what you like, you know—I'm just the spanner,
right?"

Two gassy little jets in the back of the pod gave it the minutest
fraction of a shove forward into a leisurely drift across the vacuum,
toward the satellite slowly spinning out ahead. Deke stared, red-eyed
and smiling, as the pod edged out from under the shuttle, and the
canopy of the universe above his head unrolled until the sphere in
which he sat, and his visor, and his eyes, were all filled to the brim
with the singing light of the stars. . . .

He found that he was crying and laughing all at once.

"Kalero Control, Lewis, you have company, over." *Click.*

"I wonder if he smokes."

"Repeat, over." *Click.*

"Never mind." Deke watched the Soviet orbit hopper arriving on
the far side of Ecto.

The cosmonaut's name was Yuri Popkov. A true product of *glas-
nost,* he was a fan of the Chicago Cubs and of the Bears, and of all
American pop music, but especially of Prince. He'd been on Mir for
six months, and was kind of yearnsome for new company. Now
true, the Americans were pretty touchy these days, walking out of
Geneva and Vienna in an inexplicable huff, and hanging about
pointing lasers at you all the time—but there was no harm in at least

offering to help. And besides you never knew, they might have some books to trade, or a spare pair of Levi's. . . .

The world watched the president's motorcade pulling up outside the stadium. He greeted the match officials, then swept into the complex amid a crowd of security men. The lieutenant with the black briefcase scurried along behind him.

Archimedes, Flor, Garrapatal, Chiriqui, all the team waited jogging on the spot, touching toes, bouncing balls on heads and feet, and taking small nervous sips at their drinks. Singani moved among them, spreading confidence. The coach strode in to tell them, "The president's here."

Cameras followed him into the room, and he hustled around slapping shoulders, shaking hands. Finally, he was isolated by the cameras with Singani, parked on preset marks before a backdrop of flags and Kalero logos. The camera lights gleamed blinding down off the tiled walls around them; Singani wondered when anyone was going to let him actually think about playing soccer. He was beginning, in the sudden melee of all this entourage and press, to feel a little woozy here. He took another sip of water from his plastic cup.

The president was entirely unfazed by the lights, smiling at the world, and slipping like the professional he was into newsbite-sized delivery.

"My fellow Americans and all freedom-loving people—welcome.

"I'd just like to tell you—I'm backing my team.

"These fine young men are proof, I say proof, that America continues, the land of opportunity, open to all."

He turned to Singani and said, "So let me just say, your president will be praying to the Good Lord for your success.

"Now go out there and thrash 'em."

"Si, senor," said Singani, and led his team out to the tunnel.

On his way up to the president's box, the president hissed urgently at an aide, "Who's that buncha spics playing out there anyhow?"

"Ah—I'm not sure, sir, hold on." Hasty confabs ensured, then the aide hissed back, as they trooped up the carpeted stairways, "Paraguay, sir."

"Paraguay, huh? Where's that? Is it one of ours? Do they play baseball?"

The president's box was, literally, a box—a large cubic structure high in the grandstand, sealed and cased all around with bulletproof glass. As he emerged into it up stairs from the reception rooms beneath, speakers boomed all around the ground, hailing him, "Ladies and gentlemen, the president of the United States of America!"

The president gave a cheery wave with both arms from the front of the box around the sea of smoke bombs and flags; thousands of red, white, and blue balloons were released, and he smiled and he smiled. . . .

In an empty service corridor beneath the box, Scarskull tacked his Semtex to the inside of the air-conditioning duct, close to one of the main girders in the structure's support. He left Communist IDs for the forensics to find. Now they'd know, he grinned, how bad those Communists are. . . .

"Ladies and gentlemen," said Elmer Rayban to the swilling congressmen at the canape trough in DC, "I'm sorry to interrupt the screening just for a moment, here—but could members of the defense committee please step into the briefing room, the chief of staff would like a word."

The word was: "Interference with our orbital communications capability, gentlemen, downgrades significantly the quality of our response posture, should a first strike occur. . . ."

The congressmen all nodded in knowing agreement that this sounded pretty bad—though privately they all wondered, yet again, why these people from the Pentagon couldn't just for once speak plain English.

Yuri Popkov hopped on his space scooter, and jetted toward Ecto VII.

The teams stepped out onto the field to a redoubling of the tumult of the 144,000. Speakers blared fanatic music, "Oh say can you see . . ."

In Dollarville, Gantry grinned exultant at the screen. His eyes were snake's eyes, his face had the scales of a reptile; his tongue flickered between his razor-sharp teeth.

Poachers killed the last rhino.

Lev was underneath her, Blok was above, and both were inside her. Larkins with his camera screamed to fuck the bitch, fuck the bitch hard.
Her head rolled and shook with the pain.

Charlie and Mel made slowly down wide stairs to the fieldside executive bar. Mel wanted more champagne.
In the bleachers, Dandy bought Mr. Squalatush a beer.
Smoke and streamers and balloons drifted around the stands in livid profusion; the noise was deafening. Singani blinked at the swimming chaos of color beneath the blimps in the blazing sky. He made ready to kick off.

The work pod fired a brake jet fifty feet from the outer wings of Ecto VII. Deke stared with a vacant stoned grin at what appeared to be a dog standing on the flashing rungs of the solar power panels. "Kalero Control, Lewis, we're taking you closer. Report Russian activity, over." *Click.*
Yuri sat on his scooter, hoping as he drew nearer that the American would be friendly.
"He's coming closer." Stockton didn't know it, but Deke was

talking about the beast here now, not the Russian; and his grin was turning to fear. "Look, man, he's moving, what the fuck is this? Jesus, he's coming right at me, give me manual, give me manual on the tool arms," and his voice as the beast ran to the end of Ecto and jumped, eager eyes shining, teeth glinting, toward the pod, was now cracking with sudden paranoid alarm. "What the hell have you got me into up here . . .?"

"He's being attacked," said Rutger Mengel. "Get me the chief of staff on the line."

Deke frantically swung the robot arm up as the beast, flying heels-first to land on the skin of the pod, came within a yard—then the gangling, pulleyed and socketed strip of telescopic tools crashed into the beast's stone ribs, knocking him aside, deflecting him into a spinning earthward trajectory. The beast thought, Well, fuck you. He'd only wanted to say hello.

"Kalero Control, Lewis, do you copy, over." *Click.*

"Kalero Control, Lewis, what happened, over." *Click.*

But Deke had switched them off. He stared through his wire-laced sphere into the shiny black void, seeing—literally—nothing; his face was frozen, brain stalled trying to register what he'd seen. He thought, nah, couldn't be, it couldn't be—then there came a tapping on the hard plastic above him. He looked up with a start.

Yuri held a piece of paper facedown on the surface of the sphere. It said, "Hey, American—did you see what I just saw?"

Newsflashes announced gravely the committing by the Russians of the first recorded act of space terrorism, an attack on an unarmed allied astronaut. . . .

Word was brought to the president. When he saw the note coming, and the expression on the aides' faces, he thought, Dear Lord, what's fallen now? Tel Aviv? Manila? Tucson? He scanned the message. "I've had it," he said, "up to here with these godless sons of bitches."

He looked up, and saw Singani lining up one of those long, inch-perfect, incisively defense-shredding passes into space on the flanks for which, justly, he was famous—except, his swinging leg missed the ball altogether. It sat dead on the ground, and he fell flat on his back beside it. The Paraguayans stopped and scratched their heads. Capistrano was on his knees, pointing at his toppled captain and giggling uncontrollably. Archimedes had left his goal, and was making faces at the photographers along the end of the field. Singani stared up at the blistering sky. The silence of 144,000 descended, more deafening by far than all their previous noise.

"You don't think," said Charlie, "we used too much?"

The beast, hugely miffed at the reception he'd got from Deke, rolled on his back through the emptiness. His head was a computer-paced clicking of angles and speeds, planes and coordinates. Right, he was thinking, let's go talk to these people.

From his ore-lined gut he let rip through his diatomite asshole a powerful jet of digested and pressurized mineral gas. He ignited it with sparks from his lava blood, fired through crystal capillaries like the hot flash off the flint of a lighter, and the rocket-blast fart propelled him earthward.

"Kalero Control, Lewis, are you there, over.' Click.

No answer. Deke was holding a note faceup against the pod's transparent roof which said to Yuri, "Hi. Come over to my place."

The rock beast roared with pleasure, his body glowing red in the ecstatic blazing flame of reentry.

Early warning tracker systems charted the inbound trajectory.

The phone rang in the briefing room. A voice told the chief of staff, "Sir, we have a hostile inbound from the vicinity of our tampered satellite. It's headed where the president is. . . ."

"Fuck the president—I just sent my best divisions to that town." He slammed down the phone and turned to the congressmen. "This is it, gentlemen. Use 'em or lose 'em."

One asked, dry-mouthed, "Ah—shouldn't we be seeking the president's authorization on this?"

Scarskull radio-activated his detonator. The president's box disintegrated in a roaring cascade of fire and glass, showering the stands all about with razor-edged debris.

Billions watched the president die. Charlie and Mel stared up from where they'd fallen on the grass at the endless screaming, and the licking of flames from the blackened gashed hole in the stands.

The trampling for the exits began, raising higher the death count.

Singani smiled, watching in the bleak burnished sky the growing star of impossible brightness that was rushing toward him from the heavens.

Scarskull stood on the roof of the stadium, lobbing grenades into the VIP stands. He sprayed the fleeing mass of bodies with his Uzi; Charlie hauled Mel across the ground behind the executive bar, as bullets kicked the turf up all around them.

Marcovaloza called Gantry. "I think that ought to stir them."

"I have a feeling," crooned Gantry, "it'll stir them all the way."

The congressmen pressed forward around the chief of staff. One asked, "Excuse me, sir, but, ah—now we've got the things away—is there a bunker hereabouts?"

"See," pointed Roman Squalatush to the brilliant ball of smoking flame rushing closer and closer in the sky, "He comes."

The sirens sounded all around Dollarville, *a-whah, a-whah-ah-ooohhn* ... how will you spend your four minutes, when you're waiting to die?

Baines poured himself a stiff whiskey, and kissed his friends good-bye. And if you're lucky, you too may find there's a good man near you who can keep you calm, and stop you from screaming—because screaming won't help.

Gantry went to the roof of the tower and spread his arms wide to embrace the burning heaven.

She was on her back, head lolled helpless over the edge of the desk. Lev stood, jetting come in her eyes. Blok's knife fell again and again in her stomach. As the sirens wailed, he lay across her; he fucked the wounds, cock pumping in the blood.

Nuclear war. The ultimate snuff movie.

The map explodes.

13. CHARLIE'S DIARY

I feel it's obligatory to write this journal. It seems unlikely that any-one'll come along to read it, I know—or, at least, that anyone who does happen by will be able or willing to read it—but it's just the custom, anyhow, it's the thing you do. When you're the last man in the world, you shoot your mouth off about it.

Actually, I'm one of three last men in the world, plus one last woman and an alien too—me, who used to hope I'd just grow qui-etly old in Traderstown, herbalist to the zecks, writer of cacky videos. . . . But I always did say, it was an uncertain world. I still have the tie I was wearing, pheasant copper and swimming-pool blue, when I walked out my door.

There'll be no one growing old in Traderstown now. The towers of the Heart are stumps, and the sidewalks ash. I guess I wasn't born unlucky after all.

The others aren't much interested in keeping diaries. Mel, it's true, keeps herself busy with a thesis on the behavior of the black rhinoceros, which I keenly await—but diaries, no.

"Where's the use," says Dandy, "writing for posterity when there isn't one?"

Now don't get me wrong here, Dandy's happy—he's rigging up some machine to get us power off the river flow, we're doing OK—but his attitude to posterity, that's shared. We figure, survival will do; posterity can wait.

Anyhow, Dandy misses the point. I'm not tying stuff down for the future here. I'm just doing it for me, in the present.

It comes natural. My life was a museum already, by the end. My house was a records office; I stopped it in time, just trying to keep a hold of what I'd been and seen, trying to hang on with things in place, a picture here, a map and a memory there, so I wouldn't forget—the archival bent comes natural.

What I'm saying is, for me, in this world right now—writing is survival. When I die, it doesn't. That's all.

Now there is, of course, another point of view on this notion. The end of the world, I know, as subjects go, it ain't cheerful—but it sure as hell beats lawn mowers.

The rock beast tells me, when he crawled grinning from the smoking crater, the first thing he saw was Singani. And Singani says to him, "How many of you are there?" That still cracks him up.

It cracks him up so much, what Mel did, that he's now taken, when you're walking about the camp, to popping out from behind tents or store sheds and shouting as you jump, "How many of you are there?" And then, cackling—sounds like a cement mixer—he trots off, plotting already some next bit of peskiness.

Gets on your nerves, living with an alien.

How many of us are there? It sort of echoes when he asks it. It's like he's saying, What kind of asshole species were you people anyhow?

Hitachi, on this question, is no use. The electromagnetic pulse must have torched the whole shebang, signals cutting out just like that in Chicago, Detroit, Houston, Philly, Dollarville, Moscow, who knows how many towns? I have to wonder what that part of it was like—there's no siren where you live, say, and you're watching TV, and it dies. You get up saying, hey, wha' happen? Then the air turns to fire and comes rushing through your windows . . .

We saw it, me and Mel, the signals going down. There were screens set in the wall of the executive bar. We lay hidden on the pitchside from Scarskull's bullets, watching the column of furnace smoke rise where the beast had landed—and around us where we lay, one by one, the channels went blank.

We let the beast eat Hitachi, in the end.

A TV dinner.

Still, how many of us are there?

For a while, at first, we caught weird snatches on the radio now and then, little garbled appeals, fading away.

We don't broadcast, ourselves. We have almost everything we need; we're agreed, there's no point letting anybody know about it. We'd rather not learn what kind of people might be prowling out there.

So—there are five of us.

It seems like between us, we've got what it takes to make a go of things. We're a bit like one of those enterprise ads, earnest people striding about starting their own business—some days, you could almost call me optimistic.

For a start, old Roman, on the food-growing front—he really knows his stuff. This is, after all, his territory, tucked away in the Cordillera. . . .

It seems touch and go he'll beat the weather—it's definitely deteriorating—but he's having a game crack at it. The plots around the settlement look neat and well-tended—and lessons I learned off Les the Flower Man come in handy, too; I was worried I'd be useless. Thankfully, it's not turned out that way.

So I spend a lot of time rooting about with the old guy—we rub along pretty good. When we're not studying how best to tend the corn, the onions, the fruit trees, we go out in the forest, and he shows me the plants they always used here for medicine. I enjoy that, and I'm getting us cataloged up. We're going to need all the help we can get, let's face it; I mean, I'm not a basket case—if I say I'm an optimist, it's an optimism that comes pretty qualified.

E.g., nature has little in stock to cure the effects of radiation.

We don't know whether any fallout will come this way; maybe some already has—but what can I say? You takes your chances.

And you don't think about it. You think, hey, patting yourself on the back for your luck, we got a month's supply of tinned rations for two hundred left here by the mercenaries; you think, that'll keep us going for a while. And then you look for things to do, to keep your mind good and busy.

Memories of getting here keep the mind pretty busy.

Lying there on the pitchside grass with the flames and the screams and the shooting all about, tripping footballers making lurching stumbling efforts to get away from a smoldering alien trotting around trying to find someone to talk to him, Scarskull abseiling from the grandstand roof to vanish among the panic and stampede—it sure did feel like the end of the world.

It was Roman who made friends with the rock beast; he wandered onto the pitch through the crowds, Dandy uncertainly in tow. And then, "Look," he says, "you're scaring people, just calm down, sit still. You really didn't," he tells him, "pick a good time to come."

"Then why," says the rock beast, "were you praying for me to come?"

We've since explained to the beast the nature of his misunderstanding. But it seems hard, all the same, to duck the conclusion that in other ways, we really did ask for this.

If we feel good, in these conditions, I better say also how a lot of that comes down to Mel. I wouldn't know what leadership's about, it was never my bag—but whatever it's about, she's got it. When we met in the tents strung up around the Alka-Seltzer van, the frantic streams of people spilling away all about us, it was she who, on hearing of this place, was most decisive that we should come here. People, she said, would go north, not south.

And so, it seems, from the radio's little spurts of information, it has proved. I have this image of a whole continent being looted up there. . . .

We found six bodies when we arrived. Dandy's guess is the last few mercenaries had themselves a rampage, before making north for the grand scavenge. There can only have been a couple of them—they'd not taken with them one twentieth part of the camp's supplies—and now Roman says, the rest of his people must be out in the forest. He wants to go look for them; but Mel's persuaded him it's best to wait, and tend their crops. They'll come back, she says, of their own accord.

Burying the bodies was bleak. Luckily, Dandy and I found them before Roman did, and managed to cover them so he'd only see the faces. We dug the grave ourselves, too, and kept him away from the work. We didn't want him to see the mutilations.

He said a few words, when we'd filled the hole, and we stood about shuffling; there didn't seem many words that would serve.

It was an unfortunate start, and we don't refer to it.

Nor do I forget it.

But then, I forget nothing. I'm a data base, disconnected: I sit here clacking with information about a world that no longer exists—a past without a future.

And when I think like this, of course I wonder, going about grinning at each other in a kind of competition to see who can be the most optimistic, whether all we are, in fact, is just collectively crazy. But what can I say? We keep busy.

Whether crazy or not, the group's determined bonhomie is much tested by the rock beast.

I always wondered, since I was a kid and got my first atlas that had the pictures of the solar system, what life on other worlds might be like. So the beast's a major disappointment. He behaves, basically, like a bloody delinquent.

Imagine, for example, Mel and I sitting contented like an old farmer couple (we don't have rocking chairs, but you know what I mean) on the *jefe*'s screened verandah—and suddenly, out beyond the perimeter wires, there's this god-almighty explosion. The little bugger gets a kick, it seems, out of walking on land mines. If you look up quick enough (and you do tend, I tell you, to look up pretty quick) you can catch a glimpse of him, cartwheeling with a sort of hooligan whoop through the air on the blast, amid the smoke and flying dirt.

Once I stormed off over the drill ground, meaning to yell at him, really bawl him out—but when I got to the inside of the rolls of wire, I lost heart. He was nuzzling around for hot bits of shrapnel to nibble at, and he looked up so—well, so *plaintive* . . . it was like he was saying, look, I'm a rock beast, we just come this way, I mean, what did you expect? ET?

And I guess, if you visit a planet, and the inhabitants go and blow the place up before you've even started to look around—I guess you might feel pretty peeved.

I wish he wouldn't moan so much about his diet. How does he think we feel about ours? The crops are hardly bumper, and the skies grow steadily more dirty, more gray, the winds more chill.

We fed him the surplus weaponry that we'd not, between us, be able to use, should there come any call for us to use it—but our generosity, given fears of who or what might be out there, was far from promiscuous. We only let him have, for example, one grenade. He went about muttering that we were stingy for days.

I assume, however, that he grudgingly accepts our case—basically, because I also assume he could probably take anything he wanted;

I've seen him morosely spitting acid at the trees, and wouldn't like to tangle with him.

When, eventually, I confronted him on the issue, he just said, "Rock beasts aren't violent, OK? We're not like you people."

The *jefe*'s shack is two rooms—a bedroom and an office—with the verandah along the length of the front. It's yielded a few treasures: a case of Flor de Cano, a box of cheap thrillers, some fancy boots—they fit me perfectly, which is a great relief; my own zip-and-buckle affairs, having perhaps sensed that the adventure's now over, are disintegrating in sympathy with the climate.

But the best find by far is the atlas.

It's inscribed, "To My *Jefe*. One day, it will all be ours—Marcovaloza." (And I guess you could say he was right).

But I don't, anyhow, much concern myself with who owned it before, in what I think of as the preworld. The atlas is too beautiful to waste my time remembering them, when there's the whole world on its pages to be remembered.

I stare at the maps for ages, and roll the names around my tongue.

The colors, also, make me want to take up painting. Roman is teaching me how to make dyes from the plants of the forest; it would be good to illustrate these words. I've already attempted crude portraits in charcoal—the beast was an unconscionable fidget and I've done him from memory, but the others were patient. We are learning patience.

We are learning, also, what being hungry is like.

There was snow the other day. We now rarely see the sun; when we do, it's a watery disk. Occasionally there are storms, and the wind beats through the treetops, and the rain turns the earth to a morass. But it's reassuring, as the storms come in, to hear the monkeys howl; we figure, if they can make it, so can we.

I hope the wind don't bring cancer on its breath. I pray that it doesn't—I've taken to using the camp chapel. I don't pray to any god there, particularly—I just pray. Perhaps if the weather gets better, I'll go out with Roman and we'll look for some real gods.

This evening I was reading the index of the atlas—we're through all the thrillers. I'm reduced to this shivering litany, sipping rations of rum to warm an aching stomach, trying not to think how long the stores will last, or how long winter will be, or how deep.

And I came, inadvertently, through Wiscasset in Maine and Wischhafen on the Elbe, to Wisconsin. State, river, lake, dells. I went on quick to Wiscoy in New York State, to Wisdom, Montana, and Wise in Virginia—but she stopped me, one hand out of the blanket on her shoulders coming to rest on mine. We went back from the index and looked at the map—all those places. "I wouldn't," she said, "want to know what the winter's like there now."

The optimism tournament is over.

We've started sleeping together. We don't often make love, though when we do it's tender and attentive and enormously reassuring—she has a smile that shines.

But mostly we sleep together for the warmth and the company. Night's a dead time, empty. We're low on energy, and we cling together, not talking—just remembering our memories, thanking god we're not alone.

I know she's a blood risk—but what's there to lose? Better short happiness than none.

The rock beast's cleared off. We kind of miss him.

Beneath the thinned leaves of the forest I saw spirits this afternoon, dancing in small flashes of colored flame over the surface of a pool. A stream rolled in and out of the hollow under the icy rocks, making as it passed this sheltered pond, hidden from the barren sky. A misty dust hung in the air, bleak light drifting through it like a curtain of butter muslin slightly shifting in a draft, and on the surface of the water, the spirits twisted and shimmered.

I called to Roman, and he threw out some kind of powder on the rippled face of the dark water. Fishes, stunned, floated to the top.

I believe this was a miracle.

It doesn't make us less thin or our prospects less meager. But it was a miracle all the same.

This is the first I have written for forty-seven days.

There has been a second miracle: Roman's people are returned. They have between them five pigs, and soon we shall eat.

I believe also that the weather is, sporadically, easing. I saw stars last night, like a bright memory returning. Roman is talking about planting some early crops.

Dandy says, with the extra manpower, he can channel the river to much greater effect. He says we may get to have lights at night. That would be remarkable. We could be a regular little township.

I have read the index of the atlas seven times now, turning each time from Zyrzyn and Zywiec back to the River Aa between Flanders and Artois, to Aach, Aachen, Aadorf. There are 160,000 names.

That's more names than there were warheads. They can't have killed us all. . . .

We have survived winter like the first colonists in Virginia, brought through it in the main by the kindness and knowledge of the local people.

To pass the time, Dandy now teaches science; me, I teach history and geography. In daily matters, Roman is our chief minister; for judgment and leadership, we look to Mel. We will be a model settlement—though I fear, among the 160,000 names of the earth, whether others will be likewise.

I am making something special, for the party at which we'll celebrate five years of our survival.

In the *jefe*'s office he had sheets of acetate—for briefings, presumably, or presentations to his backers, who cares?—and I've cut them into small squares. I'm making primitive slides, outline maps in bright colors of different regions of the world, working gloopy lines and blobs of the gritty color pastes onto each frame in glowing miniature detail. It is long, fiddly, and absorbing work—but I expect to put on a good show.

Mel will speak. She will remember for us Roman Alberto Squalatush, who died of skin cancer, whose funeral was a year and three months ago; he is part of our public ritual. And she will speak of our common gratitude, for this our pocket of the earth.

She looks radiant; she is pregnant with our third child—watching her, I no longer think, I now know, that we're going to make it. There have been more births than deaths; we have a good and pleasing life, with time to work and time to think. I've even written two novels. Mel tells me, if I write a few more, they might eventually get readable.

When she finishes speaking, we turn off the main lights, and the bright one inside the magic lantern in the marquee ceiling comes on. From the sealed disk all round it in which they're set, my slides shine out in many colors and forms around the white-sheeted tent walls; the shapes of the world flicker across our skin as we dance in the lantern light, tripped out on datura, and on the patterns of the planet all about us. . . .

Well—it's all we have to worship, let's face it. The previous batch of gods didn't have so hot a track record, you know what I mean?

Whereas talking to the people here, you get to thinking that just the world will do, respected as it is and not grandiosely, arrogantly, blindly fucked with.

Roman was the starting point; but Mel and I now seem, teaching geography and ecology, inadvertently to be developing a new religion, a sort of conservationist animism. I even swear by the continents; if I bang my thumb with a hammer, I say, "Oh Antarctica."

We had a good party. Sorry you couldn't join us.

I got the rock beast on the radio today. We told him when he left, we'd have a half-hour trawl around the airwaves every Sunday, if he wanted to send us any little rock beast messages, or sermons—but he never did, until today.

He told us how he came on the abandoned control rooms on the Stockton Plateau, some of the power still eerily on, console lights blinking, tapes turning, monitors hissing blank white noise. One audio tape, endlessly rerunning in the empty bunker, played the voices of two stoned astronauts, blearily singing away their oxygen to the sound of some old Prince song, "'U turn on the telly and every other story is tellin' U somebody died,' *huh-aah*," mimicked the rock beast, "*dah-dum-dum-dooh . . .*"

Imagine what that war must have looked like from space.

The beast had other news.

He said, in Miami, he came upon a creature of warts and hair and scales with horns and flashing eyes, a lithe and gleaming animal-man fizzing with radiation in the murk of the ruined city, feeding off the millions of scorched and rotted corpses in the wasted suburbs. And, said the beast, he was following this slouched thing; and he was coming our way.

I'm not sure what we'll do about this.

We'll work something out.

September 1985, Amsterdam–January 1989, Washington, D.C.